MEETING HER MATCH

MEETING HER MATCH

JUSTINE ELYOT

Published by Xcite Books Ltd – 2012
ISBN 9781908086150

Printed and bound in the UK

Cover design by Madamadari

Chapter One

IT IS A TRUTH universally acknowledged that a single dom in possession of a whip must be in want of a sub.

Or is it? Leaving aside my problem with the depersonalising labels of dom and sub, it seems far from truth and very far from universal acknowledgement. Even to identify oneself as a person with an interest in the kinky side of things is a risk many prefer not to take. We lurk behind the vanilla lines, looking wistfully over at the dungeon parties on the other side, getting our thrills by internet proxy.

This was how I came to find myself at a hopelessly vanilla, horribly *Sex in the-City*-esque speed dating event at a bar in Gunwharf Quays.

'I'm really not sure about this.'

But Louisa was already at the bar, ordering white wine spritzers.

'So what are you going to do? Sit in your flat for ever more? It's been six months, Chez. I bet Gareth's met someone else over the summer holidays.'

'I couldn't give a toss. In fact, I hope he has. Some cheerleader type who's happy to stand on sidelines in all weathers. No, I mean I'm not sure about speed dating. It's not very … organic.'

'Neither is this wine, but that doesn't seem to bother you.'

'I mean, it's a bit forced. Desperate, even.'

'Yeah, well, I am desperate,' said Lou, necking back a big swig of wine. 'If I don't get a shag soon, I'm going to start hanging around the dockyard gates in a basque and suspenders.'

'Ah, all the nice girls love a sailor. But do sailors love nice girls?'

I looked out through the window at the warship radar towers looming in the distance.

'I'm not a nice girl,' pointed out Lou. 'Not like you.'

Oh, if you only knew.

But I couldn't tell her, and I couldn't tell Gareth, even though a large proportion of my reasons for fancying him centred on his size and breadth and large hands and capacity to fling me around like a rag doll. Not that he ever used it. He crushed me to a pulp in the missionary position thrice weekly, panting for five minutes then roaring, 'You're fucked, girl,' before indulging in some target practice with the condom and the wastepaper basket.

When I found myself planning a lesson on composition theory during sex, I realised it was time to send Gareth and his vast collection of rugby shirts back into the world of singledom.

'So, what's the talent like?' wondered Lou, casting her eyes around the room. 'Anything take your fancy?'

I shrugged. It looked like the usual selection of chancers in cheap suits to me. I wanted to choke from the miasma of conflicting fragrance in the room.

'I'm guessing Hugo Boss is here somewhere,' I said, sniffing. 'I bet he's worth a few bob. Plus, I like his name.'

'Hugo?'

'No. Boss.'

'You like a man who wears the trousers?'

Ooh, close to the bone. I have to deflect this line of reasoning.

'Yeah,' I said lightly. 'Though I wouldn't rule out Eddie Izzard either. Or even Grayson Perry.'

She laughed and a bell rang. It was time to speed date.

Time to start a dozen abortive, pointless conversations with strange men.

Eleven of the conversations went like this:

Him: Hi, I'm Jim/Joe/Harry/Kamil.

Me: I'm Cherry, pleased to meet you. What do you do?

Him: I'm an insurance salesman/physiotherapist/paralegal/electrician. How about you?

Me: I'm a teacher.

Him: (leering) Oh yeah? I bet you could teach me a thing or two.

Me: headdesk.

The twelfth took a different course.

Him: That's a lovely choker.

Me: Oh, thank you. It's one of my favourites too.

Him: I've often wondered how those feel, around your neck. Do they constrict your breathing at all?

Me: Not really. You are sort of aware of it all the time, though.

Him: (smiling dangerously) I like the sound of that.

Me: (speechless, suddenly quivery, giving him a long, hard second look)

Him: It's a good present from a lover, isn't it? Like having his hand wrapped around your neck all night. His mark on you.

Me: (gabbling) Are you a possessive type, then?

Him: Oh yes. Not particularly jealous, though, and certainly not in an abusive way. But if a girl likes to feel possessed, then I'm happy to oblige.

Me: How do you … make her feel like that, then?

Him: I'd love to show you.

Me: (quailing beneath keen grey stare, predatory curl of lip, broad shouldered swoop forward) Oh. Really?

Him: Yes, really. Come with me.

A direct order. I can never defy one of those, and I didn't want to anyway. His suit was well cut and, while he must have been in his forties at least, he had that still, calm air of authority that floored me and filled my dreams.

He stood, gesturing me up, and I followed him to the bar, where he bought me – without asking what I would like – a mineral water, plus a whisky for himself.

'I don't want to be accused of taking advantage of tipsiness,' he told me, nudging the water glass down the polished bar top. 'Now, let's sort a few things out. You strike me as curious about certain aspects of human sexuality, am I right?'

I coughed into my glass, feeling as transparent as the crystal waters within.

'Is it obvious?'

'To me it is. Probably not to the world in general. How curious are you?'

'Moderately.'

'There's nothing moderate about what I do … What's your name?'

'Cherry.'

'Stuart.'

'Pleased to meet you.'

'Well, Cherry, I like to be master in my own bedroom, if you catch my drift. Does that interest you?'

I gulped. What should I say? I rather thought the fiery spreading blush on my face was saying it for me.

'It might,' I muttered.

'Does it or doesn't it? I don't have time to waste.'

His stern tone caught me right between the thighs.

'Yeah. I suppose it does,' I admitted, a mite sulkily.

'Good. Though I think we'll need to discuss your tone, young lady.'

Oh my God, he was killing me. "Young lady". I was positively pre-orgasmic, especially when he raised an eyebrow in a way that couldn't say "you're getting spanked" any louder or clearer.

'Drink up,' he ordered. 'Are you here alone?'

4

'No, with a friend.'

'Good. You can tell her you're going home with me, and that you'll call her by eleven so that she knows you're safe.'

'I'll ... tell her that.' I looked around the bar for her, finally locating her in a darkened alcove, snogging some guy with a beard like a King of Leon. Sex on fire indeed.

I passed on the message, slipping it between her and the hairy one like a credit card of information. Her reply was a swallowed grunt.

'I'll be at home then,' I reminded her brightly, feeling a broad hand descend on my shoulder. SM Stuart was not about to let me get away. I had been hooked like an unsuspecting fish, and now I was in the net I wouldn't get out until I was being sizzled over the flames of his fire.

'Where do you live?' he asked, yanking me backwards, away from the bar.

'Near South Parade Pier.'

'Good. Not too far.'

It wasn't until we were in the taxi that the insane foolishness of the idea hit home. Taking a strange man home for kinky sex – how on earth would that stack up on the risk assessment form? Not well at all, I realised with a sickening lurch of the stomach.

But then he pulled me towards him and into a long, hard kiss, and the lurching became something else, something much sweeter and less easily dismissed, something that squeezed all of my good sense into a tiny ball and batted it down between my legs, which were trembling.

It was mad and it was stupid, but I wanted sex – real, good sex – so much that I was prepared to follow my cunt wherever it led me that night.

Stuart's mouth was firm and hungry, and his hand landed with a wondrous heaviness on my thigh, edging up the hem of my skirt, kneading its way to heaven, regardless of the taxi driver.

Luckily, the ride was not long enough for him to reach my stocking tops. The skirt was mid-thigh when he paid the fare, helped me out of the cab, and escorted me, hand on elbow, up the path to my apartment block.

Once inside the door, he held me out at arm's length and said, 'You're wearing stockings and suspenders, aren't you?'

I nodded.

'Sounds to me like you were out looking for somebody to take you home and fuck you. You don't wear stockings if you don't think they'll be seen.'

'They make me feel sexy,' I defended myself.

'You want to feel sexy because you want a good seeing-to, Cherry. Am I right?'

I chewed my lip, avoiding his eye.

'Maybe.'

'I'm right. And what kind of girl wants a good seeing-to, hmm?'

He pulled me closer, sliding one hand down my hip and around to pat a bum cheek. Oh, I could see where this was heading. And I liked it very, very much.

'A bad girl,' I said softly.

His lips quirked, and his hand fell a little harder on my quivering bottom.

'That's right, Cherry. A bad girl. And what do bad girls get?'

Good sex.

'They get punished?'

'Try adding a "sir" to that.'

'They get punished, sir.'

'Nice. And true. They do get punished. But first, since you're dying to show off your naughty underwear, I want you to stand over by that chair and lift your skirt for me.'

He dropped my arm and nudged me back a couple of feet, so that I was in a good position for him to rake his eyes from my bob-cut hair to my strappy sandals. Standing with his arms folded and his brows gathered, he waited for me to follow the instruction.

I felt like laughing and shivering at the same time, but I did as I was told, turned up the hem of my skirt and lifted it coyly to my waist.

'Oh yes, I see,' he said. 'Very nice. And do you call those knickers?'

I stared down at my shaking hands on the fabric. They weren't exactly substantial, it was true. I was glad I hadn't opted for the Spanx tonight after all – though, on second thoughts, they would at least have been appropriate.

The knickers I was wearing were tiny breaths of lacy air, patterned with glittery starbursts. I only knew they were there at all because they were soaking wet at the crotch. I wondered if the damp patch was visible. If not, it was certainly sniffable. I could smell myself all right.

'Turn around,' he said, and I was grateful to remove myself from the intense scrutiny and present my back view instead. The knickers weren't thong-backed, but they stretched tightly across my rear, almost transparent, so that he would be able to follow each curve to its conclusion.

'That's a lovely bottom you have there,' he commented, moving up behind me. 'No, don't let go of the skirt.' He put a hand on my lacy cheeks and rubbed them slowly up and down. I let out a tiny moan, bending my spine infinitesimally forward to give him optimum access, hoping for a quick dip between my legs. 'And one that needs a lot of attention, I think.'

He removed his hands and sat down in my armchair.

'Now put your lovely bottom over my knee, Cherry, where it belongs.'

Christ, I was more turned on than I'd ever expected to be outside my horniest fantasies. For a dizzying moment, I thought this was worth any risk, even though my rational mind knew that only a brain-dead, sex-crazed zombie would entertain that thought.

I drooped over his lap, trying to work out how to get over it in the most dignified manner, though God knows what any remnants of dignity were doing in my fevered brain at that point. Unable to compute logistics, I kind of threw myself across the middle section of his thighs, kicking my legs in the air until he smacked them down so my toes brushed the carpet.

'Now, think about where you are,' he said softly, his hand renewing its hypnotic circular pattern across my exposed bum cheeks. 'Take a moment for the full humiliating reality of your position to sink in. Where are you, Cherry?'

I clenched my thighs, his low, authoritative voice tickling the space between them like a sonic vibrator. I wished I'd had more to drink. It would have made the verbal aspect of this scenario so much easier.

'I'm over your knee.'

'That's right. But you missed a bit, Cherry. An important little word.' His palm hovered dangerously over my rear curves.

'I'm over your damn knee?' I hazarded, with an irrepressible snort. Oh dear. It seemed I was discovering a hitherto-unknown minxy side of myself.

The smack was swift and remorseless. I yelped, quivering beneath his hand.

'I'm surprised at you, young lady,' he told me. 'I see I'm going to have to deal with you quite thoroughly. No, the missing word you are looking for is "sir". Now, repeat the sentence for me, Cherry.'

I couldn't say it in my natural voice. It came out in a sort of sing-song comedy Deep Southern drawl.

'I'm over your knee, sirrrr.'

'That's right, but who is this fugitive from the Grand Ole Opry I seem to have acquired? Where is Cherry?'

I humphed and tried to kick a leg, but he secured it with a well-placed foot, waiting, hand poised.

8

'I'm over your knee, sir,' I ground out, a mite sulkily.

'Much better, Cherry. I think we're in for a long session at this rate. Now, I need you to tell me why you think you are over my knee?'

My God, this man must have had forebears in the Spanish Inquisition. Stuart was not a particularly Spanish name, though. Perhaps his surname was. I didn't know his surname! I was over the knee of a man whose surname I didn't know.

'I think something's going to happen,' I said.

His hand began to pat my rump compulsively.

'Yes,' he conceded. 'Something is going to happen. But what?'

'I think you might have some dastardly kind of plan to … spank me … sir.'

'That's almost the right answer. Less of the dastardly, though, eh? You're certainly setting yourself up for a seriously sore bottom, young lady.'

'Oh dear,' I moaned, squirming deliciously.

'Yes, "oh dear" is a valid response,' he taunted. 'Last question. What are you going to be spanked for?'

I was stymied. I had to come up with a reason for my own erotic punishment? Was "because I want you to" also a valid response?

'For …' I gave it some thought, which was difficult with the ever-present hand gliding across my buttocks, occasionally following the line that separated them, almost to the wet spot at its base. 'For taking strange men home to my flat, sir,' I said, inspired.

'Very good,' he said. 'That definitely deserves quite a firm spanking, I would say. Now then. Let's get this bottom nice and high. How long will it take me to turn it red, I wonder? I do like a physiological experiment.'

His physiological experiment began with a series of sharp slaps, falling quickly on each cheek in turn.

'If it gets too much for you, or you decide this kind of

fun is not for you, just say my name. You promise you'll do that?'

'Yes, sir,' I sighed, gyrating my hips to push my bottom up higher, revelling in the firecracker sparks he rained down on me.

'Good girl. Or rather, bad girl. Flaunting yourself in that bar and taking strange men home for kinky sex. You need a sound lesson, young lady. Believe me, your slutty behaviour will be dealt with.'

His hand felt harder, the smacks loud as pistol shots. Would the neighbours hear? I began to suffer a little, feeling the heat build.

When he stopped, after about fifty of these strokes, I flopped, exhaling deeply. But he had not finished, not by a long chalk.

'I think we'll have these knickers down now,' he decreed.

With exquisite care and attention, he edged the barely-there lace down over my stinging hindquarters, making sure the elastic dragged, awakening little darts of extra sensation on the way. Down my thighs they travelled, only to be brought to a halt at the buffers of my suspender snaps. But that was far enough for Stuart's purposes, and he left them there, moving his palms back up to rest briefly between my legs.

Oh yes! I wriggled welcomingly, hoping he would part those lips and dive in.

Instead, he dabbed his fingers in just enough to coat them in my scent, then moved back up to my warm pink bottom.

'Dirty girl,' he whispered. 'You like being spanked, don't you?'

'No, sir, honestly!' I protested, but I was caught red-handed. Or red-arsed.

'Don't lie!' he said sharply, making my bottom feel the weight of his displeasure. 'Lying will earn you extras with

10

my belt, young lady.'

Oh, his belt! Leather, smooth and cold, the image of him unbuckling and snapping it through the air. I wanted to move my hand down to my clit at the thought, but he wouldn't allow that.

'Oh no, I would hate to be whipped with your belt!' I moaned. 'That's a lie, by the way, sir.'

He wanted to laugh, I could tell, but he simply spanked me harder and faster, so that I jerked and squeaked about on his lap as if electrically shocked, his large hand covering every inch of skin from my stocking tops to the rounded crest of my bum until it all burned with uniform heat.

'You have a lot to learn about submission,' he informed me, smacking away merrily. 'And it would be so much fun to teach you.' I sensed a "but", but I didn't want to hear it, so I ignored it for the moment, preferring to focus on this gorgeous ocean wave of pleasure-pain.

'No begging for mercy so far,' he noted, giving his arm a rest. 'You're made for this. And so is your arse. Perfectly spankable.'

I felt like reminding him that my cunt was also perfectly fingerable and lickable and fuckable, should he choose to further his experimentation, but I didn't want to lead the scene. Something told me that would be contrary to etiquette. So instead, I merely raised my hips and parted my thighs a little.

His hand began to slide, so slowly, so tantalisingly, down the crack of my bum and into that humid delta beyond. When it hit the swollen target of my clit, I gasped and jiggled furiously.

'Have you never been spanked before?' he asked, incredulous.

'No. I've wanted to. But never had the nerve to ask, or bring the subject up.'

'You need it so badly. You were built to be spanked. Every day, good and hard. Your arse just looks wrong unless it's red.'

'Oh, I know.' His fingers were manipulating me with firm expertise, bringing me closer and closer to that ultimate surrender.

'I don't know what you do for a living, love, but I think you need to tell your boss, every day, that you can't go home until he or she has spanked you hard, just the way you need it. Put you in the corner with your knickers down and your red bum out until the caretaker comes in to lock up.'

I was bucking now, so close, so close, but his words made me giggle amidst the pre-orgasmic groaning.

'I work in a school,' I told him.

'Oh, interesting. So your headmaster might have one of those old school canes hiding in a cupboard somewhere. Six of the best would do you the world of good.'

'Oh God, you're evil, I'm going to come …'

He pulled his fingers out and I reached back blindly, trying to catch his arm.

'Please!'

'Not yet, you oversexed little brat. You have some business with my belt first.'

'Oh, you're so mean!' I sounded like a child denied sweets, but I obeyed his command to stand up and get my pert red bottom over the arm of the sofa nonetheless.

The heat on my bum didn't seem to last particularly long. It was already fading as I watched him take his sweet time unbuckling his wicked-looking black leather belt and removing it from his trouser loops. My skin was still pleasantly tight and a little sore, though.

When Stuart looped the belt around his fist and began whipping it down into his palm, I began to consider the wisdom of my actions. The very sound of it was fearsome, the sight of it knicker-wettingly sexy, but was it all window-dressing, softening me up for a pain I might not be capable of bearing?

While I didn't want Stuart to be disappointed, the wobbling of my legs betrayed me. I was really scared.

Stuart put a hand on the small of my back, stilling me.

'Hey, little girl,' he said softly. 'Nobody is going to make you do this. If you want to stop, or try something else instead, that's your prerogative.'

His words steeled me. My calves tautened and I pushed out my bum. This might be beyond my endurance, but I wouldn't know unless I tried, would I? And all I had to do to make it stop was call Stuart's name.

'You will stop if I ask you, won't you?'

'Of course. Just say the word. Brave girl.'

He patted my back and then stepped behind me.

I felt the leather dangle over my behind, brushing its crimson blush, slipping smoothly between my cheeks and stroking downward. I welcomed its cool caress, lulled by it, even though it added to my torment of unsatiated lust.

Then it was gone. There was a moment of tense silence, then a whoosh, then a crisp, sharp crack across the width of my still-warm arse. I jolted forward, my face finding a cushion to howl into, my fingernails tearing at the upholstery.

'Oh, ow!'

'Painful, eh? So it should be. Ten of these, young lady, should teach you a lesson in good conduct. Push your bottom back out, please.'

I took a moment to recover, then did as I was told, enjoying the spreading afterburn of the first stroke far too much to deny myself the rest of the leathering.

He laid each stroke with deadly accuracy, below its predecessor, moving down my bottom until it was evenly striped, then placing the final four on exactly the same spot – the meeting of arse and thigh, just where I would feel it when I sat down.

I pouted, I snivelled, I hopped up and down on my tiptoes, I pressed the cushion to my face and howled for the last two searing scorchers, but I was never once tempted to cry out his name and end it all.

The tenth stroke delivered, I lay panting and triumphant, buzzing with endorphins and seething with lust. I had been soundly and thoroughly dealt with, and it felt a lot like falling in love.

Stuart put his hand on the small of my back again, then pressed his other palm into my burning, ridged backside.

'You took that so well,' he said thickly. 'God, your arse is on fire, girl. Spread your thighs wider.'

I obeyed, while he took the cushion I had been drooling into and replaced it beneath my hips so that my bottom was even higher up and my feet left the floor. He used his thumbs to open my sex lips and crouched behind me, breathing on them before giving them one long luscious lick, all around my needy clit.

'So you want me to fuck you?' he asked gruffly. I heard him pat at his suit jacket before throwing it off, then his trousers came down.

'Please, sir,' I whimpered.

'Just as well. Because a good seeing-to is what you're getting.'

I heard the snap of the condom, smelled its latex tang, then Stuart's hands were on my hips, holding me still. Ah, there it was. The tip of his cock, butting my soaked cunt, stretching it until he was all the way in.

The warmth and tightness of my arse, rubbed against by his pelvis, added a delicious dimension to the feeling of fullness and I pushed myself back, squeezing my muscles around his cock, holding it there for one long second of inescapable penetration.

Then he uttered some strangulated sound and he was off, pumping and thrusting while I clutched the sofa cushion and yelped into it. I hoped the downstairs neighbours would not be disturbed by the jolting of the sofa on the wooden floor, but then he placed a thumb on my clit. I forgot all about the neighbours, concentrating only on getting my bottom higher and my cunt wider and my clit square on the pad of his thumb tip. I was in a boiling mess of shame and submission, lust and vulnerability. I was getting a proper hard fucking from the man who had just lit up my arse like the lanterns on the Promenade. It was heaven, hell, and everything in between. His weight pushed me forward, guiding his cock unerringly to my G-spot. I came, sobbing and thanking him in a frenzy over the knock-knock-knock of the sofa. He parted the cheeks of my bum and pressed a finger down into the crack before coming himself. I squealed at the rudeness of it, thrashing a little, but incapable of moving much underneath his solid bulk.

We slumped forward, on to the sofa, where he rearranged me into his half-clothed arms and stroked my damp forehead.

'There. Was that what you wanted? What you expected?'

'It was incredible. Blew my mind.'

He laughed. 'Good. That's what I was aiming for.'

'You've done this a lot, I guess.'

'Every time I get the chance. My ex-wife wasn't keen, so once the divorce was final, I suppose I got out there and made up for lost time.'

'Wild oats in reverse.'

'I suppose.'

'Is that what split you up?'

'No, no, God, no. There was much more to it than that. Divorce is very common in my line of work. But I'd prefer not to talk about that now, if you don't mind.'

'Oh. OK. Do you want a drink?'

'Maybe a glass of water.'

I staggered to the kitchen and admired the state of my arse in the shiny glass of the cooker door before making with the cups and taps. Wow. It looked angry. Dark, dark red, with a kind of self-stripe effect, slightly raised from the belt.

The sight of it turned me on again. I wondered if Stuart would be up for a bit more, perhaps minus the spanking this time, or I would be standing for the whole of the first week of term, and teaching was hard enough on the legs as it was.

'Can you stay?' I asked, handing him the glass.

He put an arm around me and pulled me close to him before replying.

'I can't, I'm afraid.'

It was a blow, I can't deny. Between filling the glass and offering it to him, I had constructed a rosy fog of kinky romance around us, imagining that I would be spending the rest of the weekend tied to the bed with my legs spread-eagled.

But I didn't know this man, when it came down to it, except at this peculiar and intense level of our mutual enjoyment of BDSM.

'That's a shame,' I said tentatively. I wanted to ask why, but equally I didn't want the answer.

'Yes.' He sipped. 'It is.'

'Maybe …'

'There's an awful lot I'd love to teach you, Cherry. But I just can't. Because I won't be here. My ship sails for the Persian Gulf tomorrow, you see.'

'Oh! You're a sailor.'

'Yes. A medical officer.'

'So is that why you split up?'

'Yes, pretty much. I retire in two years as well.' He shrugged.

'Two years isn't such a long time.'

'I hope you're not offering to wait for me, young lady. Because that wouldn't be fair on you.'

He kissed my forehead.

'Go out, find a good man with a good whip, and seize

your fun while you're young. Perhaps if you're still single and still interested in two years' time … but you won't be.'

'I might be.'

'You won't be.'

'Well, if I am, I'll be at that bar in Gunwharf Quays, two years from this date. Yes?'

'OK. It's a date. Of sorts. So you aren't angry with me?'

'Oh, this is one of my favourite teacher lines. I'm not angry with you, Stuart, I'm just a bit disappointed.'

He laughed loud and long, squeezing me tight.

'I'd love to do detention with you,' he said. 'Who knows? Perhaps one day.'

He tapped my shoulder, then extricated himself.

'I really have to go. Forgive me for taking advantage of you.'

'You didn't take advantage of me. I wanted to do this – I've always wanted to do it – and now I know how it feels.'

'Good.' He stood, looking around for his coat. 'Well, thank you, Cherry. You've made my last night of shore leave very memorable indeed.'

'*De nada*,' I said, awkward now. How does one wrap up a session of this nature? Is there a formal etiquette?

He put on his coat and then pulled my nearly-nude body to his, imprisoning my head between his hands for a long, luscious kiss.

'You're gorgeous and you deserve better,' he whispered. 'But I'll be at Gunwharf Quays in two years, if some other lucky bastard hasn't snagged you by then. In the meantime, get out there and get spanked.'

I giggled, but the giggle wanted quite badly to mutate into something embarrassing and tearful.

'I'll try.'

'See that you do. Or I'll have to come back and spank you myself.'

'That would be awful.'

'Hmm. Goodbye, then.'

'Take care. Don't get sunk. Don't get scurvy. Pack plenty of limes.'

'I rarely have to treat scurvy these days, but I'll bear it in mind.'

'Watch out for pirates.'

'I will. And now I really must go.'

And he really did go.

Chapter Two

I WENT DOWN TO Spice Island the next day and watched Stuart's ship sail, kicking myself for my pathetic sentimentality. The crew were lined up on deck, waving back to their families at the dockyard. I wondered if Stuart had anyone to wave to. I couldn't make him out amidst all the uniformed men and women, though I squinted hard enough to send me cross-eyed. Off he went, past the Isle of Wight and away to hotter, more dangerous climes. Would he come back? I waited for the hulk of greyness to disappear, along with the onlookers, and went home to plan my first week's lessons.

Two days later, I was back at work. We were to be eased in gently with a teacher training day, so the usual crowd of scuffling, high-fiving kids was nowhere in evidence as I cycled through the high-rise canyons and into the school grounds.

After locking – or rather, double-locking, given the area the school is in – my bike, I turned around and ran slap-bang into exactly the person I had most hoped to avoid.

'Oh, Gareth,' I flustered, picking up my bag and the Biros that had spilled out on to the playground. 'Have good holidays?'

'No,' he said, in his hurt voice, the one that reminded me of a plaintive buffalo. 'I had a lot on my mind.'

'Oh well. Good weather though. I expect you played lots of cricket.'

'It was only the cricket keeping me sane.'

'Cricket therapy, eh? The crack of leather on willow.' I had to stop. Leather. Willow. Mmmm. Leather.

'Stop being so flipping flippant, Chez. You know you broke my heart.'

'Oh Gareth,' I said in a hand-wringing tone. There didn't seem much else to say. I was not about to apologise, or soften, or give him a fight, which were the three options he was hoping for me to choose between. 'Have you met the new head yet?'

'What do you think? I've only just got here.'

Thank God, thank God, we made it to the doors, and I staggered into the entrance hall, almost sobbing with relief to see Louisa with some of the other girls, comparing suntans and timetables.

I left Gareth to it and was welcomed back into the fold.

'Hey, Chez, go up to the staff room and get your timetable,' advised Lou. 'We're just waiting for the Big Intro to Mr Superhead. He's going to be speaking in the hall in about ten minutes.'

'Right.' I peered at her timetable. 'Ouch! 11VY and 9KS. Double whammy! Commiserations.'

'Tell me about it,' she mourned, but I was springing away upstairs to the place of orange and brown refuge known as the staff room.

My timetable was the same as ever. I'm the only music teacher in the school, so I get all of them, in small doses, then two small GCSE groups for eight hours of the week. In an area like this, few children are interested in learning about notation or the great composers, but the modules on Popular and World music are slowly drawing a few more to the studio each year.

I raced back down, just in time to see the curtain pulled back from the hall doors and the assembled staff invited in. We sat on the moulded plastic chairs, staring at the lectern on the stage, breathing in beeswax, waiting expectantly for this miracle worker to do his stuff. And he was going to have to be a miracle worker, frankly. Most of the staff had job applications pending elsewhere, and finding replacements for them would be the proverbial hunt for hen's teeth.

We clapped, not quite knowing why, when he appeared before us. He didn't look anything like Jesus, but the air of authority was there, as well as the expensive suit and well-cut hair.

'Not bad,' whispered Lou. 'Better than Gilmour.'

'Anything would be better than Gilmour.'

'True.'

The Superhead – Patrick Marks, as he liked to call himself – spoke a few words of conventional introduction before launching into his spiel.

'Here at St Sebastian's, we all face a substantial challenge. We've seen the statistics, and we know the score. Unless we can turn this school around in two years, we close down and the government re-opens it as an Academy with a new staff. Two years. That's all we've got. We need to sail this ship together, one crew, one purpose.'

God, nautical imagery again. Everyone who comes to this city thinks they have to do that. All the same, his voice was exceptionally … something. Lulling? Reassuring? Arousing!

He had the world's sexiest voice.

How very distracting.

Now I wanted to scrutinise him more closely. I leant forward in my chair, noting the aquiline features, the long, lean nose, his height and elegant bearing. Nice hands. No wedding ring.

He was quite a speaker, using his extraordinary voice to full effect, lowering it to utter words of cunning flattery, raising it to ring out the rhetoric. It was like music, using cadence and rhythm to create an irresistible flow.

It was too tempting to imagine it murmuring wicked

words in my ear. I sunk into reverie, missing the entire section on targets, picturing myself bent over at his mercy while he paced the room whacking a riding crop against his thigh and lecturing me on my misdeeds and their penalties.

Oh, he had finished. Applause, a standing ovation, filled the hall, and I hauled myself to my feet with the rest.

'That voice,' I whispered to Lou.

'I know! Don't you want to have sex with it? His wife's a lucky woman.'

His wife. He was one of those guys who didn't wear a ring. Old school. Did that mean he was more or less likely to spank his partner?

The conundrum defeated me. I warned myself against developing a crush on this man, telling myself that he would be too busy to have much to do with a lowly music serf such as myself.

We trickled off for tea and biscuits, girding our loins for a long session of putting our classrooms to rights for the new term.

'If you are under 18 or offended by alternative sexualities, please leave now.'

I wasn't under 18, and I certainly wasn't offended by alternative sexualities, but my finger was positively shaking over the "Enter" button, as if I expected a flashing light to go off at the local police station the moment I pressed it.

'Pervert alert,' the desk sergeant would say laconically. 'At 11B South Parade Gardens.'

'Oh really?' His colleague would look up, eyebrows raised. 'But she's a schoolteacher, isn't she?'

'Yeah. St Sebastian's.'

'Well, they're all a bunch of oddballs up there. All the same, the *Evening News*'ll be interested. It'll make the front page.'

'Yeah, better call the news desk. I'll get over to her flat

and see about confiscating her computer.'

'Right you are.'

Argh!

I retracted the finger, my heart beating fast.

Counselling myself to stop being so silly, I replaced it. There was no police link to this website for consenting adults to meet up with other consenting adults who shared their particular kink. This was not a school laptop, watched over by Techno Mo, the head of Information Technology. It was my personal laptop, on which I was absolutely entitled to conduct my own personal business. Any personal business, barring criminal acts.

No policemen were going to roll up at the door wielding handcuffs. Though actually …

But I didn't have time for cop fantasies.

Was I going to do this, or not?

I took a deep breath and stabbed at the button. I was in. The world seemed to look the same. What next?

I cruised through a few user profiles, occasionally stretching my eyes or exclaiming, 'Wow!' at some of the photographs illustrating them. I clicked quickly past anything involving intimate piercings or close-ups of cocks or, ew, was that an enema bag? I lingered over the pretty pictures of girls in corsets, or men with whips, or pleasingly-striped female bottoms. This was what I was here for. People like me.

At the top of the screen, the invitation to create a profile and become a member kept luring my eye toward it, like Jessica Rabbit's beckoning finger. It all looked more and more exciting, the more I read and discovered. The members made cyber-friends with each other and sent messages if they thought they might have enough in common to try meeting up. I looked for members in the local area and found an excitingly long list of them. I could actually do this. Could I?

Stuart's words revolved around my head: 'Go out there

and get spanked.' That was an order, wasn't it? If I thought of this as obeying his order, it would be easier. I imagined Stuart as a benign long-distance dictator, watching me through some kind of Skype arrangement from his warship.

'Join the site,' he urged. 'Get to know a few fellow deviants. You're bound to run across one you click with. Find him and, when you do, send me a letter with all the details.'

'OK.' I clicked on "Sign up", waited for the confirmation email, then set to work creating my profile.

So. Username. What could I have? Not one of those blatant ones like Cumsucker69 or Slut4U. I wanted something demure that hinted at the submissive longings behind it. What famous submissives were there? I could only think of O from *The Story of O* – great book, but not such an inspiring name. It took me another hour to list all the possibilities until eventually, frustrated by the unwanted procrastination, I called myself AtYourService and had done with it.

Next I had to tick a vast number of boxes detailing my interests, vanilla and non-vanilla. I only ticked "music" on the vanilla, not having time for fripperies, then moved on to the interesting part. It was like those old adverts for dating agencies, only instead of "Pets" you could tick "Caning", instead of "Pubs and Clubs" you had "Multiple Partners".

Having tick-box identified myself as a corporal punishment fetishist with interests in anal sex, humiliation, and bondage, I moved on to my personal statement.

'I am new to all this,' I started, wishing I had a pencil to suck the nub of, 'so I need to be taught a great deal. Are you a strict but caring teacher?' Fuck, it sounded like something from the *Times Educational Supplement*. Should I sex it up a bit? 'If you can help this curious girl learn the pleasures of submission, please feel free to message me. Imagination and GSOH essential, intelligence and cultural knowledge preferred, looks less relevant than natural authority. Thanks for reading.'

Ugh, "thanks for reading". I sounded so … wholesome. But who was to say that would turn some of these gentlemen off? I wasn't looking for the kind of man who wanted to surround himself with Cumsucker69s. I was looking for the kind of man who wanted me. A man like … Stuart.

A picture? No. No way. I wasn't going there.

I uploaded the profile to MasterMe.com and then had to close my browser, aghast and giggling at the huge step I had taken.

In my bed, I imagined my first meeting with a shadowy dominant man. How would it happen? Would he take me to a dungeon club? Would I have to parade past a crowd of people, led by a chain attached to a collar, wearing only a PVC basque with stockings and suspenders that exposed my tits, arse and pussy? Would they slap at my bum as I passed, commenting on my appearance, expressing their hopes that they might get a turn later? Would they watch as the shadowy master fastened me into a pillory and proceeded to whip my displayed backside until it was red and swollen? Would the crowd then surge up and feel the heat, cupping my buttocks in multiple hands, moving their fingers down to wet them in my cunt, making me come in public, over and over again, oh, oh, oh …

No. It probably wouldn't happen like that. But the fantasy was strong and suddenly I felt more optimistic than I had done in months.

I still felt optimistic even after a long day of making sure none of the instruments managed to walk out of the music room by themselves between classes. During playground duty I'd had to keep the Buckland Boyz and the Somerstown Crew on separate sides of the basketball court as hostilities erupted over somebody disrespecting somebody else's lunchbox. And my Year Eleven exam group seemed to have forgotten what a treble clef was over the course of the summer holidays.

But apart from that, it was all good.

Looking out from my classroom window, watching Gareth take the first football practice of term (and getting quite angry with his team by the looks of things), I wondered what my inbox would hold for me when I got home. I had had to forcibly restrain myself from switching my laptop on that morning, knowing that my concentration at work would be severely impaired if anything interesting was nestling in amongst the Viagra spam. No, I told myself, it's too soon. You won't hear anything yet. You probably won't hear anything, ever.

But what if Sir Right was waiting for me even now, hanging on for my reply?

I giggled to myself and wandered over to my desk, sternly telling myself that I wasn't to go home until I had marked these shoddy Year Eleven listening exercises. All awful, apart from Tunde's, as usual.

Unexpectedly, the door opened after a brief knock and I looked up to be faced with …

'Oh hullo.'

Patrick Superhead Marks, looking as suave and deadly as James Bond, stood with his hand on the knob, casting his eye around my neglected lair.

'The music room,' he declared in those knicker-wettening tones. 'And you must be Cherry? Cherry Delaney?'

'Yes,' I said, thrown into confusion. For some reason, I had stood up when he entered the room, just as I used to as an inky-fingered convent schoolgirl.

He loped across, two swift swishes of his long legs, and extended a hand. Still wedding ringless, not that that meant anything. I took it, rather limply, but he shook it with great enthusiasm and I found myself wanting the gesture to go on and on. This was how handshakes were meant to be, my

26

hand enclosed in reassuring warmth and strength, given no option but to follow his lead. He really was a lot better looking than I had at first thought, one of those men whose attractions creep up and leap on your unsuspecting libido. The voice was just the fanfare for the man. I hoped I wasn't blushing, but knew I probably was.

'I'd hoped to get round all the staff a little more quickly, but you know how it is – some of them have a list of grievances that would fill the pages of the *Encyclopaedia Britannica*. Still, better late than never. Please accept my apologies.'

'Uh, of course.' You have those crinkles at the side of your eyes.

'Good. So this is your kingdom, is it?'

'Haha, yes. It's a little bit ramshackle. Needs a new king, haha.' Jesus, what am I saying? I can't think with him standing this close. He's so distracting, with his piercing green-brown eyes. I wish he'd go away.

'Well, I don't know about a new king – you seem to be doing very well. One of the few curriculum areas that's been getting halfway decent results. But I do agree that perhaps the physical fabric of your land could do with some … regeneration.'

The truth of this statement forced my attention away from him and on to my sorry domain. One piano, indifferently tuned, stood in the corner, while paint-scratched cupboards housed a variety of ancient and battered instruments. The music stands used to be blue but now they were a gunmetal grey. The shelves on the wall held music scores that were used by these children's grandparents – dog-eared, ripped and graffitied to hell.

'Music hasn't been much of a priority in the budget, traditionally,' I confided. 'It's a bit of a poor relation.'

'That's a shame. And I think it needs to change.'

I looked up at him again, catching a breath. Was he going to make me an offer?

'You've worked hard, got good results and I think you should be rewarded. Music is a subject area that could be a real success for our school – most of the kids here love music. Many of them DJ or play in bands in their spare time. Why not capitalise on that enthusiasm? I want to build a decent music suite with a recording studio.'

'That would be amazing!' You are amazing. I think I love you.

'Yes. I think it could be developed as a community resource too. It would be popular, newsworthy, give some of the disaffected youngsters a focus, perhaps.'

'I agree!' You're giving me a focus right now. A highly sexual one.

'Good. I'll put it to the Governors. And another thing, Cherry ...'

The way you say my name makes me want to come. Say it again.

'There's more?' I laughed, trying to convey in that one sound the enormity of my gratitude for his interest in me and my music room.

'I wonder if you'd be interested in putting on a production? A musical, something like *Oliver!*. Or, I don't know, what has lots of young people in it?'

'*West Side Story*?'

'Perfect! The gang theme!'

He clapped my shoulder approvingly, his gorgeously cruel lips angled up in a broad smile. I nearly fainted.

'OK.'

'I'm happy to direct if you'll organise the musical side of things. Shall we have audition posters done? I'll announce it in assembly tomorrow.'

'Cool,' I said, feeling like an inarticulate teen.

'Yes. Cool. What is it they say? Wicked.'

I wish you were.

He smiled enigmatically. If I could have gift-wrapped that smile, taken it home and ravished it in my hallway, I

28

would have done. His wife had suddenly become the most furiously envied woman in the Solent area.

'Yeah. Really wicked! Proper nang! Grimy!'

He looked at me oddly.

'Grimy indeed,' he said, then he swanned off.

Grimy? What the fuck is wrong with me? He thinks I'm insane. Oh well. I have my inbox to look forward to, if only he was in it … Stop!

I was still thinking about Marks, and wondering how the hell I was going to spend week after week working intensively with him on a school production without accidentally dropping my knickers or shoving my tongue down his throat when I logged on to my computer at home.

'Don't expect anything, don't expect anything,' I muttered to myself, mantra-like, waiting for my internet connection to power into action.

I opened the email account I had nominated for notifications from the MasterMe site, purposely looking away so as not to see the number of messages in my inbox until I was fully prepared.

I looked at the screen and breathed in sharply.

Forty-three. Forty-three messages. All from MasterMe.com.

I permitted myself a smile and a quick victory flap of the fingers, then I set to work on the weeding process.

I quickly halved the amount by deleting everyone who wasn't within an hour's travelling distance of me.

A further 11 had enclosed alarming photographic attachments. Farewell to them.

That left 11.

'I don't usually bother with subs over size eight but I might make an exception for you if you're fit.'

Deleted. Ten dom bottles hanging on the wall.

'Suck my cock, bitch.'

And if one dom bottle should accidentally fall…

The next one expressed a desire to pierce my labia and

29

hold a knife to my throat.

That left eight.

The next one – oh, interesting! – was a woman. I chewed my lip over this one for a minute, but regretfully declined her invitation for tea and a caning.

Two more were rejected for their peculiarly hostile and aggressive tone before I narrowed it down to my final five. Each one had his merits. I decided to reply to them all.

StrictButFair was an older gent claiming to be looking for naughty young ladies to tutor in good manners. His techniques were exactly as his name might suggest. It sounded like a bit of fun, if not exactly lifelong-partnership material. I proposed myself as a new entrant to his academy.

MasterAndCommander went into a great deal of detail about his wants, needs, fetishes, likes, dislikes, tastes without asking many questions of me. All the same, his wants, needs, fetishes, likes, dislikes and tastes were all perfectly reasonable and well expressed, as well as largely coinciding with my own. I wrote back with some of my own interests and hoped he would reply.

SirLancelot seemed like a lovely man, almost too lovely to be keen on tying girls up and whipping them, but he liked Vaughan Williams and the Arcade Fire, so I couldn't not respond to him, though most of what I wrote back was about music rather than masochism.

SecretSadist had a wonderful turn of phrase and a wicked sense of humour that set me a-swoon from his first sentence. He was my domcrush from the start. I suggested we exchange photographs. Keen, I know, but sometimes you have to be bold.

The final candidate, VladofWallachia, was so terse his message skirted the borders of hostility, but his photograph was so stunning I discounted this. Shallow, I know, but my eyes were tired and something so easy on them was a rare treat. Plus I needed to look at something pretty that wasn't

Superhead Marks. I needed that man's image right out of my mind's eye.

I wrote back to Vlad, thinking that I really ought to enclose a photo myself. Which one should I choose? Not one with Gareth in it for a start. One wearing my glasses or not? I went for a specs-free shot of me on the Isle of Wight ferry with my hair tangling all over my laughing face. It sounds awful, but it's one of my favourites, and makes me look almost presentable. Perhaps, though, I thought, having pressed "send", I should have chosen a picture of me looking submissive. Except I didn't really have any of those. Oh well. If he recoiled in horror and never wrote back, there was no harm done. This was fun, an adventure. I was expecting some bumps and ego bruises along the way.

I forced myself to log out rather than hang around waiting for replies and went to bed.

Wednesday morning (I wasn't able to resist this time) brought replies from all five. StrictButFair expected me to pay for his exclusive service! The nerve of it. 'Thanks but no thanks,' I trilled, dropping his reply into the recycling bin.

MasterAndCommander asked for a photograph.

SirLancelot had written a long rhapsody on a theme by Paganini. Well, not a theme by Paganini, but all sorts of impressionistic ramblings about life, art, culture, touching only tangentially on BDSM. Tangentially was good though. I could see the virtue of taking things slowly. I gave him a mental nod of approval and filed him away for later.

SecretSadist made me shout with laughter and, while he claimed to have no recent photographs, he described himself as having a devilish smirk and a nice high forehead. 'Let's get better acquainted,' he suggested, 'perhaps in one of these newfangled online relationships

before we take the plunge into (the harbour) a meeting.'
OK, you're the boss, I saluted him, reading further down
his list of attributes. Nice eyes, greenish brown. Large
nose. White shirt. Olive skin. Mmm, I think I could …

'You are pretty,' said Vlad, 'let's meet.'

Oh! So soon? Was this wise? Bugger wise. I hit "reply".

'Maybe a coffee? Saturday morning?'

'You can come to my place.'

'No, I think a coffee first would be best.'

'OK.'

Shit! Do I mean this? Do I really want this?

'So you and Superhead are putting on a show.'

Louisa sounded wistfully jealous and a mite suspicious
as she placed the Friday evening pints on our table at the
Admiral Nelson, our preferred post-school pub.

'Yeah. Auditions are on Monday.'

'I know. Sounds like half the school are going to try out
for it.'

'Good. The buzz around this is really encouraging – I
didn't think anyone would be interested.'

'All the girls are crushing on Superhead. It's because
he's directing. You'll be lucky to get any boys. And
Romilly is spitting chips.'

'Hmm.'

Romilly was Head of Drama. It was a highly
appropriate job title, given her general demeanour. She was
understandably offended that Marks hadn't left the
directing to her. Served her right for being a lazy baggage
who hadn't bothered to put any plays or performances on
for three years, then.

'You weren't here, were you, for Romilly's production
of *Bugsy Malone*?'

The legend of *Bugsy Malone* was so familiar to all at St
Sebastian's that we gave it a minute's silence.

'It was Superhead's idea anyway,' I moved on briskly.

'If she wants to be mad at someone, she can be mad at him.'

'Hard man to be mad at,' said Lou wistfully.

'Yeah, well.' I needed to change the subject. No more discussion of Mr Marks. 'I was wondering if I could ask you a favour, actually.'

'Ask away.'

'I'm meeting someone for coffee tomorrow.'

Lou squealed annoyingly. It wasn't that big a deal, for God's sake.

'Not Duncan, the new Physics teacher, is it?'

'No.'

'Aww. I think you and he would –'

'It's not him,' I said hurriedly. 'It's a guy I met on the internet.'

'Oh! Tell.'

'He's a bit keen,' I confided. 'I don't feel I know him that well, so I was wondering if you could, y'know, keep an eye on things. It's only coffee, tomorrow morning, about 11-ish.'

'Oh God, yes. I'll lurk in the wings, ready to pounce if he puts anything where he shouldn't. What's his name?'

'Er, Vlad. I think.'

'Vlad? Sounds like a vampire.'

'Well, that would be OK.' I grinned. 'Vampires are hot these days.'

'Order a garlic latte, just in case.'

'Will do.'

The weather was still warm, and there were swan pedaloes aplenty rippling the surface of Canoe Lake as Lou and I approached the waterside café.

'I think that's him, by the ice cream kiosk,' I whispered.

'Phwoar, really?'

'Yeah. You go and sit at that table at the far end. I'll follow you in a couple of minutes.'

I lurked behind the wooden structure with its smart blue and white paint job until Louisa had been gone for a while, then I peered around the corner.

Vlad's camera hadn't lied. He was stunning: cheekbones sharper than anything Mr Gillette had ever marketed, full, lush lips, piercing eyes and a fuzz of dark hair all over his perfectly-shaped head. He was wearing combat fatigues and big boots. Underneath, I suspected he was all lean muscle and sinew.

I felt embarrassed at not being a supermodel, but I swallowed my low self-esteem and showed myself.

He stubbed out the roll-up cigarette he had been smoking and stood up, offering a hand.

'Hi,' he said, unsmiling.

'Hi … Vlad,' I said. His hand was big, but there were lots of cuts and nicks on his fingers, and the skin felt like sandpaper.

'My name isn't Vlad. It's Andreu.'

'Oh, right. Well, hi, Andreu. I'm not called AtYourService either.' I laughed, but he didn't join in. 'Cherry,' I elucidated after an awkward beat.

'Ah, like the fruit.'

'Yes. Like the fruit. Hang on, I'll just order …'

'No. You won't order. I'll order. You want coffee?'

'Thanks. Cappuccino, please.'

'No. Not cappuccino.'

What? He wanted to dictate what coffee I could drink? Was that not a bit too much too soon? I watched in bemusement as he went over to the counter, then made a grimace to Lou that I hope she interpreted as "slightly odd beginning, don't go anywhere".

He returned with a cup of strong-looking tea.

'Oh, tea. Lovely.' I took a sip.

'You look like a tea-drinker,' he said, obviously considering this enough in the way of explanation.

'Oh, right. But you aren't. Andreu – what sort of name

34

is that?'

'Romanian. My mother's Romanian. Like Vlad of Wallachia.' He drained the dregs of his coffee and then leant forward, watching me intently, so intently that my hand shook and the teacup began to quiver.

'I know what to do with you,' he announced.

I put the cup down, fascinated.

'I'm going to take you to my flat. You'll get on your knees and suck me until I'm hard. I'll push you down so your face is on the floor, I'll take off my belt and whip you with it till you scream. But that's what you want, isn't it?'

I couldn't reply, my half-open mouth and shallow breaths urging him to continue.

'You want me to fuck you. So I'll fuck you, hard. You'll scream, then I'll call my boys and they'll come and fuck you too.'

I had to stop him there. 'Your boys?'

'My friends. We work together.'

'And … fuck together?'

'When there's a slut who wants it, yes, we fuck together. We fuck the slut until she screams. Come on. Come back and I'll show you.'

'Actually …' I half-stood, looking over to Lou.

'Don't play games with me.' He was snarling, reaching over to grab my wrist. 'You want this.'

'Maybe, Andreu, maybe. But not like this. Not so soon. And not with you. I'm sorry.'

I managed to free my wrist once Andreu noticed people looking at us, and I backed away over to Lou.

'You wasted my time!' he shouted after me. 'You stupid slut!'

'Nice guy!' panted Lou once we had run around the perimeter of the lake and stopped for breath by the statue of the angel. 'Will you see him again?'

'Shut up. He just … It all felt off, that's all. It wasn't right.'

'Pity. What a face. Straight out of an aftershave ad. What the hell did you say to him, to get that reaction?'

'Just that I didn't want to shag on the first date.'

'That's why I don't do internet dating,' said Lou, with an irritating air of conferring great wisdom on the ignorant. 'Too many guys sharpening their penknives for the next notch on the bedpost. Why don't you ask Duncan out?'

'I don't fancy him,' I grumped and we tramped off down the parade towards town to soothe our egos at Karen Millen.

Perhaps this just wasn't for me. Perhaps it was all my fault. Perhaps I should have been up for wild kinky group sex in exchange for one cup of tea. After all, I had been advertising my interest in such things, or Andreu wouldn't have responded.

I wrestled with the aftermath of the dating disaster, lying on my sofa, listening to Wagnerian *sturm und drang*. How safe was I in trusting my instincts? After all, I had been happy to bring Stuart back for activities most would consider inappropriate for such a brief term of acquaintanceship – why was he OK and Andreu not?

I supposed Stuart had seemed in control of himself, and considerate of my feelings, whereas Andreu had visibly seethed with all kinds of unsettling qualities. Hostility? Resentment? Hatred? Misogyny? I didn't know him well enough to understand what might have been behind his behaviour, but whatever it was, it wasn't my problem, and I wasn't about to make it so.

I lifted the lid of my laptop. Should I? Could I? Was it best if I just deleted my profile off MasterMe and … No, I was not going to ask Duncan out. No way.

And Andreu was just one man, surely unrepresentative of domkind. I would get better at this. I would learn to sort the wheat from the chaff. The masters from the twats. I sat up, put back my shoulders and logged on.

Chapter Three

'GET YOUR EGG TIMER, set it for thirty minutes, go to the corner of your room and stay there until you hear the alarm go off.'

I read through the instructions quickly then typed back.

'Why?'

'Because I told you to.'

I flipped my computer screen the bird and whispered, 'Because you're an asshole!' but I was grinning as I went to the kitchen to carry out the task.

SecretSadist and I had a thing going on, though it was probably nothing as tangible as an affair, or as respectable as a relationship. It was, at this stage, just a thing. He sent me tasks and I completed them.

I heard the little xylophoney blurt that announced another message.

'Have you done it yet?'

'No, obviously, or I wouldn't be replying.'

'I don't care for your tone, young lady. While you're in the corner, I want you to consider long and hard what you have been sent there for. I want you to imagine all the things I might have in store for you, to teach you the lesson you so badly need. When you come out, I want you to tell me what you think you deserve in the way of punishment. Do you understand me?'

'Yes, sir.'

'What are you going to be punished for?'

'Excessive levity, sir.'

'Exactly. Not to mention insolence.'

'Oh, on that subject, I should confess that I just called you an asshole, sir. Sorry about that.'

'You will be! Now set that timer and get to the corner. Thank you for your honesty btw.'

I put down the timer and put my nose in the corner, imagining SecretSadist to be sitting in my armchair, long legs crossed, hands steepled, spectacles halfway down his nose.

Now this, I thought, folding my hands behind my back, was more like it. The kind of fun that made me squirmy and damp between the thighs, without the fear or unpredictability of that awful meeting with Andreu last weekend. SecretSadist seemed to have the measure of me, gleaned from a great many evening conversations by instant messenger, during which we had pared our kinks down to the bone. They matched. And he was in no hurry to corral me into a meeting. We were going to take it slowly, see how things went.

I shut my eyes and relaxed into the feeling. I was wearing, as instructed, only my underwear, including a pair of stockings and suspenders I hadn't seen since that wet weekend in Bognor with Gareth. My nipples were teased by the chafing lace of my bra cup, held in a state of perfect stiffness, waiting for a touch, a kiss, anything to justify their engorged ripeness. Cool air drifted down my bare spine to the powder-blue suspender belt, on which my crossed hands rested, the thumbs pulling at the elastic for something to do. My thighs were goosepimpled above the stocking tops. I rubbed them together, enjoying the friction of my silky knickers against my clit. Was I allowed to do this? Was I allowed to be frisky in the corner? I would have to ask.

Perhaps it would add to my punishment. Oh, glory. Just the thought of the word, not even spoken out loud, made my stomach tighten and my knickers drench. SecretSadist was going to punish me. But how? I pushed back my bottom, feeling the silk stretch tauter over my cheeks, imagining myself bent over for SecretSadist's cane.

Oh God. How much longer? I peeked at the egg timer. Still ages to go.

How would his hands feel, on my slippery, sheeny bum? Patting and tapping, stroking and sliding and then, smack, a hot red handprint to remember him by. Would he be very angry with me if I unclasped my hands and slid a finger inside the elastic ..? I didn't have to tell him.

No, Cherry, you do.

There was no point to this if I was going to cheat. I had to follow the orders to the letter, or I might as well give up.

If I was going to make it through the next twenty minutes, though, I needed to stop thinking horny thoughts and empty my mind.

Empty your mind, empty your mind …

Was Kacey McMillan really going to cut the mustard as Maria? She had quite a good voice, but it had a strident quality that didn't really suit the gentle Hispanic heroine of *West Side Story*. Never knowingly seen without gum in her mouth or twenty pounds of gold hanging off her ears, Kacey had a bray that could be heard on the Isle of Wight. She had been delighted to win the role of Maria "'cos it's like, next stop *X Factor*, innit?' but had shown little knowledge or understanding of what winning that role might now entail. In a word, work. Hard work. Something Kacey wasn't renowned for.

At least Tony was going to be played by Tunde. As a teacher, I wasn't supposed to have favourites, but I could hardly help being won over by Tunde's natural musicality and sensitivity. Some days, he was the only person who spoke to me in more than a monosyllable. He worked hard and with genuine enthusiasm in composition lessons because, as he said, 'I need to work out how to get all these sounds in my head down on paper.' He played the French horn and the electric guitar like a pro, and he had the most beautiful mellow voice. Listening to it was like lying back in a bath of warm chocolate.

But Tunde and Kacey … Hardly the pair you'd put together.

Still, Superhead thought it would work. If it failed, he would take the rap.

A rap across the knuckles.

Chastisement.

Discipline.

My thighs squeezed tight again. No matter what I thought about, it came back to the imminence of my punishment. I was supposed to be thinking about my wrongdoings. What were they? Over the course of our week-long thing, I had been guilty of flippancy, cheek and teasing SecretSadist about his job (accountancy). When I'd found out he kept a spreadsheet balance of my bad behaviour and its consequences, I started taking his qualifications seriously. Accountants made good doms, of course they did. Who better to hold one to account?

I pictured the spreadsheet, a long list of black marks in one column and then, in the other … What? What would my punishment be?

The egg timer buzzed and my pulse raced. I wasn't ready to come out of the corner and face my fate. I needed to stand there for longer, letting the dread seep into my pores and permeate my being. But he would be waiting for me, so I padded over to the computer and typed in the words, 'I'm ready, sir,' even though I wasn't.

'Good. Did you behave yourself in the corner?'

'Yes, sir! I thought about … doing things … but I didn't.'

'Good. I won't enquire… So? Your thoughts? What might your just desserts be?'

I almost typed "trifle" but I held back, knowing that this would hardly be in the spirit of contrition SecretSadist had hoped to instil.

'I'm not sure. Maybe I should get sent to bed without supper.'

'Maybe.'

Ugh, no. Not sexy. Don't do that!

'Or ...'

'???'

'Something embarrassing ... I can't say it ...'

'Say it. Go on.'

'If you were here ...'

'If I were there ...'

'You could put me over your knee ...'

'And?'

'Give me what I deserve.'

'Which is?'

'Argh! Don't make me say it!'

'I'm not. This is typeface. I'll make you say it when we meet, though, make no mistake. So? I'm waiting. It'll be worse for you if you make me hang on much longer.'

'Damn it! You could spank me.'

'Language, young lady! Yes, I certainly think you've earned a spanking. If only I were there, I'd have you over my knee right now.'

' ... '

'I'd pull your scanty silky knickers down to your knees, miss, and then I'd smack your bare bottom hard until it glowed redder than fire.'

'Ouch.'

'And if you weren't sorry, I'd make you fetch your hairbrush and I'd apply it to your stinging rump until you begged for mercy. And then I'd spank you some more.'

'I'll bear it in mind.'

'You'll bear it on your bottom. Your bare bottom. One day. Soon.'

'Eek. (Can't wait).'

'But for now your naughtiness will have to be dealt with

41

otherwise. I can't very well ask you to spank yourself, can I?'

'S'pose not.'

'What I can do is unpick the threads of what makes a spanking such an effective form of discipline and try to apply those elements in a different way. So, brainstorm for me, what's so bad about a spanking?'

'Umm, it hurts, for one.'

'Right. Pain. What else?'

'It's embarrassing.'

'Excellent! Embarrassment.'

'And humbling.'

'Humiliation. My favourite. Anything else?'

'Makes me feel submissive and powerless.'

'Exactly. And, dare I suggest, excited?'

'When it's over.'

'It makes you wet?'

'*blush* yes, sir.'

'I like it when you blush. On both sets of cheeks.'

'So do I.'

'Do you have a vibrator?'

'No, sir.'

'Seriously? I thought everyone had them these days.'

'I've thought about getting one … Just never got around to it.'

'Well, that's good.'

'Why, sir?'

'Because your punishment is this. You will put a coat – nothing else – over your underwear and walk to the nearest adult shop. Do you have one nearby?'

I didn't reply for several minutes. I was too aghast to type. Yes, there was a sex shop in Albert Road, about 15 minutes' walk away, but, but, but …

'What if a pupil/parent/member of staff sees me?'

'It's dark, isn't it? And there's no law against teachers having sex lives, is there?'

42

'There might be. Even if there isn't, I bet there's a White Paper about it somewhere in the system.'

'You can get a cab if you want. Straight in and out, nobody will see you.'

'Ugh. I suppose so. It's such a seedy little place, though, looks as if it smells funny inside.'

'Probably does. All the better for your punishment, my dear.'

'Humph.'

'Don't sulk. Once you're inside, you will buy a pair of nipple clamps and a vibrator. But – here's the humiliating element – you won't browse the shelves for them. You will ask the sales assistant for them.'

'OH GOD NO!'

'Oh God yes. You can refuse if you want, but it'll mean Game Over.'

'No, I'll do it. But can't I go to the neighbouring town?'

'If you want to spend the cab fare, be my guest. I don't care which sex shop you go to, just as long as you go to one. And I want it to be the old-fashioned sleazy type. No "for the girls" frills and trappings. Do you understand?'

'Yeah.'

'That sounded a mite sulky, was it intended to be?'

'No, sir!'

'Good. When you've bought them, come back and message me. I'll give you some more instructions.'

'OK.'

'Not "OK", AtYourService. Do you need more time in the corner?'

'No, sir. I meant "Yes, sir".'

'I'm sure you did. Now go and get your coat and ring that cab. I'll speak to you later.'

'Goodbye, sir. Thank you, sir.'

I logged off, my hands shaking. Was I going to do this?

I picked up the phone, put it down, picked it up again. Dialled the number of the cab firm I always used, put it down again. Picked it up, dialled again.

'Hi, I need a cab to Albert Road, please. From South Parade Gardens. For Cherry. Thanks.'

I contemplated myself in the full-length hall mirror, reaching for my longest coat. The silky knickers were spotted with evidence of my arousal and my nipples formed hard protrusions through the flimsy bra cup. I was turned on. SecretSadist was evil, but he knew exactly how far and how hard to push me. Impressive. When could we meet?

I pulled on the coat and buttoned it to the neck. The satiny lining felt cold and smooth against the bare expanses of my skin, brushing my bottom where the knickers rose in a high cut, swishing around my nude thighs.

In the cab, I shifted around, finding the silkiness too slippery to settle, pinching my coat closed in case it should fall open and reveal too much to the driver.

'Just on the corner here. Can you wait for me? I'll be five minutes, ten tops.'

'OK.'

It was early evening and the street wasn't too busy. An hour earlier it would have been filled with student types seeking vintage clothing and original pressings of Led Zeppelin LPs. In about an hour, it would be filled with student types seeking beer and snogs. But for now, it was relatively safe to keep that coat hem scrunched in my fist and run, clip-clop, across the pavement to the shop.

It could hardly look less welcoming. The frontage was painted in an unattractive brown, while the window was blanked out by beige strip blinds. Parceltaped to the door were a variety of handwritten notices, including one that said "Are you over 18?" and another than forbade smoking on the premises.

I didn't dare look around me to see if I was observed, but quickly pushed open the door, finding the shop empty but for a bored-looking young woman reading a magazine.

'Can I help?' she asked.

I sighed a breath of enormous relief. Thank God she was a woman. This wouldn't be quite so bad as I'd thought.

'Yeah, uh, I'm looking for a good vibrator.' The words just came out! And nothing happened, except that she smiled faintly, revealing lipstick-coloured teeth.

'Oh right. Most of the girls like this one.' She pulled out a flesh-pink thing with some kind of mechanism at the base. 'Cos it's got, like, a clit-stimulator too, yeah? What do you think? It's our top seller.'

'I'll take it,' I said without pausing to even look at it. Hearing this woman talk about clit stimulators in her flat estuarine accent as if they were vegetables on a grocery list was making me want to giggle.

She shoved it into a brown paper bag.

'Twenty quid, love,' she said.

'Oh, there was something else.' I swallowed. Vibrators were easy to buy – they had become an acceptable thing to carry in one's handbag along with the lipsticks and breath mints – but my other item was rather less so.

She paused, hanging on to the bag, sword-like blue fingernails poised over the cash register.

I lowered my voice, hoping the words wouldn't get stuck in my throat.

'Nipple clamps.'

Her perfectly plucked eyebrows leapt.

'What sort? Clover or regular?'

'Oh … I don't know …'

'Hang on. *Steve*!' She bellowed through a doorway hung with a plastic strip curtain.

Could I leave with just one of the items on the list? Could I just slap the twenty down and snatch the bag and run?

A huge man in dark glasses appeared. Behind the glasses it was entirely possible he was checking me out.

45

'Customer wants nipple clamps but she don't know if she wants clover or regular. Can you get the display ones out to show her?'

'Sure.' He took a key from his jeans pocket and unlocked a cabinet under the counter. 'Are they for you?' he asked, producing a box of little silvery tormentors.

No, they're for my aunt's Christmas stocking. Of course they're for me.

I nodded, staring at the objects. Should I ask for a recommendation? Horribly aware of the man's fascination, I decided to choose quickly, before he started licking his lips.

'Them!' I said, jabbing a finger at the prettiest pair. They looked like earrings with a series of crystal drops dangling from the ends.

'Right you are,' he said. 'Not the most painful. Are you new to this kind of sensation play?'

'Yes. How much do I owe you?' I really didn't want to get drawn into a conversation.

'Thirty four pounds ten,' contributed the woman.

'He's in for a treat.' Steve smirked.

'Or she,' I said primly, and then he really did lick his lips.

'Ah,' he said.

I threw down the money, grabbed the bag and made an abrupt about-face, forgetting in my confusion to hang on to the hem of the coat as I raced along the pavement to my waiting cab.

I'm pretty sure he got an eyeful of stocking and suspendered thigh.

Oh well.

I hung up my coat, threw down the bag and logged on.

'Are you there?'

'Hello, AtYourService. Did you succeed in your task?'

'I've got what you asked for.'

'Good girl. Describe what happened for me.'

I typed a brief paragraph outlining the purchase of the items.

'Was it really like that?'

'Yes. It was really like that.'

'Well, so you say, but I think it was really like this …'

I leant forward, expectant.

'Are you wearing your coat?'

'No.'

'Put it on.'

I did so and came back.

'Ready?'

'Yes, sir.'

'You pushed open the door to find the shop full of men, browsing the magazines and fetish toys. Each and every one of them looked up when you entered the room, and their greedy, lecherous eyes stayed on you as you walked to the counter to make your request of the woman there. The phrase "being undressed by a man's eyes" came into your head and stayed there, as you became uncomfortably convinced that they all knew what you were – or weren't – wearing under your coat. Behind you, you could hear whispers, even the odd hint of a growl. They were watching you. You asked the woman to show you the vibrators. She took out a selection and, while you looked at them, she asked the men which one they would recommend. One or two of the customers were behind you now, looking over your shoulder, breathing on your neck. They asked you how big you liked it and whether you needed strong or weak vibration settings. Somehow you knew you had to answer their questions, and by the time they were finished you had outlined every exquisite detail of your penetration preferences, so that all in the room knew that you liked a big cock, a hard, forceful fuck and plenty of clitoral stimulation. The woman chose the vibrator she thought would suit you, then you asked for the nipple clamps.

'Steve came into the shop with the tray.

'"We have different sizes. The best way is to try a few on," he said. "Why don't you take off your coat?"

'You hesitated, looking behind you for the door, trying to judge how quickly you could get there, but your feet wouldn't move.

'"Oh, she's shy," laughed the woman. "Boys, help her off with her coat."

'(Take off your coat, AYS.)'

I stood up and shrugged it off, my mouth dry. I saw that part of the lining was damp where I had been sitting. I sat back down on the swivel chair and typed, fingers trembling.

'Have done, sir.'

'Good. You stood in the shop, surrounded on all sides by salivating men, in your tiny silky undies, stockings and heels. Now the growling was louder, there were whistles and low-voiced comments.

'"She's come in here dressed for sex."

'"She wants more than a vibe and set of clamps, mate."

'"Look at that arse! And those tits. I hope she shows us her pussy too."

'The shopkeeper, Steve, smiled at you.

'"Lovely outfit. We've got some underwear you might like here. I think a bit of latex would suit you, actually. What do you think?"

'You told them you couldn't afford anything extra today.

'"Another time then."

'He picked up a pair of clamps, the ones that you chose.

'Go and fetch them, AYS.'

I tipped them out of the bag. They jingled faintly. Such dainty, delicate things – could they really be that painful?

'I've got them, sir.'

'Good girl. He came around to the front of the counter and sat himself down on it, facing you. You made no

48

sound, not even the teeniest little protest, when he reached out his hands and tucked the cups of your bra down underneath your breasts with his thumbs – though you did flinch just a little. Those big, rough thumbs rubbed across your nipples, finding them stiff and swollen. Pull down your bra cups, AYS, and caress your nipples for me.'

They were, as he said, stiff and swollen. The feel of my thumbs against the sensitive flesh made me gasp.

'How does it feel?'

'They're huge, sir, and very sensitive.'

'Good. By now, the customers were heaving and surging around you, desperate to touch you the way Steve was doing, but the woman urged them to be patient and just watch. Perhaps their turn would come later. Steve took one clamp, opened it, then placed it gently on your left nipple. You know what I want you to do.'

I took up one clamp, which was like a slimmer version of a tweezer, and opened its rubber-coated ends. Grimacing before I had even applied it, I positioned the suddenly mean-looking tips either side of my nipple, then let them move inward, slowly, slowly, until they touched the flesh. The pressure increased infinitesimally with each fractional releasing of my finger and thumb. I began to pant and then uttered a heartfelt "yeowch" when I let go. The crystals swayed and stroked the underside of my breast. It hurt, but I worked on controlling my panic and soon the immediate crisis receded, the pain becoming duller and more manageable.

'I'm wearing it, sir.'

'What's happening?'

'It was a sharp pain to begin with, but it's not so bad now. Just a kind of throb. Still hurts, though.'

'Good. Keep it on. Steve watched your face as the clamp bit into you with obvious satisfaction.

'"Painful, eh?"

'"Yes, Sir."

'You didn't know why you'd called him "sir" – it just slipped out. He seemed mighty pleased with it and stroked a finger down your cheek before applying the right clamp ...'

I didn't need the instruction this time. I just did it, quicker than before, screwing up my eyes for the momentary flash of hot pain, then opening them slowly.

'I have both clamps on, sir.'

'Good. Keep them on until I tell you otherwise.'

'Will do, sir.'

'Then Steve took hold of your shoulders and turned you slowly around, to show the men how you looked with your juicy little nipples trapped in the clamps. They wanted to touch them, of course, but Steve forbade it and you were relieved, because they had never felt so unbearably sensitive as this. Once he was sure everyone had had a good look, he picked up the vibrator ...'

I reached over for the plastic bag and took the pink silicone monstrosity from its box. God, did it come with batteries supplied? I pressed the button quickly and was reassured by the low buzz that issued from it. Good.

'Got it, sir.'

'Thank you for telling me. Steve told you that he was unwilling to sell you the vibrator until you had sampled it and found it to your satisfaction. When he ordered you to bend over the counter, you did so without question. The beads from your nipple clamps made a clattering sound over the glass top and you squeaked as the nipples made contact with the cold, cold surface.

'Steve pulled down your knickers, nice and slowly, so that the silky material whispered over your well presented bum, tickled your thighs and came to rest by the suspender snaps. They could go no lower, which wasn't ideal for Steve's purposes, so he took a big pair of scissors and cut them off.'

'Oh!'

'Don't cut yours up. Just take them off.'

'OK.'

'Then his big, rough hand slipped between your thighs and his fingers dipped into your displayed cunt, finding it soaking wet. He ordered you to spread your legs as wide as they would go, then he held up his shiny, coated fingers to the rest of the room, so that they all would know just what a horny slut you were.

'"I think she needs this, lads."

'They cheered and jostled forwards, all eager to see your tight wet pussy and your fat, red clit.

'Steve picked up the vibrator and began to insert it, with torturous slowness, up inside you. You were gasping and mewling with need, begging him to stuff it in and fill you up, but he took his time, inch by inch, opening you up in front of everyone until the silicone cock was up to the hilt and the clit stimulator rested against your little button. Shall I give you a minute?'

I was puffing and panting with the effort of squeezing the vibrator up inside me, leaning over the computer desk with my knickers down and the nipple clamps swinging merrily. Once it was all the way in, I felt almost ready to come then and there – something about its design meant that it maintained pressure on my G-spot and was holding me in a state of near-climax right from the start. This story might be ending sooner than SecretSadist intended.

'Are you still there?'

One shaking finger typed, 'Yes.'

'Close?'

'Yes.'

'You will not come until I say so. So … there you were, bent over the counter, clamped and spread-legged while Steve rotated the vibrator inside your clenching cunt. He invited each of the men in turn to come and see your exposure at close quarters. They would crouch, sniffing at your juicy pussy, seeing the pink latex thrust in and out, looking further up the curve of your arse, which jiggled and wobbled. Steve gave them each permission to touch your arse while he continued to handle the vibe firmly. Their hands petted and patted and parted your cheeks, unfamiliar fingers sliding inside the crack and poking at the little pucker. You came hard, over and over again, with a different man's finger up your arsehole each time, pushing back on them, begging for mercy, begging for more. You may come now.'

It was too late. I already had, about halfway through the paragraph, as soon as he got to the bit about the strange men sniffing me. I slumped over the keyboard.

'isaht;oiahn;ogihnwo;aihnoei,' I typed.

By the time I was able to raise my head, having pulled the vibe slowly from my still-spasming pussy, he had typed quite a few more lines.

'That's the effect I was aiming for.'

Then, 'AtYourService?'

'Where are you?'

'Have you passed out? That's one good vibrator.'

I put my elbows on the desk and hit the keys slowly and haphazardly.

'I camw reiauly harkd.'

'So it seems.'

But now I had a confession. I had not waited for his permission. Should I tell him? Should I earn further punishment? Or would he appreciate my honesty and let me off? I waited for my fingers to stop doing their impression of leaves in the wind and pressed my lips together.

'I have to apologise for something.'

'Really? What's that? Don't tell me you faked it.'

'No, no, I did everything you said. To the letter. But I didn't wait for your permission to come. I was already coming when you gave it.'

Seconds ticked by. I bit down on my forefinger,

desperate for the little bleep heralding an incoming message.

'I'm very sorry, sir,' I typed into the silence.

Then, 'I understand if you want to punish me.'

Ah, a response.

'You have many lessons to learn, AtYourService, but I'm a patient man and I like to teach. If you were the fully formed submissive, I would have no challenge, and I would be bored. So don't worry about needing instruction. I can give it.'

'Thank you, sir.'

'Now, you'll need to be taking those clips off. And do it slowly. You'll find the sensation quite intense.'

I shook my head, astonished that I had forgotten all about the clamps. The dull throb of my nipples had faded into the background once my lust had flooded in.

SecretSadist was quite right. My nipples roared back to painful life as soon as the little tormentors were removed and I danced around the room on tiptoes, making every grimace under the sun, relieved that nobody could see me.

'OUCH!' I typed.

'Ha. Painful, eh?'

'Very.'

'What do your nipples look like?'

'Red alert.'

'I'll bet. So, you mentioned a punishment. Well …'

Oh dear. The ellipse stretched out to the crack of doom.

'Today is Saturday. Until next Saturday, nothing will touch your pussy. I am sentencing you to a virtual chastity belt.'

'No orgasms?'

'That's correct. Just goodness and virtue, for a whole week. I shall expect you to check in with me every evening at approximately nine o'clock, when I shall weave you a filthy fantasy in which you will star. But you will not touch yourself, just read it and weep. Or squirm.'

'That's awfully cruel, sir. Brilliantly cruel, in fact.'
'I know. Goodnight, AYS. Behave yourself.'
'Goodnight, sir. I will.'

It was an arduous week. Every day I worked hard, every evening I did my marking, did my planning, then logged on to read another of SecretSadist's gothically kinky sex fantasies. I felt my clit swell and my pussy flood, my knickers grow wet and my nipples grow hard, but I kept my hands on the keyboard, as ordered, throughout.

Afterwards, I would take a shower, a vain attempt to wash away my arousal, but the silky, soapy shower gel felt so sensuous and the steam so humid that it made it worse. It would take just the stroke of a fingertip …

I took to wearing a pair of those tight figure-fixer knickers to bed, just because they were so damn hard to wriggle a hand inside. I would lie on my front, thighs clamped together, hands raised up above my head, face pressed into the pillow, trying to think about anything but SecretSadist and when we might meet and what might happen at that meeting.

My dreams were vivid and overblown with sensual imagery. I was tied to a tree; I was lying in a bath of feathers that tickled me beyond endurance; a hairdryer was being blown all over my body; a thick snake parted my thighs and pressed its head to my pussy lips.

I think I must have had orgasms in my sleep. It certainly felt like it. But I couldn't be held accountable for those, could I? I couldn't definitively say they had happened. My chastity was intact.

By Friday's *West Side Story* rehearsal, I felt drugged with the need to come, heavy and thick-headed with inescapable sensuality. How on earth I was supposed to shake out of it before Superhead rolled up with his sharp suit and sexy voice I just didn't know.

The kids did their best for me, though, scuffling in a

corner of the hall so that I had to get my mind out of my knickers and into firefighting mode quick smart. Always a reliable bromide, the little charmers of St Sebastian's.

I was reading the riot act to CJ and Lanh when Mr Marks glided on to the scene, causing a deathly hush to fall on the previously overexcited audience.

'Can I believe my eyes?' he asked with deceptive calm, switching a stern gaze from one boy to the other. 'Has Ms Delaney, who is giving so generously of her free time so that you can enjoy the privilege of taking part in a performance, had to break up a fight at a rehearsal?'

'He dissed the Buckland Boyz,' muttered Lanh.

'He … Are you serious? He dissed the Buckland Boyz? Well, so do I. I diss the Buckland Boyz, if this is their idea of acceptable behaviour. Are you going to fight me too?'

I held my breath. This was a high-risk tactic. There were plenty of boys who would stab a teacher under less provocation than this. But Lanh simply shuffled his feet, pouted and shrugged.

'Take your places for the first scene.'

Lanh trudged off to join his fellow Sharks at the back of the hall while CJ took to the stage with the rest of the Jets.

Carnage averted. And – action.

'It was OK,' I muttered to Superhead, heading for the pile of music scores on the piano. 'I had the situation in hand.'

'I'm sure you did,' he said. 'But I'm the head. I have to stride in with my cape flying, ready to unleash the superpowers. That's my job.'

I laughed out loud. He had to know what his nickname was.

All that and a sense of humour too…

'I'm just glad I've got such a terrific Lois Lane,' he said, turning away while I caught a breath.

Lois Lane?

No. He just meant that we were a partnership in the

production of this musical. That was all. I wasn't going to cradle him in my arms while he was fatally weakened by Kryptonite. Neither were we scheduled to fly through the stars over the bright lights of Metropolis. Alas.

'More like Robin,' I said to his back and I saw his shoulders shake before he looked back at me.

'Holy self-deprecating humour!' he said.

I'm in love.

I picked up the scores and began to distribute them, hardly able to speak for the rest of the rehearsal.

I deliberately avoided Superhead at the end, leaving with a gaggle of overexcited faux-Latinas clicking fake castanets after the first run-through of *America*.

I rode my bicycle super-heroically fast through the Friday evening traffic on Albert Road, whizzing past the sex shop of my shame without giving it a second glance until I was home and ready to throw something into a saucepan and log on.

It was only half-past six. SecretSadist was offline.

I picked up my phone and read Lou's text again. There was a good film on at the cinema. Did I want to meet her at All Bar One at seven for a drink beforehand?

Or did I want to come?

What a choice. Go to the flicks or – flick.

I decided to email SecretSadist and tell him I was going out, so was it possible to reschedule our "date".

By the time my pasta had reached boiling point, he had replied.

'Of course. As it happens, I'm busy later too. Shall we wait until tomorrow?'

Tomorrow?

'But I'm dying of frustration!'

'Excuse me, AtYourService, you seem to think a week lasts six days. You don't get to come until tomorrow.'

'Srsly?!?!'

'V srsly.'

Oh, the despair. I prayed for no sexy scenes during the movie, but there were several moments when I had to shift uncomfortably against the velvet and cross my legs tight.

Back in the bar afterwards, I thought about getting drunk. Would that make things worse or better? I sniffed at my first gin and tonic, seeking out traces of ardour-dampener and finding none, when suddenly the biggest ardour-dampener in the world strolled up and inserted itself right between me and Louisa.

'So how was the film, ladies?' it asked with a misplaced chortle. Had anyone said anything funny? I thought not.

'Duncan!' gushed Lou. 'How lovely! Who are you out with?'

'Oh, nobody. Just a Friday night out with my favourite person.' He chortled again. Why do people chortle? It's so unattractive.

'How do you know we've been to the cinema?' I asked, suspicion of Lou's motives evident from my tone.

'Saw you come out,' he said. 'Followed you. What did you see?'

OK, that seemed to let Lou off the hook, though I supposed even Duncan wasn't incapable of a spot of light subterfuge.

'*All the Single Ladies*,' said Lou, beaming sweetly. 'Kind of appropriate for Chez and me.' I wondered if she was going to nudge him and wink next.

'God, can't believe you're single,' he said with a disbelieving shake of his puppy-like head. 'What's wrong with the men around here?'

'Most of them are sailors,' said Lou pensively.

Duncan did a weird kind of snorting thing.

'My mates warned me against coming here when I applied for the job,' he said. 'Said it was rough. But it's fine! Can I get you ladies a drink?'

'So you're single then, Duncan?' Louisa moved ahead with her scheme.

One excruciatingly tedious hour later, I left Louisa and Duncan alone, the alcohol plan having failed to dull my need for orgasm.

Just another night.

In my bed, I relived Duncan's conversational techniques in order to dampen my ardour. He was a man who enjoyed doing poor impressions of celebrities and saw no purpose to speech other than to try and make its recipients snigger. His singular unfunniness stopped irritating me after a while, and I began to feel sorry for him, which in turn irritated me again. I didn't want Duncan in my consciousness, either as an annoyance or a figure to be pitied.

Beside my bed, my phone bleeped.

'Y did u go home? Me n D goin 2 TigerTiger, come on, dont b a killjoy x'.

They'd end up snogging and then she would regret it and there would be an awkward atmosphere between them for the rest of the academic year.

'Gone 2 bed. B careful x.' I texted back, wondering how I had the gall to advise somebody else on self-preservation when my own life seemed such a high-risk enterprise these days.

SecretSadist took pity on me in the end and didn't make me wait until nine o'clock at night to end my orgasm ban.

Instead we arranged to "meet" online at three o'clock that afternoon.

I had to get a messy, hungover Lou off the phone by five to, which was difficult, because she had many lamentations on the theme of having just kicked Duncan out of her bed to express.

I invented a hair appointment and promised to meet her for brunch the next day, then sat down at the computer and waited with bated breath.

I was wearing my favourite underwear set, for some

reason, with my Chinese silk wrap over the top, barefoot and perfumed. It felt like an Occasion, so I'd even put on a necklace and some lipstick. I wanted SecretSadist to see me. I wanted him to watch this. I decided to ask about Skyping with webcams as a next step.

When he started things off with 'Good afternoon, AtYourService,' I replied quickly and eagerly, tapping with manicured nails.

'Good afternoon, sir, I wish you could see me now.'

'Why?'

'I've dressed for the occasion.'

'Oh good – what are you wearing?'

'Very little. I have my silk wrap on – it's red with a pattern of blue butterflies and pink and green flowers, and some black and gold around the hems. It's very delicate and very thin. I can hardly feel I'm wearing it.'

'And is it all you're wearing?'

'No. Underneath I have my new red and black bra and knickers. They're mesh fabric – like fishnet – with tiny red bows at the front and red ribbon ties at the side of the knickers.'

'Easy to undo, then.'

'Very easy.'

'Stockings?'

'Sorry, no stockings. Didn't have a matching suspender belt. I can put on some hold-ups if you like.'

'No, don't worry. I'm picturing you. Take off the wrap.'

'Yes, sir. I'm wearing dark red lipstick too, and a thin silver chain around my neck and wrist. I wish you could see me.'

'So do I. But for now, I want you to spread your legs wide so they dangle off the corners of your chair.'

'Yes, sir.'

'I'm going to tell you a story. And you aren't to come until the very end of the story. But, while I'm telling it, I want one of your hands inside your bra, playing with your nipples, and the other down the front of your knickers, pressed up close to your clit. Can you do that for me, AtYourService?'

'Yes, sir.' But could I? Could I wait until the end, in that position?

I found one of my warm, hardening buds inside the bra cup and fiddled with it while my other fingers slipped down, every knuckle visible through the mesh, burrowing into the humid wetness between my pussy lips.

'Are you ready? Then I'll begin.

'You have been sent to my house tonight, knowing nothing about who I am, with an envelope to give me. When you left the bureau after your case conference, the taxi was called for you and all you had to do was get inside and be driven to the destination predetermined by the court. Sitting in the back of the taxi, you are nervous, butterflies in the stomach, hands folded neatly in your lap, neck twisted to your right so you can look out of the window without having to face or converse with the cab driver. You were in an isolation booth while the caseworkers met to discuss your fate, so you have no idea of the sentence they have handed down. It could be a compulsory work order. It could be period of detention. It could be – something else.'

I bet it's something else.

My clit swelled, pushing into my fingertips. I didn't dare move.

'You are wearing a simple prison-issue smock dress, short and white, just about covering your bottom and skimming your thighs, with flat white tennis shoes and bare legs. You keep your knees tightly together in case the cabbie is perving on you. If you parted them, he might see the plain white cotton briefs that are the only things standing between your cunt and the curious eyes of the world.

'After a ten minute drive, the cab pulls into a wide gravel drive behind a high brick wall. You crane your neck,

60

spying a house at the end. The house is large, but it doesn't look institutional. It looks like someone's home, with welcoming lights in the windows and hanging baskets by the door. Could this be where you will pass your sentence? It seems so ... nice.

'The driver opens the door for you, and you step out on to the gravel, preparing to climb the steps. But before you can make a move, he holds out a hand. "You'll need to give me your knickers," he says.

'"Excuse me?" You sound indignant and ready to argue, but he simply crooks his fingers, cold and implacable.

'He'll be watching, and if you disobey, he'll be harder on you.'

'He?'

'You look up at the windows. There is movement behind an upstairs curtain. You are being watched.

'The night is chilly and you feel the draught travel up beneath your brief skirt as you reach up to remove the knickers. You pull them down awkwardly, holding your skirt pressed to your thighs with your forearms so that the motion is stiff and tricky and you almost fall sideways, but eventually the knickers are off and you hand them to the taxi driver with a sulky grimace.

'He feels the gusset between thumb and finger.

'"Damp," he says with a grin, then he takes a good long sniff. "He'll like you."

'Fear replaces your outrage.

'"Who is he? What is this place?"

'"Go in. You'll soon find out."

'He watches you from the side of the taxi while you try to ascend the steps without letting your tiny skirt ride up and show him your bum – not an easy task.

'There is no doorbell, nor a knocker, but when you touch one of the wooden panels of the door it swings open and you step into a large, empty hall.

'You look around at the curving staircase, the parquet

61

tiles, the handsome coat and umbrella stands, the antique desks and furnishings. A vase of lilies stands on a table at the foot of the stairs and you are drawn to its heavy fragrance.

'"Stand still and put your hands on your head." The voice comes from the top of the stairs.

'You are still carrying the envelope, so it flaps over your hands as you stand waiting and watching me descend. When I reach the bottom, I ask you to hand over the envelope, which you do, before returning to your commanded stance.

'I open it and read.

'"I see," I say and you search my face for a clue to your fate. You see nothing. "Walk into the room to your right, please."

'You walk, hands still on your head, through a set of double doors into a large, high-ceilinged room. In the doorway, you stop short until I nudge you forward with a hand between your shoulder blades. The room is full of people. People you know. People you have sinned against, lied to, insulted, cheated.

'"You'll see that we were having a meeting," I tell you. "A meeting all about you. We care about you, AtYourService. We want what's best for you, just as the courts do. We are here to see that your sentence is served."

'You turn to face me, agitated. "What's my sentence?"

'"You are to carry out your compulsory work order here, in my service, performing required domestic tasks in that tiny little uniform dress of yours and completing them to my high standards. In between the scrubbing of floors and peeling of potatoes, you are to report three times a day to my office for a scheduled spanking."

'"A what?" You are aghast. Nobody has ever dared to touch a hair of your naughty little head until today.

'"A scheduled spanking, the severity of which will depend on your attitude. The sentence will end when I am

62

sincerely convinced of your improved behaviour and self-control."

"'I won't!" you cry, looking for a way out. "I refuse to accept this!"

"'You have no choice. The alternative is life imprisonment. Before that part of your sentence begins, there is one additional element, which we will deal with now."

'I take your arm and lead you to a tall stool in the centre of the room.

"'Bend over the stool now. In front of these witnesses, all of whom have been wronged by you, you will receive 12 hard strokes of the cane."

"'I can't ..." Your horror is strong, but you are slowly realising that there is no point resisting me. Not now, at any rate. You vow revenge, you determine to plot your escape, but for the moment you must bend in acquiescence.'

I am gasping. My clit is so fat now and my fingers so slicked that I consider removing the hand from my bra and typing a desperate one-handed plea for relief. But I don't want to miss the caning. God, no, I don't want to miss that.

'You place yourself over the padded seat of the stool. I call for one of your victims to bring me the senior school cane from the rack – one of my heaviest, it packs an almighty sting and leaves raised, deep red marks on those unfortunate enough to feel its weight. Your skirt is halfway up your rear cheeks, exposing the underhang and your tight cleft behind, but I push it all the way up to your waist, so no part of your vulnerable bottom is hidden to the audience. They make appreciative noises and lean forward, hungry for your pain.

"'Before I use this cane," I tell them, "I would like each one of you to come forward and lay a good strong smack on AtYourService's behind. Is that OK? One each, but make it a good one." They queue up, all 23 of them, men and women, old and young, all known to you, some very well known. Each one spanks your arse hard, some of them wordlessly, others speaking to you as they mark your cheek with their handprint.

'"You deserve this," they say, "after what you did to me." You make small yelps with each stroke, but you are determined not to give them the satisfaction of tears or struggles. As the last one retires, you are glowing all over your bum, feeling the soreness radiate out and dampen your pussy. This can't be turning me on, you think, mortified, but you aren't the only person who has noticed the telltale glisten at the split of your thighs. All the 24 other occupants of the room have seen it too.

'"You need this," I tell you, and the first stroke of the cane whistles down, catching you unprepared, and you scream as the first line throbs into life across the broadest section of your bum.

'I make you count, and I make you thank me for each breathtaking stroke. By six, your resolve is wavering, and by nine you are wailing and sobbing while the audience murmurs approval, some of them laughing and calling out to you. "About time you got your come-uppance," they say. Nobody seems moved by your misery and indeed, after I lay the twelfth and final stroke, some of them insist that you should get more.

'"I'm sure she'll get more," I tell them. "Just not today. I think she's had enough for an introduction. But don't worry. I'm accountable to you. This girl will be punished until each one of you feels she has repaid what she owes you and the rest of society. You will each be intimately involved with her ongoing discipline. Trust me." This satisfies them and I invite them up in turn to closely inspect your throbbing welts, feeling them with curious and delighted fingers, pinching and prodding.

'Once the last witness has gone and only you and I remain, I place a damp cloth over your bottom, pressing it close and caressingly to your burning flesh. You are crying. I stroke your hair and murmur words of comfort. After all, you don't know what's coming next.'

Yes, I do! I am!

There was a hideously tense silence and I began, beside myself, to rub at my clit. Say the word, please say the word.

'OK,' he typed. 'I'm not going to drag it out any further. I've been cruel enough, haven't I? You may come.'

I doubled over in ecstatic gratitude, working my fingers harder than they had ever worked, pinching my nipple so hard I yelped. My orgasm lifted me out of my body and threw me around the air, bump, bump, bump, until I fell back to earth with my forehead on the computer desk.

'Thank you, sir,' I said.

'YW,' he said.

Chapter Four

SPIRITS WERE EVEN GIDDIER than on an average Friday afternoon, and my last lesson of the day was more or less a write-off, a sacrifice to the gods of the impending half-term. I put on a video recording of *Glee* and let 8KY get on with it while I planned the next rehearsal of *West Side Story*.

It was going well. The Jets and the Sharks were slowly taking shape, while the girls couldn't get enough of the dance scene, imagining themselves in the circle skirts and neckerchiefs, clicking their fingers at their bequiffed admirers. The nasal timbre of Kacey's voice was receding, replaced by a pretty serviceable soprano. Tunde was excellent as ever. And Superhead was ... Well, he knew how to direct. He was a man who understood the mechanisms of control, using his voice, his stance, his body, his hands ... I shook my head. Daydreamer. Forget it.

There was a vacancy in my fantasies, ever since I spooked SecretSadist by asking for webcam contact. I hadn't heard from him since – four weeks had passed.

It had been a blow, of course. We had been messaging a matter of a couple of weeks, but in that time I had grown so strangely close to him. Perhaps that was the problem. Perhaps I came across as needy or suffocating. Don't make excuses for him, Cherry. He's married, or in a long-term relationship of some kind. He's unavailable and he played with you. But that's hardly surprising. That's what you let yourself in for when you get involved in this – kind of thing.

This kind of thing.

I should just accept that my sexuality, my kink, was always going to be taboo, sordid, disgusting, sleazy. But what could I do? I'd tried vanilla, and it hadn't worked. Was I going to have to settle for a life of self-love?

It looked like it from here. I'd tried a few other doms on the site, but the correspondence had been desultory, the connection nowhere near as instant and killer as what I'd had with SecretSadist. Pale shadows. Should it matter who whips you, so long as somebody does? This was a question I couldn't answer.

I'd given up for the time being, left MasterMe.com alone for a couple of weeks and switched all my focus to the musical and the plans for the new studio. Of course, this wasn't entirely safe. It left me open to my stupidly adolescent yearnings for the man whose click of the fingers had furnished all this wealth. Super, stupefying, Superhead Marks.

He was waiting for me when I arrived in the hall, dropping music scores here and there on the scuffed parquet in my wake.

'Somebody help Ms Delaney,' he ordered, shaking his head at the collective apathy of the performers, and Tunde stepped in, gathering the papers up like confetti in reverse.

'I ain't singing this,' said Kacey, thrusting her copy into my face.

'Why not?'

'I ain't saying I'm gay.'

The hall erupted into mirth.

'What are you talking about?' Superhead asked long-sufferingly.

'The lyrics say "I feel pretty and witty and gay". I ain't saying that. I ain't no lezzer.'

Superhead raised an eyebrow. 'If it's what's written

down, then it's what you'll say.'

'It's OK,' I flustered, rushing to Kacey's rescue. 'Those scores are rather old. Most productions use an alternative version – "pretty and witty and bright". Then they substitute "today" with "tonight"' for the rhyme.'

'Well, I'll sing that then,' said Kacey, mollified.

Superhead looked slightly askance at me and I trembled pleasurably beneath the weight of that severe brow. Should I have forced Kacey to sing words she wasn't comfortable with?

'Fine,' I said. 'Though there's absolutely nothing wrong with being a lesbian, as you know perfectly well.'

'I know that, Miss. Just wanted to be clear. I mean, Maria's straight anyway, innit, or none of this killing and stuff would have happened to begin with. Thought it might be confusing for the audience.'

Well saved, Kacey. Superhead's brow unfurrowed and he began directing people to their places for her song.

'I feel pretty,' she sang with such a magnificent glottal stop that I had to remind her she was playing a Hispanic girl, not Eliza Doolittle.

'Are you a lesbian, miss?' asked Yousef from 11JG.

'No way, man,' Lanh answered him, 'cos, like, Mr Sim's balling her, innit?'

'Get out,' growled Superhead. 'Come back when you can show a bit more respect.'

They slouched off while I died a thousand deaths. Now Superhead would think that Gareth and I were still an item. Not that it mattered, I supposed. Kacey and her girlfriends twirled around the imaginary fabric store, dancing with imaginary dummies, and Superhead moved closer until he was able to talk to me without being heard by the kids.

'Are you off anywhere this half-term?'

'Me? No. How about you?'

'Off to London tomorrow. Family visit. Look, do you have time for a drink after the rehearsal? Bit of a wind down?'

I looked up at him, needing to see what his face looked like when he asked me out. It looked like a normal face, handsome but normal. He wasn't anxious for my reply. It was merely a friendly request. I wasn't sure whether that was good or bad.

'Yeah, that'd be nice,' I said, striking a balance between nonchalance and biting-off-of-hand. At least, I hoped so.

'Good. Not the local, though, eh?'

'They don't let you in without Pompey dots.'

He laughed at my reference to the favoured local hardman tattoo.

'Somewhere south of Albert Road then?'

'Perfect.'

'So is that where you're from then? London?' I asked, once he had set down a wine spritzer for me and a real ale for him at a pleasant pub with a roaring fire just off the main drag.

'Yes,' he said. 'I suppose you know I was at a school in Camberwell before coming here?'

'Oh, we all heard the stories. From lawless no-go area to top of the league tables in three years. Very impressive. You can already see that St Sebastian's is starting to pull itself up by the bootstraps too. I got all the way from the canteen to the staff room without having to break up a single fight yesterday.'

He smiled, gratified no doubt by my blatant fangirling.

'It's a challenge, but I like challenges,' he said.

'Hence trying to get the kids into musical theatre,' I said. 'Shall we go for opera next term?'

Oh God, don't look at me like that! It was a kind of indulgent, avuncular look, but there was something else in it, an interest that was just keen enough to make my heart constrict as if bound in rubber bands.

'We need more teachers like you on the staff,' he said.

'Positive. Interested in the children as individuals. Fostering high expectations.'

I was too flattered to speak.

'Oh,' I said, taking an interest in my wineglass. 'Is that unusual, then?'

'Strangely, yes. At least, as far as St Sebastian's is concerned.'

'It isn't true,' I blurted, cursing myself for saying the words before they were even out. 'About Mr Sim. Gareth, I mean. We aren't ... I mean, we were, last term, but we aren't ... any more.'

He took a draught of his pint and nodded.

Say something! I waded into the silent breach.

'Is that OK? I mean, do you frown upon relationships between staff members?'

'No,' he said, leaning a little bit further forward, 'not necessarily.'

I was about to ask him if his wife was a teacher when a loud beery sound from the doorway made me look away.

'Oh God,' I muttered.

'Well, look who it –' Gareth was on the verge of making a spectacular fool of himself, but he processed the identity of my drinking companion in the nick of time and turned his declamation into a brisk nod and a formal, 'Headmaster. Cherry.'

'Gareth,' said Patrick unenthusiastically. 'Come and join us. We were just indulging in a bit of a debrief session after our rehearsal.'

'No, you're all right,' said Gareth. 'I'm here with the rugby boys. Thanks, though.' He skulked back to his broad-shouldered group at the bar, casting occasional glances over said broad shoulders for the remainder of our conversation.

'You don't have to explain yourself to him,' I said. The atmosphere had switched from warm to awkward. I couldn't stop looking over at the bar.

'I know. I wasn't. Er, so, you were saying …'

'What was I saying? I've forgotten now. About you going to London? I'm not going anywhere much. Might visit my mum.'

'Does she live locally?'

'Nah, abroad.'

'Really? What country?'

'The Isle of Wight.'

He frowned at me for a thrilling moment before crumpling divinely into laughter, in which I joined with gratitude.

I had the feeling that, were it not for the hostile man-mountain at the bar, Patrick would have been offering to buy another round of drinks, but instead he picked up his scarf and made an apologetic face.

'Well, best be getting my bags packed if I'm on the road tomorrow. Thank you for the company – I needed it after the half-term I've had.'

'Oh, not a problem,' I twittered, cheeks glowing from more than the effects of the coal fire. 'Any time.'

He put a hand on the inner part of my elbow as I rose to my feet. I had to shut my eyes.

'I appreciate it,' he said softly. 'Can I … Should I walk you home?'

'No, no, I'm fine. I only live a couple of streets away.'

Idiot, idiot, idiot!

'Right. Well, have a great half-term. You've earned a rest.'

'You too.'

We were at the door. The back of my neck burned, probably from death rays sent out by Gareth's eyes.

Outside on the pavement, Patrick took a step back – figuratively, it seemed, as well as literally.

'See you in November,' he said, raising a hand before turning and half-running, head down, into the slow dawning of another Friday night.

Perhaps a few days in the 1950s – I mean, Isle of Wight – were exactly what was called for. My mother was keen to know if I had 'met someone' – my break-up with Gareth had disappointed her, though she was good enough not to show it – but I couldn't exactly give her the love-life lowdown. One one-night stand, a flurry of internet messages and an unattainable crush. It didn't amount to much.

Sitting on the grass on a windy, stormy day, looking out at The Needles, I tried to analyse my relationship with Patrick Marks. Was it more than professional, or was I deluded? What he'd been saying when Gareth interrupted us that last night ... Wasn't it something to do with workplace romances? What had he said? I tried and tried to call the exact words to mind, but the threads wouldn't disentangle. And besides, if he was married ... Oh, it was no good.

I would go home, draw up my lesson plans up until Christmas and return to work with renewed professionalism and efficiency. Perhaps I would get a twinset and wear my hair in a bun, go for full-on librarian chic instead of the slightly messy, distrait image I tended to present to the world.

And then Patrick could unpin my chignon and take off my glasses and ... But, Ms Delaney, you're beautiful ...

God, I'm a twat sometimes.

I took the hovercraft back on Hallowe'en, a Friday this year, and braved the gathering gloom along the promenade, past the kids in *Scream* masks shaking hollowed pumpkins full of candy, until I arrived at my cold, unheated flat.

I switched on the computer before I attended to the boiler – for some reason I had this itchy premonitory feeling that SecretSadist might have a new message for me, but I was wrong.

Sitting down with a cup of tea and a chocolate Hobnob, I found the usual stream of messages from hopeful pain-inflicters on MasterMe.com. Delete, delete, delete. My finger hesitated over something different, some kind of flyer or general invitation.

'Come to the first Solent area Munch!'

What the hell was a Munch? I thought of *The Scream*, then some kind of picnic affair, before clicking out of idle curiosity and reading on.

'Do you despair of ever being able to meet and socialise with like-minded local people? Well, now you can cheer up and get your spank on, because the first ever Solent area Munch is scheduled for Sunday 9th November at 1 p.m. In the Mason's Arms, Itchin Lane.

'Come for a drink and a chat – no obligations, no pressure, discretion assured. Dress code = casual. No school uniforms or latex please!

'We hope to see you soon!'

Interesting. The message was signed by one Soton_Spanker. A little bit of rummaging around MasterMe.com revealed him to be a male aged 30-40 with interests in corporal punishment, fantasy role play and astronomy. A kinky geek! The side of me I had planned to squash bounced back in full effect, my deviant synapses firing once more.

A smidgen of additional detective work dulled my overactive libido, though. He was in the "in a relationship" category, with a cute-looking girl called BadLilBunny.

All the same, the invitation was intriguing. What did a group of spanking fetishists look like in the field? Somehow, I didn't think I'd be able to resist the temptation to find out.

The first week back at school was rough, both weather-wise and in terms of workload. I staggered through the Friday rehearsal without Patrick, who was at a conference, before falling into a pit of vodka with Lou.

I was still mildly fuzzyheaded on the Sunday morning, though the worst excesses of the hangover had receded and I was at least able to eat.

The storm appeared to have finally blown through and the sun made itself known for the first time in some days. I could do this. I could have brunch and then get on the train. It wasn't a long journey, and it was in the neighbouring city, which boded well for my anonymity. Could I really do it?

I logged on to the computer and messaged Soton_Spanker.

'Is the Munch still on?'

I'd eaten my toast and was on my second cup of coffee when the reply pinged in.

'Very much so! Are you coming?'

'I hope so. Will try to make it.'

'Excellent – we'll be in the corner furthest away from the dartboard. Look forward to seeing you.'

There it was. A commitment. Not unbreakable, of course, but it put a weight of motivation beneath my idle curiosity, heavy enough to send me to the cupboard for coats and scarves and make sure my railcard was in my purse.

All the way on the train I entertained a stupid fantasy of Stuart, my spanking surgical sailor, being one of the parties lurking in the corner of the snug. A reunion, all the more passionate for being unexpected – he would bend me backwards over the table for an extended kissing scene, then he would bend me forwards and bare my bottom, right there in the pub, while the Munchers looked on and applauded.

By the time the train pulled into the station, I was struggling with an inconvenient heat between my thighs, wishing that I had been a) alone in the carriage and b) wearing fewer than four layers. Under my coat, my jumper

74

dress, my tights, my knickers, a furtive humidity radiated out, soaking my underwear, demanding attention I couldn't give without criminalising myself.

The vibration of the engines beneath the prickly seat had almost tipped me over the edge, so it was a relief, in a contradictory kind of way, when they ceased and I was able to step out into cold, head-clearing air and concentrate on finding the pub.

It was in a quiet backstreet close to the dockyard. The row of sleek, shiny motormonsters lined up outside denoted a bikers' pub – a nice choice, I thought. There might not be an actual correlation between bikes and BDSM, but the two seem to rub along together quite well.

I stopped halfway across the gravel car park and looked behind me. Should I stay or should I go? I could just nip off over to West Quay and go for a browse through the shops instead. Catch a movie at the neighbouring multiplex, overdose on popcorn and self-loathing, go home.

'Nice boots! I think I saw some like that in last month's *Elle*.'

From the doorway, a snub-nosed blonde laughed over at me, beckoning madly. I recognised her from her MasterMe profile – BadLilBunny in the flesh.

I didn't move. 'Thanks,' I said. 'They're only from the market.'

'Shepherds Bush?'

She had stepped down and was crunching across the gravel towards me, still beaming, a naughty little angel in Seven jeans, with an Australian accent.

'Shepherds Bush?' I repeated, not understanding.

'You know. The fetish market. I love that Victorian lace-up style.'

'Oh, no, no, just the market under the old Tricorn centre. Sorry, are you ..?'

She held out a hand.

'Maz,' she said. 'Aka BadLilBunny. And – you're going to think I'm insane if you're not – but I'm guessing you're AtYourService?'

'Umm,' I hedged. This was my last chance to back out. Say, 'No, certainly not, I'm a churchwarden called Gladys,' and make a run for it. But her smiley, welcoming aura won me over. 'Yeah, that's right. Keris.' I took her proffered hand and shook, congratulating myself on my presence of mind. After all, how many Cherries of my age could there be in the area? I didn't want any curious Googling fingers linking my bare spanked arse to St Sebastian's. Keris could be the bare spanked arse. Cherry could be the rest of me.

She giggled and pulled me rather abruptly into a hug.

'I'm so excited to have another girl in the group,' she confided. 'The guys are going to love you. Come on. I'll buy you a drink – newbie privilege. What do you like?'

'Uh …' Did I necessarily want to lose my inhibitions today? Maybe not. 'I'll have an orange juice and lemonade, thanks.'

The pub was dark and creaky and, despite the smoking ban, there was a kind of tobacco-laden feel to the air inside. I wouldn't have been at all surprised to find out that the ghost of a pipe-smoking Harley rider sat by the fireplace on the night of the full moon.

Maz pushed me into the corner furthest from the dartboard with an explanatory chirrup of, 'This is Keris, guys, do your gentlemanly thing,' before flitting off to the bar.

A lanky guy in spectacles and a Killers T-shirt leapt up and offered me a place on the bench beside him.

'Hi,' he said effusively. 'Are you AtYourService?'

I nodded, blinking around me. There were two other men there – a massively bearded man in dusty leather trousers and a older gent in a smart shirt and chinos combo. It seemed Maz and I were the female contingent.

'Yeah,' I admitted. 'You must be – Soton_Spanker?'

'Justin,' he said with a nod. 'This is Rev and this is Lawrence.'

'Rev?' I looked at the biker and snickered. 'You don't have a dog collar.'

'As in revving a bike,' he explained, raising an eyebrow. 'No holy orders taken. Though I might be in possession of a collar or two. I don't wear them myself though.'

I experienced a frisson, hyper-aware of the fact that I was a submissive girl surrounded by doms. Daniella in the lions' den.

'You're new on the scene,' remarked Lawrence.

'I didn't even know there was a scene.'

'Oh, there's a scene,' said Justin confidently. 'You can participate in it as much or as little as you like, but it's definitely there. So you're new to kink?'

'I suppose. I've had a … I haven't done much. I've been interested for a long time though.'

Maz appeared with the drinks and I exhaled deeply, hoping she would dilute the scrutiny I appeared to be subject to.

'Yay, a total newbie,' she said. 'You've been so brave, coming here alone. And it's a great first step – we're all friendly and experienced. Even if you don't want to play with any of us, we've got loads of advice and help to offer.'

Play.

The word didn't fit. My secret fetishes had always seemed so dangerous, so serious, a deadly delicious poison infecting my bloodstream, threatening my chances of a sane and ordered future. What was frivolous about that? But perhaps, after all, it could be no more than a game.

Weirdly crestfallen, I gave Maz a weak smile.

'I'm glad I came,' I said. 'You're all very – approachable. This is quite a scary thing for me to do.'

'I can imagine,' said Justin. He had a kill-you-stone-dead sexy smile, all lips and teeth. Maz had chosen well. 'And I bet you were expecting a load of guys in leather carrying whips in their holsters. Well, I suppose Rev is a bit like that …'

We all laughed, Rev more than anyone. My disappointment faded – why would I be disappointed at meeting people who understood me at last? I decided to cheer up and embrace the opportunity. If nothing else, it would be a learning experience.

And I learned a lot that day.

I learned that Maz had come over on a student visa and stayed after meeting Justin through the MasterMe website two years earlier – she was an A&E nurse working at the general hospital. I wondered if her nursing skills ever came in handy in her private life, but I refrained from asking. I learned that Rev was recently divorced and "back on the scene" after taking a break for a few years. I learned that Lawrence had been a spanking fetishist from boyhood, but only with the advent of the internet had he been emboldened to explore his interest, having suppressed it for fifty years. Our generation was lucky. We could take our sexuality and run with it, let it evolve and develop instead of stuffing it under the bed and putting on the stiff upper lip. I was moved by his story.

'Don't be like me,' he said. 'Don't try and deny who and what you are.'

'I won't,' I promised.

'You wouldn't dare,' said Justin with a devilish wink. 'Not now we're on your case.'

Ah, Justin. An interesting man. A lecturer in astrophysics at the local university, he looked wholesome and earnest but Maz assured me that he wielded the meanest cane this side of the Thames. And whenever he smiled "wholesome and earnest" flew off his face, replaced by "filthysexygorgeous".

By two o'clock, both Lawrence and Rev had left, pleading other commitments, but Justin, Maz and I got another round in, and this time I felt comfortable enough to let go of my tight-reined self-control and order a bottle of Mexican lager.

'It's a shame your web dom disappeared,' Maz sympathised, having been regaled with the story of SecretSadist. 'But hey. His loss is our gain, eh, Justin?'

I looked rapidly from each to each. In what sense?

'She means,' said Justin, putting the drinks down, 'that you probably wouldn't have come to the Munch if you were still in touch with him. Steady on, Maz, it sounded like you were trying to seduce poor Keris here then.'

'Shit, sorry, didn't mean it to come out like that!'

Justin left a beat, putting a contemplative finger to his lip before speaking again.

'Though if you were interested, of course …'

The beer bottle was slippery in my hand. I put it down.

'Interested? In what? You're … I mean … You're together, aren't you?'

'Sure,' said Maz, taking an insouciant chug of her alcopop. 'We're together. But we aren't exclusive. We're poly.'

'You're …' For some reason, the only image that sprang to mind was acres of agricultural polytunnels flapping in a field. 'Poly?'

Justin laughed. 'Polyamorous.'

'Polyamorous? Is that like, bisexual?'

'No.' Maz was delighted, enraptured even, at my naïveté. 'It means we have a kind of open relationship. But not the kind where we go off individually and sleep with other partners. We like to include other people in our relationship, I guess, is one way of putting it.'

'Oh. How does that work then?'

'It's complicated.' Justin smiled charmingly. 'But then, so are we. So are you, I think. We have a network of close

friends and playmates. Some of them are lovers, in a full
sense. Some of them just like to come along when there's a
big group scene planned. Horses for courses. Horsewhips
for friendships.'

'Heh.' The chuckle was a punctuation mark. I had no
idea what to do with this information. Did I have to do
anything with it?

'So, J is just saying,' Maz took up the baton. 'If you
found yourself needing a bit of action of any kind, you
know, we'd be happy to oblige. Either or both of us, if you
see what I mean.'

'I'm sorry.' Justin put a hand on mine and I flushed all
over. 'We've frightened you off, haven't we? Look, forget
it, Keris. Some people are cut out for monogamy and some
aren't. No judgements. If you're a one-man woman, that's
cool. We just thought it would be a shame, if you weren't,
to let a gorgeous unattached submissive woman like you
slip away without mentioning the possibilities. Still
friends?'

I flicked my eyes up at him. His pout, his spectacles, his
ruffled brown hair, his taut man's arms.

'I'm not frightened,' I said. 'Just curious.'

Maz shuffled up closer to me, her denimed hip nudging
mine.

'Curiosity is good,' she said. 'We can work with
curiosity.'

'What sort of thing … I mean … How would it work –
if I was to – in theory …'

Justin stemmed the flow of verbal diarrhoea, squeezing
my hand.

'It would work any way you wanted. We can fit around
your fantasies, unless they're further out there than ours –
which is unlikely, if I'm honest. Whatever you've never
done, whatever you've dreamed of doing … Just say the
word.'

What an offer. The remnants of my common sense

suggested that I thank them politely for their interest, take their mobile phone numbers and make my goodbyes. The rest of me, plus beer, had different ideas.

'Well, you know, I've come to a Munch. I think the interest in spanking is a given,' I said coyly.

Maz giggled and did a sort of excitable wriggle beside me.

'We kinda figured, and believe me, Justin is the best spanker around. He's a thinker – I reckon thinkers make great spankers, don't you?'

'It's the appliance of science,' he said, with yet another knicker-soaker of a smile.

Oh God. Apply that science to my backside. Apply it good and hard.

'So ... I might be in the market,' I said haltingly. 'For a, y'know, just something to tide me over while I'm waiting for something more permanent.'

'A stop-gap.' Justin pouted cartoonishly. 'Aww.' He brightened, winking. 'No, that's cool. Absolutely. I can do that. So ... Do you want to fix a time and place? And do you want just me, or is there any way Maz can get involved?'

'Well ...' Fuck. Now the contract was on the table, I didn't know what clauses I wanted to include. 'Why don't I invite you two round for supper? Friday night. We can take it from there.'

'Terrific!' Maz squeaked. 'I can't wait. We'll bring our toybox, right, J?'

Play? Toys? Was this just another way of deferring adulthood? I didn't know. And right then, neither did I care.

Chapter Five

BY FRIDAY NIGHT, HOWEVER, I was beginning to care.

Superhead invited me for a drink after the rehearsal again but I had to turn him down, so absorbed in getting to Sainsbury's and stocking up for the night's festivities was I. What did kinksters like to eat and drink? Kittens and absinthe? I settled on an easy pot-roast recipe, followed by a light pudding of mixed berries and cream. Didn't want everyone too replete to – er, whatever. And an Australian Shiraz, to make Maz feel at home. Presumably they would bring a bottle or two themselves, and I had a few sticky bottles of old spirits knocking around the flat in case wine wasn't a popular choice. Once again, it wouldn't do to be getting too tipsy too quickly.

Back at the flat, I fell into a frenzy of decluttering and organisation of space. How should the furniture be arranged, if there was going to be kink? Should the floor be clear? Should I move the coffee table? Was there any free-standing piece of furniture to which handcuffs could be safely affixed?

I forced myself into the kitchen to attend to peeling vegetables instead. If things happened, they would happen. Trying to predict the evening's events would just drive me into a state of nervous collapse. I needed to relax, take it easy. Maybe a glass of that Australian Shiraz …

By the time the bell rang, the flat smelled delicious and I was equally fragrant, dressed in a slinky black halterneck dress and stockings. Even if nothing happened, it seemed best to be prepared.

Justin and Maz were kitted out for a smart Friday night, Justin in a blue shirt and dark trousers, Maz in knee-length boots and a stretchy tube dress, her blonde hair swept up in a spiky topknot. They could have been any couple on the dinner-party circuit, were it not for the classic brown leather doctor's bag Justin hefted on to the coffee table once I'd ushered them into the living room.

'Is this OK?' he asked, as I took their coats.

'Oh, fine,' I said, eyeing the bag with mingled curiosity and alarm. 'It looks as if you're here to give me a medical. Is there a stethoscope in there?'

Maz laughed. 'No stethoscope, but plenty of things to get your pulse racing.'

'Perhaps we should leave the contents of the bag for after dinner,' cautioned Justin, but I was not sure I could wait.

'Can't I just have a sneak preview?'

Justin smiled evilly. 'You want to start with a little bit of headspace play before dinner? Well, why not? OK, this is how it's going to be, Keris. We do nothing that you aren't happy with. As soon as things seem to be headed in a direction you don't like, you stop by saying the word "Mars".'

'Mars?'

'Well, yeah, it's Maz's safeword, so we tend to use it when other players join in too.'

'OK. Mars. The god of war.'

'Right.' He smirked. 'Before we start, I'll explain a few things about us. I'm a top. I'm always a top. That's what I am. Maz, on the other hand, is a switch. Usually, she's submissive, but occasionally, especially when third, fourth or fifth parties are involved, she will top, either alone or with me. Is this clear so far?'

'Wine?' I offered the bottle, filling three glasses when they both nodded. 'Er, yes. You always do the spanking and sometimes Maz joins in, if she's in the mood, or she might prefer to take the pain instead.'

'Exactly.' He sat down, and Maz and I suddenly felt able to do the same. Justin had the strange knack of making you want to follow his lead. 'So, if you want two spankers, you can have that. Or if you want somebody to share the pain, Maz is your girl. But tonight, since you say you're new to all this, you'll probably just want a one-on-one scene, and that's fine. We don't have any expectations, so there's no pressure. Was there a particular script, so to speak, that you wanted to follow tonight?'

I thought about this. A script. A role play scenario. For me, part of the spanking fantasy was having responsibility for my sexuality taken away from me, so I was a little nonplussed at the idea of having to dictate the action. I was being asked to take control of my loss of control. It was almost too paradoxical to contemplate.

'I kind of always fantasise about the idea of punishment,' I told him. 'Like, I've done something bad – or I'm just a bad person. A dirty girl, or whatever. So ... something like that, I suppose.'

'Something like that? Or that?'

Justin tipped back his glass, eyes narrowed behind the specs, and suddenly he looked so cold and severe that I shuddered.

'I'm sorry, I'm not used to talking about this stuff, I ...' I shrugged and hugged my arms around me, intimidated and yet thirsting for more intimidation.

'No, let's get this clear,' he said, putting down his glass. 'You want to be punished.'

'Yeah,' I whispered.

'So your fantasy involves an authority figure who is displeased with you?'

'Uh-huh.'

'And is this authority figure a person who is close to you in your life? I mean, is he administering loving

84

correction? Or is he a sadist who just gets off on hurting you?'

'Sometimes one, sometimes the other.'

'Right. Some submissives like the whole Daddy thing –'

'Oh, no, no. That's not for me. If it's loving correction, it's a boyfriend or husband in the fantasy.'

'OK, so that's clear. Which one is it going to be tonight?'

'Tonight, well, there's dinner, isn't there? So I think, uh, you're my boss. Somebody I work for. Maz might be your secretary, or your wife. Either way, I've been invited to account for something. Maybe some problem with my expenses … and after dinner, it's understood that I'm going to be punished. Is that …? I mean, it's a bit ad hoc, but could that work?'

'That could work very well.' Justin picked up the bag and unlocked it. 'You're my secretary. Maz is my wife. I'm coming round tonight to get to the bottom of some missing petty cash, and Maz is my witness. You will call me Mr Masters – or sir, of course.'

I had stopped listening. The bag was open. Pandora's Bag.

Spilling from the worn brown leather were paddles, straps, whippy things with many strings, hairbrushes, riding crops, the full de Sade works. Only the cane was absent, presumably because of its impractical length.

He snapped the bag shut again and my mouth followed suit.

'Shall we begin?'

I nodded. Maz came around to stand beside Justin, her sweet, open face suddenly grave.

I actually gulped, like somebody out of a Fifties comic strip, but Justin had the air of suppressed authoritative menace down to a fine art.

'So, Miss Delray,' he intoned, folding his arms. 'You may not have realised, but I have an ulterior motive in coming here tonight. I've been checking the petty cash supply.' He paused, eyebrow raised, waiting for me to fall into the big hole he was digging for me.

I think I probably paled. It all seemed so real. Ersatz, but no less effective, guilt crept into my consciousness, knocking all the confidence out of me.

'Oh,' I said.

'Oh? Is that all you can say? I'm finding it a little short. Actually, more than a little. Short to the tune of 57 pounds and 33 pence. How do you account for this?'

'I'm not an accountant,' I pleaded.

He sneered.

'So you're saying it's a mistake? A question of poor arithmetical training?'

'Uh, probably.'

'But I know there was more than a hundred pounds in there three days ago, Miss Delray. So I'm not entirely sure you're being honest with me.'

Oh. So I was dishonest rather than incompetent. In that case, I needed to come up with some bluster.

'It, hang on, I think, um, yeah, the fan broke so I had to buy another! That's right! I remember now.'

'You had the fan on in mid-November?'

'I, um, just felt a bit hot, you know?'

'No. I don't think I do. Why am I paying for central heating in your office if you're turning on the fan? This gets worse by the minute. You incriminate yourself every time you open your mouth. If I were you, Miss Delray, I'd stop digging.'

I put down my metaphorical spade and dropped my eyes to the floor. Something bad was coming. Something good-bad-good. My pulse raced and a wave of nausea rocked through my body.

'I'm still waiting,' he said stridently, 'for a word of apology. Even if you can't be honest with me.'

'Sorry, sir,' I whispered.

'You will be. Now, you are going to serve us our dinner and, while we eat, I am going to consider the thorny problem of how to deal with you.'

'Shit! The veg is boiling over!' I exclaimed, racing to the kitchen.

Maybe not the best end to that particular scene, but it was true.

While I dished up, I let my heart rate return to normal, retrospectively admiring Justin's diabolical knack for this kind of thing. I had lost my appetite and didn't want to think about digesting the French peasant-style chicken thing I was ladling on to the plates. Considering I had been ravenous since the rehearsal, this was quite an achievement.

What was he going to do to me? Did we have to stay in role throughout the meal? How was I going to?

'Smells gorgeous.'

Maz had crept up behind me, smiling in a very non-irate-boss's-wife way.

'Thanks. Are we …?'

'Justin thought we could drop the role play for the first course and get back into it during dessert. Pretty harsh on the old digestive system otherwise.'

'I was just thinking that.'

I allowed myself to breathe in the heavenly aroma of the food. My appetite returned. This sex-play stuff was like magic. Powerful, psychic enchantment.

As we ate our casserole, we chatted about work and kink.

I hadn't been able to tell my guests that I was a schoolteacher - I feared the response it evoked in people and besides, I felt the need to keep my new friends at arm's length, at least initially. Self-preservation of a sort.

But they couldn't fail to notice the upright piano in the corner of the room, so I told them I gave private music lessons.

'Are you like James Mason in that movie?'

I laughed.

'*Seventh Veil*? I can't tell you how often I've watched that. He's so exquisitely cruel in it. I longed for a piano teacher like him – I was warped even as a youngster. But instead I had a lovely kind old lady. The disappointments of life, eh?'

Justin and Maz smiled sympathetically.

'You always knew you were kinky?' Maz asked.

'I think so. Flipped through my Enid Blytons for the spanking scenes, felt funny when people got tied up on television, all of that. I don't know why. I tend to think it's either innate or something that happens in the wiring long before we know about it.'

'It'd be interesting to find out,' said Justin with a nod. 'I suppose the psychologists are working on it as we speak.'

'I wish they'd come up with a conclusion,' added Maz. 'I wish I didn't feel the need to keep this under wraps. It's not something I chose – it chose me.'

My eyes filled with tears.

'Oh, sweetie,' said Maz, putting out a hand and patting mine. 'Are you OK?'

'Yeah, fine.' I choked them back. 'Just… It's weird … and wonderful to know I'm not the only person who feels this way.'

'You're welcome, hon,' she said. Then she turned to Justin. 'We could do a piano teacher scene sometime. How awesome would that be?'

'Oh, I'd love that!' I said. 'Why didn't I think of that before?'

'We've got all the time in the world,' said Justin, laying down his knife and fork. 'We can play every scene you ever imagined.'

'Then you're going to need all the time in the world.'

All this amicability and bonhomie was forgotten at the advent of the summer berries with their frosting of confectioner's sugar. The thump of the accompanying jug of cream on to the table was like the knell of doom.

Justin pushed his glasses back up his nose, and Maz went from vibrant to muted in the time it took for me to pour. Switch was a good word for her. She seemed able to turn it on and off at will.

I sat down and pushed some blueberries around in the cream with my spoon.

'May I ask, sir,' I faltered, daring to eye Justin from under my drooping brow, 'what you mean to do?'

'I mean to eat my pudding,' said Justin severely. 'How about you?'

'No, I mean to me. What do you mean to do to me?'

'So you accept that you deserve punishment?'

'No! I didn't do anything! I didn't steal the money. I bought a new fan, like I said …' My words were cutting no ice. I wondered about wheeling out the tears, but I wasn't great at emotional scenes, so I simply pouted and tapped my spoon on the side of my bowl in a rebellious manner.

'I won't be scowled at over the table,' said Justin quietly. 'Put down your spoon and place yourself in the corner, beside the piano. Nose to the wall.'

What should I do? Should I play the malcontent and refuse? I thought about the dynamic – boss and secretary. I had to have respect for him – he paid my wages, after all. Besides, I saw enough sulky bratty behaviour at work and it rather bored me. I decided to obey.

The corner. The place to be. A place I had often dreamed of being.

Now I was there, it wasn't all that. The wall was cold, numbing my nose, and it was boring. The boss and his wife didn't seem to have much to say to each other, so my only entertainment was the clinking of spoons against china and my own furtive imagination. What was Justin going to do to me? Would he send me back here afterwards? How would I be feeling? How long would it go on for?

The clinking stopped and Justin spoke – his voice low, only just loud enough for me to pick up.

'So, what do you think, Marianne? What's a suitable punishment for our light-fingered miscreant?'

'Well, she needs a firm lesson,' said Maz. 'That's for sure. She still hasn't admitted her fault, or apologised for it. It'll have to be harder because of that.'

'I'm inclined to agree.'

A prickly silence fell, during which the heat and wetness between my legs clamoured for attention I was not able to give. Being discussed like this, in my hearing but without any respect for my presence, was so very arousing. The tension was building too far, too fast. I wanted to let out a moan. But then I might miss their next words.

'She needs a good, long spanking,' was Maz's verdict. 'Several implements. Maybe the strap and one of the wooden paddles. Get that bum good and red. To be honest, perhaps we should have done this in front of the other staff – made an example of her.'

'Well, perhaps if the offence is ever repeated … Though I hope any thought of that will be long gone, by the time I'm finished with her.'

Another gulp. A throb of the clit. Breath coming hard and fast. Cold nose, warm cunt. Is that the saying?

'Well, then.' Chair legs scraping back, footsteps, something being placed on the floor – most likely that same chair. 'Come here, Miss Delray.'

I turned around to see Justin sitting on the chair, the medical bag at his side, palms flat on his thighs, leaning forward a little. Maz stood behind him, smiling grimly.

As I walked across the floor, Justin rolled up his shirtsleeves.

The moan came out. I couldn't help it.

'Over my lap, Miss Delray.'

Justin's lap was narrower than Stuart's, his legs longer and bonier, so I drooped a little more on either side of him.

The position was not uncomfortable, but the embarrassing consciousness of it – and of Maz's eyes on me – was.

'I don't suppose you thought, when you helped yourself to our petty cash, that it would land you up in this position,' said Justin, his hand making patterns on the fabric of my dress, pulling and stroking it over my proffered rump. 'Ready to be spanked like a naughty little girl, while my wife watches. That's what happens to employees who behave badly in our company, Miss Delray. They get this one chance to learn from their mistakes. Believe me, if it happens again, you will have the full audience before you get your cards. Warehousemen, cleaners, the lot. They will all witness your shame. So learn from this. Are you ready?'

'I'm sorry,' I blurted out of nowhere.

'At last!' said Maz brightly. 'But I'm sorry too, missy. It's too little too late. Don't spare her, J.'

'I won't.'

His hand fell, hard and abrupt, on the thin material of my dress. I knew then that this was going to be long and it was going to be hard. I would be glad of that second glass of wine with its mild analgesic property.

After a series of smacks, maybe twenty in total, all over my thinly-covered bottom, Maz urged Justin to lift up the dress.

'Lovely panties,' she said, once they were on view. 'They'll have to come down later, of course.'

'Of course,' said Justin, caressing the lace, sliding a finger underneath to test the warmth his hand had imparted to my skin. 'Nowhere near hot enough yet.'

Another volley of cracks penetrated the frothy laciness, causing my flesh to jiggle and my teeth to grit. I did not want to make a sound until I absolutely had to. I wanted to show these people that I was no lightweight and they didn't have to go easy on me.

I curled my toes and my fingers, held my breath tight

and still in the centre of my ribcage, but eventually I gave way and had to gasp.

He chose that moment to pull down my knickers.

Strange man and strange woman looking at my arse, checking it for heat and redness, could it be real? My overthinking head interfered with the scene, refusing to allow me to let go and swim into the fantasy. I could only think of the absurdities and practicalities. I was not in the headspace.

Perhaps if he spanked my bare flesh …

Soon my thoughts were broken up and overwhelmed by the intensity of the pain. Stop, don't stop, racing through my head in a rhythm that echoed Justin's swats, small squeals coming thick and fast.

He began to lecture me, and then it happened – then I fell. I was the secretary, being punished, learning her lesson, thinking about how much I deserved this and how determined I was not to let it happen again.

'I can see by your compliance that you're starting to feel penitent,' said Justin. 'Am I right?'

A low, suffering 'Yes,' fell from my lips. I was beginning to jerk right and left across his lap, trying to angle my bottom away from his endlessly descending hand, but my room for manoeuvre was small and I was doomed to failure.

'I hope that, every time you open and shut that petty cash box, you think about what's happening today. I don't want you to be able to handle cash without remembering how sore your bottom was. And remember, we will both be watching you very carefully from now on. Imagine this happening in front of everyone in the company. That will be the next step in the disciplinary procedure.'

'I'm sorry,' I panted.

His hand fell for the last time.

'I hope so,' he said.

He rubbed my skin, in a slow and thoughtful manner. I

remembered that I was incredibly turned on, something I had forgotten amidst the pain, and tried to clamp my thighs tight, hoping I hadn't given myself away.

His continuing scientific survey of my hot behind did little to help my concealment of this, however, and I almost wanted him to start spanking again, to deflect attention from it.

'Good,' he said at last. 'You're starting to understand that your actions have consequences. But I'm afraid I'm not finished yet. I have to be satisfied that you have truly learned your lesson first.'

'I have,' I said quickly, but he chuckled and patted my rear in an indulgent fashion.

'Still trying to pull the wool over my eyes?' he said. 'No. Go and bend over the arm of the sofa, please. Marianne, can you find me the short leather strap?'

Oh, woe was me as I bent my spine in the recommended pose, gripping the arm for dear life. Stuart had me like this when he used his belt on me. The memory strengthened me, a little something to hang on to.

The sting, once it was imparted to my flesh, was like a sweet reminder. At least, it was for the first few strokes. If I shut my eyes, I could imagine Stuart behind me, flexing that doughty naval forearm, strong fingers gripping the thick leather.

Oh God, I wish you'd come back. You're the sailor, but it's me who's at sea here.

By the fifth or sixth slap of cowhide on girlhide, the sweet memory was fading, replaced by the immediacy of the burn. The heat was penetrating below the protective outer layers of my skin, sending a throbbing alarm call from my arse to the rest of my body. Particularly those that were implicated in sex.

I began to yell with each stroke, losing my grip. What was that word? Mars. No, I didn't want to use it. Not yet.

Justin gave me twenty then dropped the strap.

'Not so cocksure now, are we?' he said. 'What do you have to say to me now?'

'I'm sorry,' I whimpered, again. I was a shivering mess, my face pressed into the sofa. It hurt, but it hadn't hurt enough yet. I needed more. I needed the pain to obliterate me.

'You're doing very well,' said Maz reassuringly. In role or out? I couldn't tell any more. They were both tormentors, regardless of what act they put on. They wanted to hurt me. They wanted to see me suffer.

I wanted them to see me suffer.

'Just a little bit more, just to make sure,' said Justin, and his voice was gentle. 'We need to finish the job off properly. Marianne, the paddle.'

I didn't know what to expect, never having felt anything wooden against my buttocks before, but the first stroke soon shook me out of my doubt.

I screamed.

How many of these could I take? Surely no more than three? Unlike the elegant sting of the strap, this packed a brutal punch, settling itself straight down into my deep tissues and staying there. I would be bruised in the morning.

'Oh my God!' I yelled. 'That hurts.'

Justin laughed, and Maz joined in.

'Looks like we've found our implement,' said Justin. 'This is the one to use when we want to send a serious message.'

He slapped it down in the centre of my bum, harder than before.

'How many before you crack?' he mused.

I made it to seven, somehow, by a combination of violent wriggling, shrieking and kicking, but I had to invoke the god of war when I found myself vaulting over the sofa arm away from my varnished wooden nemesis.

Maz's face was bright with delight while Justin slapped

the paddle into his hand, shaking his head in mock-disappointment.

I knelt on a foetal position on the sofa, clutching my throbbing bottom.

'Get back into position,' commanded Justin.

I raised bleary eyes to his.

'But I said the –'

'I know. The spanking is over. I just want you back in position. OK?'

Reluctantly, fearing some kind of trick, I moved back. Were they going to turn out to be serial killers after all?

Justin's hand felt my bottom, stroking it all over.

'I just need to ask you something, Keris,' he said softly.

'Oh, what?'

'Sometimes people just want a spanking. Sometimes they want a little bit … more. Now we can stop right here, or we can … It's up to you.'

His hand on my arse sent waves of need along the channel and into my pussy. How should I answer this question? It seemed my cunt wanted to answer it for me.

'I like to be touched,' I whispered.

'OK,' he whispered back. 'I can do that that. Unless you'd like Maz?'

'You.'

His fingers walked a slow path from the crack of my bum past my perineum, stopping to glide a light circle around my vagina before finding my clit.

'Oh yes, you're very wet,' he told me, unnecessarily. 'You're definitely the kind of naughty girl who needs our attention.'

He kept one hand on the small of my back while the other continued its explorations, settling into a firm fingering rhythm that made me rock and twist beneath him.

From the corner of my eye I could see Maz, transfixed, one of her hands pressed into the front of her smart skirt, the polished fingernails sliding gently up and down.

95

'Spread your legs wider for me,' instructed Justin and I obeyed instantly, pushing my wet sex on to his busy hand, feeling the cheeks of my arse open to give him the full view. 'You really needed this, didn't you? This is the kind of treatment that works for you. A sound spanking followed by a good fingering, in front of my wife. We'll have to make this a regular event – perhaps your work performance will improve if we do this every Friday. What do you think?'

I didn't think anything. Thought was out there somewhere. I was all sex, all submission, all dirty little slut. And it felt like where I was meant to be.

'That's definitely what we should do,' said Maz, in a lower voice than usual. 'She needs it hard and often.'

I came, half-sobbing, hiding my face in a cushion.

Well satisfied, Justin withdrew his fingers and patted my bum with them, leaving a sticky cold patch on the residually warm globes.

'Do you want a hug?' he asked.

I nodded and he came to sit beside me, pulling me into a tight embrace on his knee, stroking my hair. My bottom hurt when I sat on his thigh, but it was a wonderful, glowing kind of hurt that I hoped might last for ever.

'Was that everything you wanted it to be?' he asked.

I looked for my voice, which came out in a breathless rush.

'Oh God, yes. Thank you so much. It was amazing.'

'It's all going to happen at your pace, Keris. Whatever you're ready for, we can do.'

'You're so good at this. I feel like I've landed on my feet with you two.'

'Thanks,' said Justin, and Maz joined in with a little "aww" of approbation. 'That means a lot to us.'

The hug went on until I felt I could almost fall asleep, safe and tired and protected. But eventually, Justin cleared his throat and shifted slightly, so that I felt the rude protrusion inside his trousers.

'Another question for you,' he said, with an embarrassed smile. 'How do you feel about sex?'

'Sex?'

'Maz and I ... You know, we get quite turned on by spanking. If you like, you can go into the bedroom while we sort ourselves out. Or you can watch. Or even, y'know, join in ...'

'Oh, wow, I'm so sorry, I feel I've been horribly selfish.'

'Submission is a bit of a head trip,' said Maz with an understanding squeeze of my arm. 'Don't worry about it.'

'Please, I, er, is it really OK if I watch?'

'Absolutely,' said Justin. 'We love being watched. Don't we, Maz?'

'Too right. We even put footage up on the internet sometimes. With pixellated faces, obviously.'

'Well, then, be my guests,' I said. 'Since you are. Literally. My guests.'

'Cool,' said Maz. 'You get comfy there. I think the floor will do for us, if you just bung us a couple of cushions.'

Justin had tipped me off his lap and was unbuttoning his shirt. I helped Maz construct a kind of cushion-bed on the rug and retired to the sofa with my wine glass. I wondered whether to fetch my spectacles, but thought that might be bad manners. I would have to be content with a slight blur.

Maz took off her shoes and lay down, staring up at Justin as he disrobed.

'Aren't you going to strip?' he asked, unbuckling his belt.

She lifted her bottom off the floor and unzipped her skirt, shucking it off with a sensual wriggle, then set to work on her shirt. Her underwear, I was quite intrigued to discover, was made of skintight black latex, including the suspender belt. Who would have known what lurked beneath the smart dinner-party chic? I felt my clit spark into life again and had to change position, tucking a leg beneath me.

Oh God, the knickers were crotchless. I began to dampen. She had been wearing crotchless knickers at my dinner table all night. Did Justin order her to? I was tempted to touch myself, but I was too fascinated by the sight in front of me, and I didn't want to distract them.

Justin, down to his boxers, stood over Maz, nudging her feet apart with his toe.

'Now I can see how hot you are for it,' he said. 'Dirty little beast with your cunt wide open all night. How much do you want it?'

'I need to be fucked, J,' said Maz. 'Real bad.'

'Don't you? First I want you to put your fingers in that slit and show me how much.'

She moaned and moved a hand between the gap in the latex. Wasn't that awfully hot to wear? Her skin shone, but it wasn't clear what kind of heat had produced the sheen. I watched as her manicured fingers got slick and wet, her face pinkening with the effort.

'Keris is getting quite a show,' said Justin. 'I bet she's never seen a slut like you before, a slut who'll do anything with anyone. You'll have to tell her how many people have had you sometime. Mind you, she'll catch up with you one day, I guess. I think she needs a bit of what you're going to get. Get those legs really wide, show her that soaking cunt of yours.'

Maz, gasping, did as she was told.

Justin dropped his boxers, his cock stiff and thick. I wanted it inside me, but I had to let Maz have her reward for services rendered. I would just have to watch and wait my turn, if I was to be allowed one.

'OK, enough of that,' he said. 'Get on all fours and push that arse out for me.'

Maz rolled over and knelt up. The split in the latex crotch continued up the back of the knickers, exposing her bottom in a broad circle. It seemed wrong to call them knickers, somehow, since they didn't do the job. What would be a good name for them? Sex pants, maybe.

Her pert white bottom gleamed between the boundaries of wet-look blackness, while her shaved pussy was well spread and juicy. Even I wanted to fuck it. If only I had a strap-on.

'Now, I want you to ask me nicely,' said Justin, kneeling and taking his cock in hand, preparing for the penetration.

'Please, sir, may I be fucked?' moaned Maz.

'You may.' The tip of his cock lined up with the tiny target, butting it gently. 'How hard should I fuck you?'

'As hard as you want, sir.'

'That's right. And where should I put my cock?'

I bit my lip, too tense to breathe.

'Wherever you want to, sir.'

'Good. I'm going to use your cunt tonight, since Keris is new to all this. Keep it nice and tight for me.'

'Yes, sir.'

'Now get your eyes off the floor and look at Keris while you're getting fucked.'

She groaned, seemingly unwilling, but she lifted her head, turned it to the side and stared straight at me. It was most disconcerting. I hid my face in the wine glass, peering narrowly over the rim at her.

Justin's cock slid inside, disappearing inch by inch, until his pelvis made contact with her bum. He took hold of her hips and began to thrust, slowly at first, so that I saw his pole glisten with her juices as it made its inexorable back and forth motion.

'Oh, you are keeping it tight, good slut,' he said, reaching down to squeeze a rubber breast. 'Nipples good and hard, can you see them, Keris?'

'Yeah,' I coughed. Mine weren't exactly flat.

'I wish you could feel how tight and hot she is,' he said

to me. 'She's a fucking dream of a cunt.'

I put my glass down. It was no use. I was going to have to masturbate. My knickers were hanging off one ankle so it was easy enough to get a hand under my skirt and begin a frantic massage of my clit.

Maz looked so luscious, her face faraway and dreamy even though her eyes were still fixed in my direction. Justin was speeding up, his lean torso bent over her arched back, his cock beginning to pound.

'Of course, I prefer a nice red arse, like yours, Keris,' he said through gritted teeth. 'But I can make an exception. Oh, are you frigging yourself? You bad girl.'

He turned his head and grinned at me. My fingers pushed down harder.

He removed one hand from Maz's hips and dipped it down between her sex lips, swirling it round and round. Then he took the juiced tip of one finger and began to circle her arsehole with it.

My jaw dropped. I was going to come. This was too much.

The finger plunged inside Maz's bum and she cried out, her eyes glazed, then shut. She was coming.

My own orgasm coincided with Justin's, my watery whimper drowned by his roar of triumph.

'Mmm,' said Justin, his finger still plugging that hole. 'Keris got a really good show. She watched you getting fucked with your arse filled too. How does that make you feel?'

'Ashamed,' said Maz quietly. 'Humiliated.'

'Good. So it should.'

He pulled out the finger and smacked her bum, leaving a handprint. She flopped forward on to her stomach.

'Do you have any tissues, Keris?' he asked politely, and I sprang into action at once, hurrying into the kitchen to wash my hands and get a wad of kitchen roll for my guests.

When I returned, Justin was already back in his shirt,

while Maz lay, rumpled and gorgeous, spread all over my cushions.

They cleaned themselves up and began to dress again, utterly comfortable with themselves and their outrageous sexual habits. I envied them. Could I ever be so free?

'What did you think, Keris?' asked Justin. 'I hope we didn't alarm you.'

'No, not at all. God, that was hot. Like that underwear must be.'

Maz grinned, pulling her skirt over the questionable "knickers".

'Do you like it? I feel so frisky when I wear it. I mean, I was dying for a shag all through dinner. You should get some.'

'Maybe I will. So … That was good for you?'

Maz's eyes opened wide. 'Well, duh!' she said.

'Just … You looked as if you were about to cry at one point. And then you said that stuff about feeling ashamed and humiliated.'

'That's what gets me off.' She sounded a little put out.

'Yeah, of course, I'm sorry. It's just that I'm used to those words having negative connotations. It's odd to hear them used like that, in a sexual context.'

'Oh yeah, you get used to it,' she said offhandedly, buttoning her shirt. 'Or at least, you will if you want to keep on with this stuff. Do you?'

'I think I do,' I said.

'Good. Maybe we can do something next weekend then?'

'Maybe.'

Chapter Six

'YOU HAVE TO UNDERSTAND how important it was to keep it secret. Their relationship could never be made public. Have you never had a secret, Kacey?'

''Course.' Kacey shrugged, then made the elementary mistake of moving her jaw in a manner that betrayed the chewing gum within. Patrick pointed long-sufferingly to the wastepaper basket and she trudged over to throw the offending gum away.

'How do you expect to be able to sing and chew at the same time?' he scolded. 'Anyone would think that stuff held your bones together. You seem quite incapable of going without it for more than ten minutes.'

I grinned, watching the little scene from the piano. Chewing gum has been one of the top ten bugbears of my life, ever since I had to write off a school violin whose strings were coated in the stuff. Hilarious joke.

'Anyway, returning to my original point – you've got to give the audience some sense of the risk that's involved for you when you start seeing Tony. Sure, you're loved up and full of the joys of spring – but there's danger too. It's a love that dares not speak its name.'

'You what?' Kacey stared at Patrick as if he had asked her to rip out her hoop earrings and frisbee them across the hall.

'Like if a Somerstown Crew started seeing a Buckland Boi,' I suggested. Really, it was such an obvious parallel, I wondered why it hadn't occurred to Patrick.

A lightbulb pinged over Kacey's head. 'Oh, right, I get you,' she said. 'They've gotta keep it quiet or ...' She mimicked the loading and discharge of a pump-action shotgun.

'Exactly.' Patrick looked over at me and smiled, causing my heart to melt all over the white keys. 'Thank you, Ms Delaney. But which are the Montagues and which the Capulets, eh?'

Be but sworn my love, and I'll no longer be a deviant.

Stupid, stupid crush.

Besides, I had other fish to fry now, big, fat kink-fish with snappy jaws and whip fins. I had my piano lesson scene with Justin and Maz to set up, and there was talk of the three of us signing up for a big event in London at the end of the month. I hadn't made up my mind whether to go through with it yet, but I expected my new friends' arguments in favour to be persuasive.

Kacey and Tunde ran through their balcony scene once more, then the rehearsal was over and I prepared to leave.

'Secret love,' said Patrick, unexpectedly and rather alarmingly, having crept up to some spot just behind my left shoulder while I was rummaging in my bag.

Was there an answer to that? Did he expect an answer?

'Those were the days,' I said vaguely, though they weren't really. I'd never had a secret lover, as far I could remember. I suppose you could count Justin as one, though "lover" didn't seem quite the right word. What did love have to do with it?

'Really?' Patrick's voice blended curiosity and melancholy, but I had no elaboration for him. 'No secret lovers stashed in the instrument cupboards, then?'

'Er, no. You?'

'Not one. Actually, I was wondering whether you were free –'

A basketball crashed deafeningly across the floor, making the pair of us jump.

103

'Sorry, headmaster,' said Gareth insincerely. 'Just checking the place out for the match tomorrow. I need to ask you about a few things, actually. Are you available?'

Patrick masked a sigh. 'Of course.'

A dull conversation about team bibs and after-match refreshments broke out. I picked up my bag, nodded my excuses and left.

What had he been about to ask me? His manner had been quite intimate, almost diffident for such a confident man. Was I going mad, or did he seem to be approaching me for a – a date? An adulterous liaison! Was he really that kind of man?

The excitement of it was outweighed heavily by disappointment at his lack of integrity. But perhaps they had separated? A divorce was on the cards? She had cheated on him and he wanted revenge? They had an open marriage? But he had said that thing about "secret love" – that pointed a rather damning finger towards the adultery theory.

A million scenarios flew through my head between school and my flat, but I didn't dare pursue any one of them. I wasn't going to be any man's mistress. If I was a mistress, how could a man be my master? No, it was a hopeless case. I would keep exploring my sexuality in an emotionally safe setting and keep the love stuff for another time, if another time ever came.

We had negotiated the scene beforehand this time. We knew exactly who was playing what role, and what body parts were going where and in whom afterwards.

Maz, in severe tweed and a tight bun, was my piano teacher, tapping my knuckles with her baton whenever my fingers strayed on to the wrong keys. Once I had made three successive errors, I was told to bend over the piano stool while she lifted my skirt and petticoat, lowered my old-fashioned bloomers and spanked me hard with the conductor's baton. It didn't hurt very much, being similar in length and width to a knitting needle, so she switched to using her hand, which was pretty hard considering it lacked the size and firm quality of Justin's.

Once my arse was reddened to her satisfaction, she pulled the bloomers back up and I sat back on the stool and continued with the piece.

But it still wasn't good enough. My hands were wrenched off the keys, the lid put down and I was led by the hand to the next room, where "Professor Stern", the head of the conservatoire, kept his office.

'Enter,' said Justin.

I had to freeze my facial muscles to avoid smiling when I saw him. He had found a dusty old black schoolmaster's gown from somewhere and was holding it at the lapels, pacing up and down my hastily-rearranged bedroom.

'What appears to be the problem, Miss Cross?'

'This lazy girl hasn't practised since our last lesson,' said Maz.

'That's not true,' I protested, but their combined wrathful looks soon drove my rebellious spirit back inside me and I listened mutely while they discussed my poor performance.

'I've spanked her once already today, but it seems to have done no good,' complained Maz. 'The girl has had to bare her bottom every day since we started – she is by far my laziest student. I think stronger measures are called for, Professor.'

'I see. Well, Miss Delray, it's a very long time since I've had such a recalcitrant student as you. I'm not sure the conservatoire is the right place for you any more.'

'Oh, please, sir, don't expel me! The shame would kill my mother!' I exclaimed, hamming it up for the non-existent gallery.

'I'm going to offer you another chance,' said Justin.

'Oh, thank you, thank you.' I wondered about sinking to

my knees, but held myself in check as Justin opened my wardrobe door.

'Don't thank me, Miss Delray, until I've finished with you. I might not be expelling you, but it's clear that some extraordinary measures are needed to encourage you to develop your self-discipline.' He emerged from the wardrobe wielding a rattan cane.

My first caning. I goosebumped all over, curling my toes inside the Victorian lace-up boots.

'I haven't used this in many a year,' he said, bending the cane reflectively. 'I hoped I would never have cause to again. But you have brought it out of retirement. Miss Cross, I will need your assistance. Please pin up her skirts for me.'

'Oh no,' I wailed miserably as Maz crouched to grab my hem and lift it up, taking some pins from her hair and using them to tack the material up at my waist level.

'It's a sound six of the best, or you leave this place for good,' Justin reminded me, whipping the cane through the air. The sound was terrifying, alluring, terrifying again. 'Bend over, please.' He pointed his cane at the footboard of my bed, and I gripped it hard, watching my knuckles whiten.

'I'll practise, I promise,' I whimpered, listening to the tap-tap-tap of the rattan in Justin's palm.

'Yes,' he said. 'You will. Miss Cross, kindly lower her drawers for me.'

For the second time in that half hour, my bottom was exposed, pushed out and positioned high, the focus of everyone's attention.

'I see you had to spank her quite hard,' said Justin. His hand touched my right bum cheek, finding it warm. 'Your arm must be tired.'

'It is,' said Maz.

Humph. All the sympathy for her arm – how about my backside? I twinged and let out a hasty breath as the long, thin rod was laid against the plumpest section of my cheeks. It felt so innocuous, just a whisper of cool, a light, sweet thing …

Its soft kiss ended and Justin drew back his arm.

I clamped my jaw and tensed my shoulders.

The air split and sang and a streak of heat branded my behind.

It hurt. A second passed, and then it hurt much worse. I couldn't hold back my cry. This was pain beyond imagining, beyond expectation, and yet I didn't say the word. Instead, I let the agony sear its path through my skin and tissues until it became pleasure – the process took no more than half a minute.

And then I wanted another.

'Please, sir,' I whispered.

'Yes,' said Justin. 'You may have another.'

He gave me it. And again, laying them on swiftly and briskly until six angry lines barred my bottom.

'Good shot!' said Maz on the sixth, while my knees buckled and I let go of the footboard, spouting some incoherent noise that might have been swear words. I was red hot and throbbing, at my outer limit, my fingers pressing anxiously into the expanding welts, as if touch could soothe them, which it could not.

'Hands on your head,' barked Justin, grabbing my wrist and yanking it away from my rear.

I stood – just about – by the footboard, skirts up, drawers down, presenting my freshly caned and scorching hot arse to whoever cared to look at it.

'That's a job well done, Professor,' said Maz, in a passable cut-glass accent.

'Take a closer look,' invited Justin.

I winced as Maz ran her long fingernails across each sensitive mark, pushing them in, pinching cruelly.

'That should concentrate her mind,' she said.

'Yes. You know, Miss Cross, I'm thinking that we

should make this a regular fixture. Perhaps on a weekly basis. I imagine it would improve her concentration no end.'

'What a good idea, Professor. Six of the best at the beginning of each week, to start our sessions off as they mean to go on. Extras as necessary, throughout the course of the term.'

'That's agreed. You'll present yourself in my office every Monday morning at nine o'clock sharp, Miss Delray. And from now on, all piano practice is to be done bare-bottomed, so you're ready for extra spanking when required. Is that clear?'

'Yes, sir,' I snivelled.

'Good. Now march back into the practice room and let's try that piece again. No, don't pull up your drawers. Like that will be fine.'

I shuffled haltingly, ankles constricted by the linen bloomers, back into the living room. Arriving at the piano I could not quite believe Maz meant for me to sit down on the stool. Couldn't I play standing up?

But my glance of appeal was met with a firm shake of the head and I lowered myself gradually on to the uncomfortable velvet pile, whimpering with pain as my sore bottom made contact.

'Now, let's have that *Étude* again from the beginning, Miss Delray.'

I began to play, heat and pain raging through my arse while something else raged in my pussy. I needed to be fucked. Oh God, let this piece be finished so I can get fucked. I played it so fast I missed out half the notes, squirming furiously on the unforgiving stool.

Maz laughed as I reached the end and slumped forward, plunging my forehead on to the keys with a grand discord.

'To be honest, Keris, I don't think that caning worked at all. That was awful!'

But she stood beside me and bent down to kiss the back

of my neck, indicating that we were out of role and ready for the real fun to start.

'It worked,' I muttered into the ivories. 'Oh, it worked a treat.'

'Can I check?' whispered Maz, a flirtatious hand on my thigh.

'Uh-huh.'

Her fingers skimmed my bare pussy and she giggled.

'I see what you mean. Wanna come through to the bedroom? I bet Justin's ready for you.'

'Damn right I am.'

I looked up and screamed at the sight of him – stark naked but for the dusty old black robe, his cock pointing optimistically at the ceiling.

Maz, quick as a flash, was back in role.

'Professor Stern!' she rebuked. 'Now, if I remember correctly, there is a further task for Miss Delray. Go through the bedroom, Miss, and disrobe. Wait for us in the corner.'

I heard Justin and Maz kissing and giggling from beyond the bedroom door while I took off my drawers, my high-necked Edwardian blouse, my chemise. I took my naked body to the corner, still preoccupied by the scorpion-sting pain in my bottom. I rested my forehead against the wall, dreaming of cool lotion, a cold flannel, anything to take the heat away. But I knew that the heat was the point. I had to keep the heat and the sting, or the sex wouldn't hit the heights I wanted and needed.

The door opened and closed behind me and their footsteps moved softly over the carpet.

'Good,' said Justin. 'Now get on to the bed on all fours please, bottom raised nice and high for us.'

I obeyed immediately, my heart racing, remembering what we had agreed over IM during the week.

'Miss Cross, take up your position.'

I heard Maz unzip her skirt and let it fall to the floor.

109

She climbed on to the bed and sat down in front of me, spreading her legs in their sheer stockings and nude suspenders so that her pussy gaped wide just beyond my nose. Her upper body was fully clothed in a mint green twinset and pearls and she'd managed to achieve a hair and make-up look that aged her by about twenty years.

I swallowed hard. I knew what I had to do, but it was my first time. I hoped she would be firm with me.

'Well, girl,' she said. 'What are you waiting for? Service me or the cane comes out again.'

Exactly right. Gratefully, I bobbed my head down, pushed out my tongue and gave her lower lips a tentative lick.

Maz put her hand in my hair and pressed my face into her hot spread.

'Don't hold back,' she said gruffly. 'Eat it.'

I breathed her in, my nose squashed into her clit, my tongue working at identifying her taste. It was far from unpleasant, a salty, subtle tang, and I began to relish my task, poking and probing into her intricate folds of flesh.

'Good girl,' she said heavily. 'Don't you dare stop.'

Her free hand reached down to cup a breast and fondle it.

Then there were larger hands, on my hips, and I knew from the tipping of the mattress and the approaching warmth that Justin was at my rear, ready to fulfil his part of the plan.

He gave my sore bottom a few hard slaps, causing me to moan into Maz's cunt, then lined his cock up, quickly and neatly, with my wet pussy and pushed it in without ceremony.

'Aaaah,' he gasped appreciatively. 'Nice and tight, and so hot. Nothing like fucking a girl who's just been caned. Nothing better in the whole world.'

He proved his point by thrusting brutally so that his pelvis slapped my bum, exacerbating the sting in a way that drove me half-mad.

Maz, bucking her pussy hard into my damp face, laughed and kissed him over my bent spine. They seemed to hold the kiss, on and off, for most of the time it took Justin to fuck me, breaking off to call me a slut or tell me I needed this and it would be my arse next time.

I cowered beneath them, their creature, their slave, existing to satisfy their sadistic urges, their whipping girl, their fucktoy.

Justin powered into me, over and over, pushing me further into Maz's greedy quim until I came, my muffled grunts lost in my mistress' clit, and then she spent into my mouth while Justin's cock emptied its load inside me.

I lay curled on the duvet, feeling utterly submissive and used, my bum still burning, my pussy stretched, nipple sore, face shiny with Maz's juices. I felt good. Ecstatic, even. This was all I had hoped for, and more.

So why were there tears rolling down my face?

'Hey, babe,' said Maz softly, cradling my head in her lap and stroking my hair. 'Was that too much?'

Justin returned from disposing of the condom and sat on the other side of me, looking down with sad brown eyes.

'Melissa was like that too, remember?' he said to Maz. 'The first time.'

'Yeah, I remember. Hey, talk to us, Keris. Are you OK?'

'I'm fine, I'm fine, ignore me, just … You know. A reaction.'

'A good one or a bad one?'

'That was incredible. My mind's blown. I think this is what happens to me when my mind is blown.'

'Hey, J, you get the lotion and I'll make Keris a drink. Maybe a brandy. Do you have brandy?'

'An ancient bottle in the kitchen somewhere.'

'Cool. Hold it right there.'

Justin, in the meanwhile, found me a tissue and then

rolled me on to my stomach before retrieving a bottle from his bag. Oh, the lotion was heavenly on my cane welts, calming and soothing. I began to sniff less and sigh more.

'So what were the tears for?' he asked, circling a lotioned fingertip around the hot spots.

'I think … gratitude,' I said. 'I'm doing things I've only dreamed of and finding them even better than fantasy. I expected it to be sordid and awkward, but it's even more powerful than I imagined.'

'It's addictive too,' commented Justin. 'I'm pleased we've opened this world up to you. Another job well done. Perhaps we should ask for a testimonial.'

'How many people have you done this with?'

'Oh God, I don't know. Dozens. We're part of a wider scene, like I've mentioned.'

Maz came back in with the brandy, which she put to my lips as if I were a child and she my nurse. It was instantly comforting and I sank back into the pillow, floating on a sense of being cherished and cared for.

'So it was OK?' she asked anxiously.

'Honestly, brilliant,' I mumbled.

'We haven't put you off?'

'Quite the opposite.'

'Oh, I'm so glad.' She clapped her hands and sat down beside me on the bed. 'You're really a born submissive. I know so many doms – male and female – who would just love to play with you.'

That wider scene thing again. Was I ready for it? Could I consider it?

'And I can't believe you'd never gone down on a girl before,' she babbled on. 'That was awesome! Right up there with the best.'

'Wow, thanks.' I was genuinely flattered. And it was true, I had enjoyed it.

'It's us that should be thanking you,' said Justin. 'Another outstanding scene. Listen, it can be hard to come

112

down from intense sex like this – we'll stay with you as long as you like, OK? Maybe run you a bath. Put on a DVD.'

I wanted to cry again. It felt like an age since anyone had considered my needs. Gareth, the selfish fucker, had been one for rolling over and snoring immediately after his substandard version of The Deed. These people were like sex fairies, granting my every wish.

'I'm so glad I went to that Munch,' I yawned.

Later on, all curled up together on the sofa watching some Friday night nonsense, the talk turned to the Big Event in London.

'So what is it? Do you think I'd like it?'

'You might,' said Justin. 'You might not. But it'd be interesting to find out, don't you think? Besides, you don't have to do anything if you don't want to. If you just want to watch, that's fine.'

'There'll be all kinds of people there,' said Maz, 'into all kinds of different versions of kink. Some of them live it as a lifestyle, others just play now and again. Some are into big group scenes, others strictly couple-focused.'

'Hang on,' I said. 'You said some of them live it as a lifestyle. What, you mean, they have kinky sex all the time? How can that be?'

Justin lifted my wrist and kissed it. 'Of course they're not having sex 24/7. But they're living a Total Power Exchange lifestyle.'

Total Power Exchange? It sounded like a hair metal band.

'What's that when it's at home then?'

'A master/slave dynamic,' said Maz.

'Really? Like, real life master and slave?' I was fascinated. 'That would be …'

'Would you like to do something like that?' asked Justin.

'No. No, I couldn't, could I? How could I work, or just,

113

you know, go to the shops or … anything?'

'I guess people work things out in their own way,' said Maz with a shrug. 'I've got a couple of full-time slave friends. One of them sleeps in shackles in a cage, every night. She loves it. Each to their own, right?'

'Of course. It's just, well, hard to imagine.' But interesting to imagine. And to fantasise about.

'You seem to like obeying orders,' commented Justin.

'Well, yeah, in role play. Not in real life, though. I have to give orders all day long …' I trailed off, not wanting to reveal my real job. 'And if I'd had a piano lesson like that for real, I'd have called the police.'

Maz laughed.

'I'm quite drawn to a 24/7 contract, to be honest,' she said. 'But it'd never work for me. Like you say, it just wouldn't fit around work. And I'm usually so knackered from working shifts, I'm playing scenes less and less.' She sighed. 'That's why tonight was such a great release. Not having to be a nurse. An "angel", as we get called. If only they knew exactly how angelic I really am.'

'You're my angel,' said Justin gallantly, stretching his neck behind me to kiss her.

'Aww, honey,' she said. 'So! The Gathering! Are we all going together or what?'

I bit my lip and considered it for a moment.

'Count me in.'

Justin and Maz applauded my decision and began making plans immediately.

'OK,' said Maz. 'We'll need tickets – that's easy, I can get them off Madam Malfeasance on Wednesday night. Transport, accommodation, costumes '

'What sort of costumes?'

'Oh, whatever you like. Preferably something a bit kinky, but up to you. What do you fancy?'

'I don't know. I liked you in latex last week.'

'We'll have to go shopping! Tell you what, I'll take you

114

to the fetish outfitters in London before the Gathering, sort you out with a costume that'll get all the doms circling you like a pack of whip-wielding wolves.'

'Wow.' This sounded better by the minute. 'I'm in.'

'You'll love it. I always get a bit overexcited and end up doing something a bit closer to my limits than I intended. I managed to go home with pierced labia last time.'

'Christ!'

'But nobody forced me! You just do what you feel, hon, what you're comfortable with. It's all about personal taste.'

'How many people will be there?'

Justin spoke up. 'Last year there were more than five hundred. It's held in a stately home just outside London that the promoters have hired for the night. You can book rooms there, if you can afford it.'

'Oh, let's do that this year, J! I know we can stay with friends, but I think it'd be nice for Keris.'

'Well, why not? OK.'

Maz squealed and clapped her hands.

'They have everything – a torture chamber, a flogging room, tattoo and piercing room, a massive orgy chamber, cages, a giant ballroom … Oh, it's just heaven.'

A paradise of perversion, with all the accoutrements of the Other Place. I had to see this for myself.

'And it's at the end of the month, you say?'

'Last weekend of November. Saturday night right through till Sunday morning. Last year I went as a nun.'

'A nun?'

'A latex nun. Justin was a priest. He looked so hot. I think this year I'd like to be a courtesan. Or a burlesque dancer. Maybe a pony girl.'

Decisions, decisions.

'Are you busy this weekend?'

Yes, thanks for asking, Headmaster, as a matter of fact I'm very busy. I have latex slutwear to choose and a fetish party to attend, probably followed by an orgy. Yourself?

'Actually, I'm visiting friends in London.'

'Oh.' A pause, pregnant with …something. Maybe disappointment. 'Well, I hope you have a good one.'

A good one, eh? Better than the one I'd have as your mistress, you mean?

'Thanks. Are you busy?'

'Not especially. Well, when I say "not especially" I mean, no more than usual – no such thing as a quiet weekend for a headteacher.'

'That must be hard on your wife.'

He blinked.

'Not especially. Not since the divorce.'

'Divorce. Oh.'

Let me rewind, take everything back, go to the beginning and start all over again.

I wondered if this was one of those occasions when an awkward "I'm sorry" was called for. What is the correct response when a man you fancy like mad tells you that he is not, as you suspected, married and actually appears to be making a tiny play for you, much too late, because you are now fully embroiled in the BDSM scene?

I settled for, 'I didn't realise.'

At that point, the cast and crew trooped through the hall doors and I retreated to the piano.

The lacklustre November weather seemed to be affecting everybody's mood. Our gangs couldn't muster much aggression, the Latinas' flirtatious *joie de vivre* was too low-key and as for Tony and Maria, I'd seen more passion in the sloth enclosure at Marwell Zoo.

'This is ridiculous.' Patrick acted, interrupting a rendition of *There's a Place for Us* that wouldn't have been out of place on a nursery rhyme CD. 'This is supposed to be tragic, Tunde. Kacey, your one true love is dying. You look as if you're resigned to the fact that you've missed the bus to town. We need agony here.'

Kacey shrugged. 'I ain't never known no one what's died, innit? Except my nan and I was only three then.'

'Well, then, think about it. How do you think you'd feel?'

'I dunno.'

'Look, it's like this … Ms Delaney, perhaps you could help out. Why don't you be Maria and I'll be Tony and we'll try to give Kacey an idea of what she should be aiming for?'

Me? He wanted me to grieve dramatically in song over his pretend dead body?

The chorus sniggered as Patrick feigned a long, slow stagger, clutching at an imaginary bullet hole in his chest before thudding to the woodblock flooring.

Trying not to laugh, or cry, I hurried over and crouched at his side, searching for the opening note in my head and hoping this gave me enough of a preoccupied air to make me look convincingly devastated.

His hand, large and long-fingered, lay across his expensive shirt and rumpled tie, chunky watch weighing down his wrist. His eyes were shut but the lids fluttered a little and his cheekbones twitched. He was trying not to breathe too hard, trying to look as if the life was draining out of him, but all I could see was energy, vigour, health and potency. He worked so hard, and yet he never seemed to tire. He was so attractive, and yet he was lonely. How could such a man be alone?

I put my hand on his, and the contact was mildly electric. I didn't need to force the quiver into my voice when I sang the first few notes of the song.

There's a place for us.

Is there?

Leaning over him, singing, I could feel his warmth, what they call the vital signs. His pulse, bumping in his wrist, his heartbeat so close to my ear. The melodious, melancholy promises I made sounded sincere, a forlorn hope genuinely held. A place for us, for me and for him.

At the end of the song, the students cheered. A few of them whistled.

Patrick sat up straight, grinning, and clapped me himself.

'Exactly what I mean. Real emotion, Kacey. It is possible to sing the right notes and act at the same time. Want to give it a try?'

The moment of eye contact when he found his feet was fleeting, but powerful. It probed inside me, turned me inside out, examined every hope and wish I had for my personal life.

He had moved on to stage-directing as soon as the fuse was lit, but I was still feeling its slow, deadly fizzle when I arrived back at the piano.

I think I'm actually in love. Am I? Is it?

Perhaps I could cancel the weekend plans. I pictured myself strolling around some breezy marina with Patrick, picking out yachts for some reason. Yachts? Why? I was beyond analysing myself. A dinghy would be more our budget.

The tumult of youth shooed into the weekend world and Patrick came to join me in returning the scores to the cupboard.

'Are you leaving tonight?' he asked. 'Do you have time for a drink?'

Only the rest of my life.

'A quick one.'

Was this wise? Throughout the rehearsal I had been cautioning myself to hold back, to be enigmatic, not to let him think I had any more admiration for him than was seemly from a member of staff to her supervisor.

All the same, it was with a giddy sense of being flung on the breeze like an autumn leaf that I followed him to the same pub we had visited that last time.

'So,' he said, drinks bought and packet of crisps ripped

open for free consumption on the table. 'You were saying, a while back, that you had no secret lovers in the music stores. Is that still true?'

Wow, straight to the heart of the matter. Was he really going to ..?

'Um, yes, last time I looked.'

'So you're single.'

'Technically.'

Oh fuck! What kind of a stupid response was that? Why didn't I just say "yes"?

He frowned. I had just more or less admitted that I was indulging in a festival of commitment-free shagging.

So what? I thought, with a hint of libertine irritation. My sex life was my own affair. Just because I was having sex outside a conventional relationship, did that make me a pariah?

'What does technically mean? Either you're single or you aren't.'

Wrong again, mister.

'I mean, y'know, Gareth's obviously still not over everything and I'm –'

'Oh. Gareth. Right.'

'He keeps calling me.'

'He wants you back? Do you want him back?'

'No. I'm ready to move on.'

'So don't let him hold you hostage. He's a grown-up.'

'Yeah. I know.'

My cagey tone wasn't winning me any romance points here. I could see the "Is this worth it?" sliding behind Patrick's eyes, feel the unsighed breath before it came out. I couldn't possibly cry off the ball; I would be letting Justin and Maz down badly. It was one weekend. Give me one weekend …

But it didn't look as if he was going to.

'OK, the time's not right,' said Patrick enigmatically. 'Story of my life.'

119

'Time's not right? Right for what?'

'Anything.'

He drained his pint, stood and gathered up his belongings.

'Patrick, I'm not sure what I've done to upset you.'

'You haven't. You haven't done anything to upset me. Forget it.'

'If I knew what "it" was, I could try.'

He was almost out of the door though. The "it" to be forgotten had not even been identified. How was I supposed to put that from my mind?

'Have a nice weekend,' he called over his shoulder.

He was gone before I could utter the polite, 'You too.'

Chapter Seven

'DON'T YOU THINK THAT would look cute?'

'I think it would look insane!'

'No, it would suit you! You've got the figure for it.'

Maz had made it her personal mission to persuade me to dress up as a slave girl for the ball in little more than a metallic-looking bra, knickers and padlockable collar. Now, my body confidence might not be the worst in the world, but that was a flesh-flash too far for me. I'd had some kind of black rubber maid's outfit in mind, something that at least covered most of the stuff that wasn't legal to show in public.

Maz and Justin were firmly in Roman mode, though, rifling through togas and tunics to find something that would give them the required patrician air.

'Instead of those knickers, you could have a gold belt with some material hanging from it, just between your legs, say,' said Maz. 'Kind of a skirt, but not. Do you know what I mean?'

I didn't, so she showed me an example. It looked even more obscene than the knickers on their own.

'That's perfect,' said Justin, looking over from his helmet-fitting. 'Go for that. We're a Roman couple and she's our slave. We just need to get a few bunches of grapes for her to feed us, and a whip or something.'

'Try it on,' said Maz, holding out the apparel.

'Are you sure a Roman slave would have worn this?' I asked dubiously, weighing the items in my hand. They were so light, I would hardly know I was wearing anything, the "metal" really no more than moulded plastic. 'Looks more like Princess Leia when she was Jabba the Hutt's prisoner to me.'

Justin snorted.

'OK, OK,' he said. 'That might just be a little fantasy of mine come true. Go on, Keris. We'll love you for ever if you wear it tonight.'

Eternal love was quite a good payback for a few hours freezing my arse off in a skimpy costume. I removed my underwear and let Maz help me clip on the bra. When I say "bra" I'm using the word loosely. It appeared to be a pair of golden strips, plunging in a V-shape to just cover my nipples while the rest of the cup was sheer spangly gauze.

Around my hips sat the gold leather belt, two swathes of spangly goldy stuff falling between my thighs at front and back. Behind the waterfall skirts – nothing. I was bare. A hand would only have to brush the material aside to display my naked bottom or pussy. I would need to tread carefully, that was for sure.

The outfit was completed with slave bands for my wrists, ankles and upper arms, and – of course – the *coup de grâce* of the lockable collar with chain lead.

'Mmm,' said Justin, drawing near and grazing his knuckles over my collarbones, just where the chain links hung. 'That's you. Stripped, chained and ready for use. And boy, are you going to get used tonight.'

The shopkeeper knocked at the fitting room door.

'Is everything OK in there? Do you need any help?'

'Shall I ask for his help?' whispered Justin. 'Shall I ask if he wants to inspect you?'

'No!' I hissed back, to my friends' amusement.

'You might not get the chance to say no tonight,' Maz warned me. 'Not if you want to stick to what we discussed during the week.'

What we discussed during the week. My chest tightened

underneath the tiny bra top and my clit woke up.

'We've picked our costumes,' Maz sang out. 'Just coming to pay for them.'

In the hotel room, we dressed again, this time surrounded by luxury and history instead of cheap felt carpeting and plasterboard walls. Justin had bought a new martinet at Shepherds Bush Market and was swishing it to and fro while Maz rubbed gold-flecked lotion all over my bare flesh, which took some time.

'So you're feeling brave?' Maz asked gently, reaching deep down into my cleavage and working the ointment in. 'You want to go through with what we talked about?'

'I think so. Dressed like this makes me want to even more. Funny how just changing clothes can get you into a mindset.'

'It's good, isn't it?' Justin grinned, wrapping the leather fronds of the whip around one of the bedposts with a flick of the wrist. 'How something as simple as showing a lot of skin can make a person feel submissive. And when you add collars and cuffs to that ...'

'It's a bit like magic,' I agreed. 'Before a word's been said, I want to kiss somebody's feet.'

'Kiss mine if you like,' offered Maz, giggling.

They were cute feet, toes wriggling in gladiator sandals, but I decided to pass for the moment.

'Maybe later. You look great too, by the way.'

In her abbreviated silk toga and richly-jewelled cloak, she looked imperious and impish at the same time. I supposed that was the trick of switching. The opulent cloths were mistressy enough, but the teeny toga hem was perfect for flipping up and delivering an impromptu spanking. She could go either way tonight.

'Right then, you two,' said Justin, bored of practising his whip hand on the bedposts. 'Bend over the end of the bed and let's give this a proper trial run.'

'Both of us?' squealed Maz.

'Of course. Bottoms bared, please. I want you both going downstairs with noticeable markings. Besides, I think a little warm-up is a sensible idea, don't you?'

I exchanged a glance with Maz and we both giggled, adjusting our skirts as required before lining up at the foot of the bed and bending at identical angles.

'Ten from this side and ten from the other should give you a nice even glow each,' surmised Justin.

He started off on Maz's corner, which meant that my bottom caught the stinging knotty ends of the lash, heating it more quickly than my partner-in-submission's. It was sharp but manageable, as lashes go, and quickly transformed to a spread of warmth that permeated both cheeks. I hissed and wriggled my hips with each descent of the whip, while Maz seemed to be positively enjoying herself, sighing and pushing back to heighten the sensation.

'I won't have my slave girls let me down tonight,' said Justin in a low growl. 'So let this be a warning. You will remember to be well-behaved, obedient and submissive at all times, unless I give you explicit permission to dominate another slave – which only applies to you, Marianne. As for Keris – you are here to serve tonight, and you needn't forget it.'

He laid the tenth stroke, a sizzler, then changed positions so that he stood just behind me. Now Maz was getting the evil ends of the martinet while I found the throbbing in my rear enhanced and heated by the stroke of the thong tops.

Like Maz earlier, I began to moan with pleasure, wanting it harder, perhaps wanting a little spark of sting between my pussy lips. I spread my thighs and thrust my arse out as far as I could. Once Justin had dealt the final ten, he chuckled and sent his lash curling sweetly and painfully inside my thighs so that I gasped and jumped up, clutching the bedpost.

'You didn't really want that, did you, sweetheart?' He laughed.

'I like the idea of it,' I confessed, rubbing my swollen clit furiously.

'The reality is quite painful,' agreed Maz. 'But you'll feel incredibly turned on all night now – take my word for it. A whipped pussy is a hot pussy.'

And that's what I was to be for the night. A pussy for fucking and an arse for whipping.

All my fantasies were coming true, week by week, in rapid succession. I had to stop and remember how long I had known these people – under a month. How had I come this far, this fast? I must have wanted it badly, more badly than I knew.

For a seasick moment, I thought of Stuart, out there on the ocean wave. Would he have brought me here? Oddly enough, I wasn't sure he would.

But he had made his choice, and now I was making mine.

'Are your nipples rouged?' Justin asked us anxiously. 'And your labia?'

'Mine don't need any reddening now,' I said, pressing tentative fingertips against the inflamed flesh.

'I guess not. Is your collar OK? Not too tight?'

'It's fine.'

'Are you nervous?'

'Ummm.'

'You should be nervous.' Justin's voice was stern. 'That's your role tonight. Other girls can do the bratty thing – it's not really you, is it?'

'No. It isn't.'

'So you're the nervous new slave girl, anxious to please her master and mistress in any and every way, fearing punishment if she doesn't get it right. Just like we agreed.'

I nodded, and now I really was nervous, a blend of performance anxiety and fear of the unknown. It would be

OK. Justin and Maz would take care of me. It would be OK.

Outside on the landing, we weren't the only guests ready to descend to the depths of decadence, aka the ballroom and banqueting hall. A couple came out of the room opposite and I immediately lowered my eyes to the floor, but not before I'd clocked a man in riding gear carrying a horsewhip and leading a human pony by a tight rein. I might think that I was in a humiliating position, led by a chain, collared and naked under my scanty adornments, but at least I didn't have what appeared to be a horsehair-tailed butt-plug up my bum for all to see.

Fascinated, I watched the woman pretend to paw the ground skittishly while the men conversed.

'Lovely leather,' said Justin, stroking the ponygirl's bridle. 'Where did you get it made?'

'At the SubSaddlery – do you know it?'

'Yeah, got myself a few of their riding crops. Nice workmanship.'

We turned and headed together at a leisurely pace towards the staircase. Justin and the riding man appeared to know each other.

'Who's the new girl?' asked the rider. 'Think I'd remember if I'd seen that at an event before.'

That. I was a thing, a possession. My pussy slicked.

'This is my new slave girl, Keris. Show the master your respects, please, Keris.'

This was my cue to drop to my knees and kiss the man's riding boots, which were at least shone to perfection. I saw my eyes, huge and intent, in their mirror sheen.

'Lovely,' he said. 'I'm Rider. Stand up – let me get a good look at you.'

I stood as instructed, while Justin, Maz and the pony watched on the sidelines. Over the balustrade I could see a throng of people, raising glasses and jostling at the foot of the stairs.

Rider's crop outlined my nearly-nude body, starting at my chin then moving slowly down my silhouette. He tapped my bare hip, a little painfully, then slapped the underside of my breasts in their flimsy gauze. The leather returned and slid under my skirts, tracing a path down the backs of my thighs then back up again, sawing briefly back and forth between my legs. The glorious cold and smoothness of it against my still-burning clit was a sweet relief, but I was less relieved when he withdrew the crop and inspected its flat leather tip, which was damp and slicked with my juices.

'Dirty girl,' he said with satisfaction, then he presented it to my face. 'Lick it off.'

While my tongue washed it clean and I burned with shame he continued chatting to Justin about me as if I weren't there.

'What's her form? Does she ride well?'

'She's pretty much untried, but I find her a very satisfying mount. I think she'll go the distance.'

'Does she take the whip well?'

'Again, she's new, but very promising.'

'I'd love to give her a gallop some time.'

'Well, this is her first big event, so we'll be taking it good and slow, but you never know your luck, Rider. Keep in touch. How's, um … Sorry, I've forgotten your ponygirl's name.'

'Little Miss Naughty,' obliged Rider. 'Or just Naughty for short. She's had some good rides lately and her dressage skills are so much better than they were. Mind you, it took a lot of whippings to get it the way we wanted, didn't it, Naughty?'

She whinnied. I had to double-take, she sounded so much like a real horse.

Justin tugged on my chain and we turned to the staircase, stepping slowly. Maz leant on Justin's elbow while his other arm was occupied in keeping my chain as safely short as he could. Rider and Little Miss Naughty followed us at a slow trot.

Now I could see how the huge reception rooms, so quiet and echoey when we checked in hours earlier, had been transformed by their colourful guests into a bacchanalia of lust. Skin was everywhere, including bouncing nipple-clamped breasts and striped buttocks, cocks in cages or strapped on to slim female waists. In between the expanses of bared flesh, strips of leather or latex ran cunningly, providing some form of "dress". Others were more formally attired, in flouncy ballgowns or Regency breeches, with wigs and masks, while others still swished in schoolmaster robes or flirted in tiny pleated skirts. They fell into two ultimate camps – the displayers and the displayed. The dominants and the submissives. The doers and the done-to.

'Right,' said Justin, finding a path through the crowds for us, fending off greetings and well wishes while I had no choice but to accept the curious hands that landed on my body, patting my bum, pinching my hips, as we passed. 'We need to find the Slave Market.'

'Market?'

'It's just the name they give the area. It's where all the slave stuff happens. Don't worry, I'm not going to sell you. Unless you want me to.'

'No, no.'

'We'll play the scene there – oh, right, I think I can see it. Hang left.'

We moved past a variety of stalls and small alcoves with different activities occurring in each one. Tattooing and piercing was next door to wax play followed by a mock schoolroom where two rather overgrown schoolboys had hairy bottoms bared for the cane. Small knots of people stood watching each tableau, applauding, or groping each other, as they played voyeur.

Our alcove consisted of a wooden platform on which a

128

number of men and women in varying degrees of nudity were standing, hands on head, collars around necks, while their handlers stood by waiting for … something.

'Here,' said Justin. 'Up on to the stage then, Keris. Hands on head. What you have to do now is wait.'

I stumbled up the steps, prodded in the bottom by Justin's martinet, and found myself a space between two totally naked women, one of whom had a pattern of raised welts all the way up her thighs and stomach and across her breasts. She had been recently whipped and her eyes were as red as the marks.

A flutter of fear made rapid progress from my stomach to my throat, closing it up. But Justin wouldn't let that happen to me. Not unless I wanted it. She had to have wanted it … Didn't she?

From the dim light of our niche, we got a surprisingly good and clear view of everyone that passed by. While Justin and Maz sipped at flutes of champagne, I watched as various slaves were pointed out by passers-by, brought to the front of the stage and examined. One pretty young man was taken away by a group of leather doms, while his owner followed in their wake, slapping his hands together with glee. I tried hard to forget that I was a guest at an unusual kind of house party, a Twenty-first century girl who made her own choices and decisions, and tried hard to slip into the mindset of a piece of property to be used for sex. The continuing tenderness of my whipped clit helped, as did the heat at my rear. All the bare flesh, goosepimpling a little despite the warm air, added to my rapid backward fall into meek submission. I didn't even think about taking my hands from my head, or demanding a glass of wine of my own. That's what Cherry would do. Keris is not Cherry.

I saw one girl bent over and spanked, another fingered to orgasm before my turn for the limelight came.

A tall, spare man in a Victorian frock coat and mutton-chop whiskers glared at me through his monocle, then let his eye follow the line of my chain to Justin's hand. Justin nodded amiably and the man spoke to him.

I quivered, unable to hear the discussion, but desperate to know what was being said. Maz winked at me over the rim of her glass and moved her free hand under the skirt of her toga. This was turning her on as well.

I felt the chain tauten and my collar yank me forward by the neck. I stepped up to the front of the stage, an item for inspection, watched by an increasing group of interested deviants.

The Victorian Gent stood about a head lower than me, tilting his neck to aim a dispassionate stare at my elevated body. Now that he was closer, I could hear what he was saying to Justin.

'And this is her first time?'

'Absolutely.'

'She has good posture. Have you trained her?'

'Not really. We haven't known her long, but she's a fast learner.'

'A fast learner. Hmm, I like that in a submissive.'

I didn't dare look at him. I know we'd discussed the possibility of my finding an exclusive master at this shindig, but for me it had been more a case of "remote possibility" rather than probability. I hadn't given it that much serious thought, content to bob along with my two new pervy friends until our arrangement became unviable. But a master of my own – could that really happen? So soon?

He had a gold-topped cane – not one you could use for thrashing, too solid, but it looked good – and he pointed it up at me, tapping me on the shoulder with it.

'Turn around, keeping your hands on your head,' he said.

I did as I was told, presenting him with my back view.

'All the way around,' he added. His voice was low and

authoritative, with the weight of age in it. I supposed he might be in his fifties or thereabouts, with that well-preserved, distinguished air that can make middle-aged men a more attractive proposition than their younger counterparts.

His cane prodded at the underside of a breast.

'Lower your bra cups and kneel for me.'

I knelt, knees either side of the fountain of material, my legs completely uncovered, and slowly pulled down the spangly slave harness, baring my breasts to him, and the rest of the crowd.

I had never done anything like this before. It was heady, a strangely powerful feeling, despite the ersatz powerlessness of the set-up. Anyone who wants to can see my breasts. Anyone who asks can touch them. The nipples flared with a buzzing sensation, weakening my knees so that I was glad not to be standing.

'Hmm, not in the order I asked for, but we'll address that later, perhaps.'

Victorian Gent reached out beringed hands and weighed my tits in them, jiggling them so that a low laugh rippled through the audience.

'A good handful,' he noted. 'And these …'

The pads of his thumbs moved over the nipples with tormenting lightness, round and round in teasing circles, letting them flood with a rush of need that also filled my clit and wetted my pussy.

'Sensitive, are they?'

'Yes, sir.'

Without warning, he pinched them hard and I gasped, shying away. His palm landed loudly on my thigh, leaving a print there.

'Keep still,' he said roughly, and Justin echoed the instruction with a warning tug on my collar. 'She needs more training.'

'Oh yes, she does,' Maz agreed. 'Lots of it.'

131

The Victorian Gent took my skirt and brushed it aside, tucking it into the gold belt from which it hung so that my shaved cunt peeked out, pink and still swollen from the whip stroke.

'No piercings,' he noted. I shuddered.

'I wouldn't say she was ready for that yet,' said Justin.

'OK, we'll come back to that. Turn around, girl. I want to inspect your arse.'

I shuffled around on my knees, hands still on my head, feeling the collar swivel and chafe my neck as I rotated. That heat in my pussy was becoming too much, making me want to rub my thighs together or touch my clit, but I knew I would find no relief until it pleased a master.

The curtain was drawn on my bum, which seemed to meet the crowd's approval. A hum of admiring chuckles and whistles jumbled into my ears. As soon as Victorian Gent's fingers pinched a cheek, I realised that it wasn't the fine form of my rear they were appreciating, but Justin's work with the martinet.

'You've flogged her already,' he commented.

'She needed a little preparation,' said Justin. 'Some encouragement to behave herself.'

'Good,' said Victorian Gent, rubbing at the warmest spots. 'I don't think whippings should be given only for punishment either. I think they work very well to keep a girl on track, remind her of her place. I like to administer varying degrees of whipping, depending on the intention behind them. Don't you?'

'Indeed I do.'

I had thought I was doing pretty well, holding my position, obeying my instructions without question, but then came the first real test.

Victorian Gent prised apart my buttocks, exposing my anus to the whole room. I clenched my muscles hard and felt a powerful urge to remove my hands from my head and push my cheeks back together. I rocked on my knees, so close to disobeying, so close to defying – and then I caught the eye of one of the other slave girls. She smiled at me, a smile of envy as well as encouragement, and that sudden reminder that I was here because I wanted to be calmed me. I took a deep breath and placed myself in the heart of my submission, ignoring the audience, the shame, the panic and concentrating only on the primal beat between my legs. This was what I was here for, after all.

'This looks tight,' said Victorian Gent. 'Is it virgin?'

'I believe it might be,' said Justin with a weak chuckle. 'Slave?'

'Yes, sir,' I confirmed. Not from choice, I wanted to add. I'd tried to interest Gareth, but he'd shied away from that particular orifice, claiming not to have any "gay urges". Methought he did protest too much, to be honest.

'Any slave of mine would need to give that up to me,' said Victorian Gent. 'Would that be a problem?'

'No, sir.'

He bent and I felt his breath against the tiny pucker as he examined it in minute detail.

'It's some time since I saw such a tight hole. I'm very interested.'

That's my selling point, my most marketable commodity. My unfucked arsehole. They should just take a picture of it, blow it up, hang it over my head and print GET IT HERE under the image. I began to pant, the heat in my crotch fierce and itchy now.

'Well,' said Victorian Gent at last, his words fanning my sphincter so that I squirmed, 'I daresay I can save that pleasure for a less public occasion. I do want a good feel of her cunt, though.' He released my buttocks and smacked them. 'Turn around and show me.'

I faced the crowd again. My bare breasts and pussy had nowhere to hide and now the audience was huge, people tiptoeing and stretching to get the best view of my shameful exposure.

Victorian Gent's hand shoved itself between my legs so quickly that I staggered a little, tripping forward so my pussy landed on his fingers almost accidentally.

'Ah, keep still, girl. Yes, I see. Very wet.' His fingertips massaged my clit, spreading the lips wide while I rocked on my feet, wishing I could take my hands off my head to steady myself. In my head, I could almost convince myself that this wasn't happening – that I wasn't standing in front of dozens of strangers being intimately fingered by a man I'd never met before. I could think about the stiffness gathering in my calves, the industrial music playing somewhere over to my left, Maz's laughter, my empty stomach which could do with filling, but then my cunt always overrode my mind, dragging it out of its safe place, bringing it back to reality. The reality of my humiliation and submission, a humiliation and submission that was building up in fiery layers from my groin upwards, ready to push me into that ultimate act of surrender – my unforced orgasm.

Was it possible to lose self-consciousness to this extent? As soon as I thought I was close, my mind would try to shut off and take me out of my pure sexual self.

'Shut your eyes,' said Justin.

I shut them and felt only the fingers of my would-be master, pushing up inside me while his other hand held me by one bare bum cheek in an iron grip. The fingers thrust, thick and filling, up and down inside me while his thumb kept playing with my clit. I heard the sound it made, the wet suck of my greedy cunt, wanting more, needing to be stretched and used. My legs buckled and I fell against his shoulder. He held me steady, supporting my weight without trouble, never breaking his unhurried rhythm while the crowd murmured and clinked glasses.

'She's soaking wet,' said Victorian Gent in a low voice. 'She could take a lot of cock too, though she's tight. I'd make sure this cunt was kept as busy as possible. The secret of a good slave is plenty of hard fucking, I think.'

Light flashed in front of my eyes and I slumped over his shoulder, coming with a desperate whimper that I couldn't silence however hard I tried.

'Did you give her permission to come?' asked Victorian Gent of Justin politely, while his hand patted my bottom.

'Yes.'

'Good. Because she just did. I'm sure you noticed.'

'We haven't really got as far as orgasm control.'

'Well, that's another project for a rainy day then. She's very promising. I'd like to register my interest.'

I regained some of my breath, though my throat was still dry. On opening my eyes, I saw Maz smiling. Victorian Gent allowed me to step off his fingers, readjust my clothing and leave the podium, where Maz had a large glass of wine waiting for me.

'She doesn't belong to us,' Justin confessed.

'Really? You aren't taking bids?' Victorian Gent sounded disappointed. I hadn't gathered the strength to look at his face yet.

'This was a fantasy she outlined to us, which we agreed to help her with,' explained Maz.

Victorian Gent turned to me. 'So you can speak for yourself?'

I lifted my eyes to his. They weren't as intimidating as I'd feared. I thought I could see the traces of a twinkle somewhere. I reminded myself that this man had just fingered me to orgasm in front of an audience and blushed, turning my face away.

He stopped me with a finger on my cheek – a finger that smelled of me.

'What do you say, slave girl? Would you like a master?'

'I, I'm not sure. I mean, I would, but I'm not sure how it could work. In the real world.'

'Ah, the real world.' He shook his head gravely, but the corners of his mouth curved upwards. 'Always spoiling our fun. But if, theoretically, a way of combining the real world with the fantasy one was possible?'

'Oh, then, yes.'

'And your fantasy of being put on display and exhibited for common use – does it go any further?'

'What do you mean?' I took a swig of wine.

'You let me take plenty of liberties with you just then. Would you go even further than that?'

I took a breath.

'Not tonight,' I said. 'Not in front of a crowd.'

'I understand,' said Victorian Gent. 'What you've just done must have required enormous reserves of courage and strength. I imagine you need a bit of time to wind down.'

I nodded apologetically.

'I was just going to watch some stuff now,' I said. 'But …'

I didn't want him to think I wasn't interested. A full-time master was what I had dreamed about all my life and he seemed to have serious potential.

He bent down to my ear and spoke so that only I could hear.

'I'm very taken with you,' he said. 'I think you're exactly what I've been looking for. Would you consider spending some more time with me?'

His voice was deadly, a witches brew of smoke and darkness.

'I'm very experienced,' he continued, 'and I would take the best care of you. You couldn't wish for a better master. Plenty of people here tonight can vouch for that.'

'I promised myself that I would only have sex with Justin and Maz this weekend.'

'That's fine. But would you let me watch?'

'I guess, if it's OK with them.'

He turned to Justin and Maz and suggested a tryst in our hotel room at midnight. They were happy to agree.

He nodded rather formally, made arrangements to meet

us at the staircase at the appointed hour and vanished into the crowd.

'I need to sit down,' I muttered, and Justin and Maz led me to an empty table in the banqueting hall where I collapsed on to a red velvet chair and began to cry.

'Jeez, Keris, are you OK?'

Weirdly enough, I was. I was better than OK. But I'm a hopeless crybaby when the hormones are raging, and the intensity of the slave scene needed its outlet. I sobbed for two minutes, then felt a gorgeously deep relaxation sink into my bones, whereupon I dabbed my eyes and smiled at my friends.

'Sorry. Just needed to let it out.'

Maz smiled sympathetically. 'I know a few weepers in the scene,' she said. 'But, oh my God, Keris! Do you know who that was?'

I frowned at her. Was he some kind of famous person? He had the sleek silver fox thing going on – perhaps a newsreader? A politician? A retired sportsman?

'His Lordship,' pronounced Justin with reverence.

'His Lordship? What, is he a member of the royal family or something?'

'No.' Maz giggled. 'He's not a real lord. That's just what everyone calls him. He's a major, major player on the scene. The most respected dom there is.'

Ah, OK. He was kink royalty, not the red carpet kind.

'Yeah?' I looked blearily around the room, my eyes beginning to refocus. Two people in head to toe gimp suits wandered by, connected by a pretty silver chain.

'Yeah,' said Justin. 'He's one of the people behind tonight's extravaganza. He throws all the best parties and pervy weekends – a different theme every time. Some of them are ticket events, but most of them are private, just for him and his friends. Maz and I have been trying to get into the inner circle for ages, but it's harder to break than the Enigma Code.'

Maz pinched my arm. 'And you come along on your first night out and catch his eye. What the fuck?'

'Sorry,' I said.

'No, don't be sorry,' they chorused, and Maz followed up with, 'It's cool. He's coming to our room. This is our chance as well as yours. Are you interested in him?'

I shut my eyes and thought about his ruthless fingers and dispassionate air.

'Yes,' I said. 'I think so. But like I said, real life isn't like that, is it?'

'Keris, we're at a fetish ball. We aren't in real life. Forget about that for tonight, yeah?'

'Sorry.'

'Good. Now let's go back into the fray and enjoy ourselves. Or I'll have to punish you.'

We went back to the great hall and spectated for a while. I saw a great many things, some of which I wished I hadn't, while others fired my imagination and my lusts.

A girl strapped to a wheel was turned slowly round and round while a shirtless man whipped her helpless body, the lash falling anywhere and everywhere, from feet to shoulders.

Two girls in harnesses and butt-plug tails offered rides around a small enclosure, their slight bodies straining under the mounts of varying sizes and weights who enjoyed their service. At the end, they pushed their faces into nosebags full of something – presumably not hay.

A man in a hood lay back on a bed while his mistress inflicted exquisite pain on his cock and balls.

A woman, handcuffed and on her knees, gave blowjobs to a series of men, her mouth held open by an O-ring gag.

'Is any of this appealing to you?' Justin asked.

'Not really. It's all a bit further on down the road than I've reached,' I said. 'Some of it's a bit scary.'

'Hey, you take whichever bit of the road appeals to you,' said Justin. 'There's no one way of doing it.

138

Spanking doesn't lead automatically to branding.'

'No. I guess not.'

I looked sideways at a guy in full drag being given a public enema by a woman dressed as Mary Poppins.

'Oh, Justin, can I?'

Maz was clapping her hands as we approached an alcove signposted "The Spanking Booth".

'Go on, then.'

Justin watched as Maz scurried behind an old-fashioned pillory affair, talking to the bearded man at the back of the tableau. He took out a key, unlocked the pillory and put Maz in it, so that her face wasn't visible to us – only her back view could be seen by the passing crowds.

The man walked around beside her, then lifted her little toga slip and tucked it into her belt, so her bare bottom was on display. He came to stand beside the pillar at the front of the alcove, drumming up trade.

Pretty soon, a queue of hopeful spankers had been drawn, and the first punter chose a short-handled flogger to use on the wriggling bottom he had paid to thrash.

I watched with fascination as Maz's bottom turned a luscious cerise shade under the onslaught of the suede lashes, holding on to Justin's hand and squeezing it tight.

Next Maz had to take twenty strokes of a leather strap, the pink darkening to a bright welted red in no time at all.

Before she could draw breath, a ping-pong paddle smacked hard into the centre of her furiously flushed skin, making her jump and squeal with each of the ten hard whacks.

'Don't you want a go?' I whispered to Justin, Maz's treatment turning my horniness dial back up to ten.

'I'm going to wait till later,' said Justin softly. 'Conserve my strength for when His Lordship is watching.'

I fluttered and clenched my pussy at the reminder.

His Lordship. The man who wanted to dominate me as more than a friend or a fellow in kink. The man who wanted to be my master.

What did masters expect of one? I wondered about this as a ruler paddle fell sharply down on Maz's poor bottom. If you accepted one, did that mean you had to do everything they said without question? What if I changed my mind? What if he wanted me to give up work? What if he turned out to be a complete monster? What if, what if, what if? The more I learned about this thing, the less I seemed to know.

I took a deep breath, reminded myself that I was a free agent operating in a free world. I didn't have to do anything that didn't suit me.

Maz, panting and bright-eyed, bounded away from the pillory after thirty strokes of the ruler paddle, linking her arms in ours and declaring herself "subspaced out". We ate and drank some more, then watched a Shibari demonstration. I'd thought it was a brand of kitchen knife rather than rope bondage. How wrong can one be?

The more I learned, the less I knew.

Chapter Eight

THE HANDS OF THE clock crept towards midnight. Any residual inhibitions amongst the crowd were long gone. People were making out on the stairs, whipping each other over the tables, giving head underneath them.

Somewhere in here, the Victorian Gent – His Lordship – waited for me.

Unless he'd found another submissive worthier of his time and attention. The idea jolted me more than I expected it would. Being singled out by this doyen of domination had flattered me on some level deeper than I knew, and I intended to prove that the potential he had seen in me was no mirage.

Maz and Justin had descended to bitching about people's poor grasp of fetish fashion and/or spanking technique; it was easy to slide into a state of inertia, listening to their barbed comments while the long hand of the clock moved in its inexorable circle.

'I don't have a problem with the schoolgirl kink,' said Maz, 'but once you're past fifty, you should probably move on to naughty nurse, don't you think?'

'Age is just a number,' reproved Justin. 'That remark might come back to haunt you in years to come. But that headmaster's gown is filthy. Didn't they think to run it through a wash cycle before they came tonight?'

'Ugh. Looks like it's been jizzed on.'

'It probably has,' I said, and then the first stroke of 12 rang out over the assembled heads, in their mortarboards and their gimp masks, their periwigs and their devil horns. The witching hour. Time to turn into a pumpkin. Or a bonded submissive.

'We mustn't be late,' I said, tugging at Justin's hand.

'No,' he agreed.

His Lordship stood at the foot of the staircase, surrounded by people, all of whom seemed to be clamouring for his attention. Instead of giving it, he frowned at a splendid gold fob watch, fist closed around the handle of his cane.

Justin edged through the crowd, dragging Maz and I behind him in a train. We pushed through heat and sweat, stale perfume and the unmistakable aroma of sex, until we reached our destination.

His Lordship looked up. Without saying a word, he turned and began to ascend the stairs. The groups at his feet sighed and turned away, disappointed to be the Unchosen Ones.

'You'll need to show me to your room, Justin,' he said. Justin broke his link with us and stepped up past His Lordship, leading us into the East Wing. Maz and I scurried behind them like handmaidens, making grimaces of nervous excitement at one another behind the men's backs. I was too anxious to feel aroused, though I was looking forward to getting out of the slave gear, especially the collar, which had begun to chafe.

Justin opened the door and stretched out an arm, indicating the giant four-post bed, big enough for six people and so very convenient for tying things to.

His Lordship watched Maz and I sidle in and stand on the other side of the door, looking down at the carpet.

'What's your name?' he asked me, reaching out a finger to tip my chin up. 'Not that it's important.'

'Keris,' I lied, used now to splitting identities between my day self and my night self.

His forefinger and thumb pinched my chin. I realised

I'd forgotten something.

'Sir,' I added.

'Very green, aren't you, Keris? If we decide to take this further, I'll give you a different name. How would you feel about that?'

'It would be fine, sir,' I said. 'I'm not sentimental about my name.' My false name, that is.

'Good. What if the name I gave you was obscene or insulting, though? How would you feel about that?'

'Oh, well, it would depend what it was, sir. Context is important too.'

'Yes, yes, that's true. Context is important.'

His eyes were keen and the angles of his face sharp, giving it an ageless quality. He was capable of looking cruel, but when his muscles relaxed, he had an elegant, insouciant air. His face alone was the most complex thing I'd ever seen. I couldn't imagine how long it would take to really know a man like this.

Something about that excited me.

'Are you looking for a master, Keris?'

I decided to be honest.

'I don't know what I'm looking for, sir.'

'That's quite common with submissives. Until they find it. Do you think you'll know it when you find it?'

'I hope so, sir.'

'I hope so too.'

His voice was hypnotic and his fingers, now splayed across one of my cheeks, held me still and calm. My breathing had evened out and my nerves had gone. I felt expectant and safe.

'I think you and I could work together,' he said. The way he looked at me made me think he was using his eyes as camera lenses, photographing me in zoom-close detail. 'You have the intelligence I like and the docility I demand. But I'll need to see a bit more of you. Justin, I'll hand this over to you for now. Put her through her paces for me.'

His Lordship's hand dropped and I put my own fingers to my cheek, missing his contact immediately. Something about his touch had made me feel like clay, waiting to be moulded. I needed to feel it again.

But instead Justin came forward, patting my backside with his martinet, chivvying me over towards the bed.

His Lordship sat down in an armchair in the corner of the room while Maz knelt at his feet.

'Strip,' ordered Justin, and my grateful hands went immediately to my collar. Justin shook his head. 'No, not the collar. Or the cuffs. Everything but them.'

Damn. In a slight sulk, I released my breasts from the slave-bra then unclipped my belt with its concealing skirts. In those two swift moves, I was naked but for the restricting buckles and chains at my neck, wrists and ankles.

'What would you like to see, Your Lordship?' asked Justin, running his whip handle down my spine.

'Well, let me see. I've already handled her, and seen her come under my handling. I think I'd like to see her whipped and fucked, Justin. Could you oblige?'

'Of course. Bound or unbound?'

'It would be a shame to waste those pretty cuffs.'

'Agreed. On to the bed, Keris, on your back, please.'

I laid myself on the paisley-embroidered covers, wondering if Justin intended to whip my breasts and belly. I hoped not. It wasn't something I'd tried, or really ever fantasised about.

'Wrists,' said Justin, and I held them out to him. From a bedside drawer, he took two lengths of stretchy black twiny stuff with clips at one end. The clips attached neatly to the buckle of my cuffs, while the other end of the twine was looped and securely knotted around the bed posts, spreading my arms in a starfish style.

I supposed the same scene would be played out with my ankles, but Justin surprised me by grabbing both legs at the knee and pushing them back over my torso until my bottom was almost completely lifted from the bed. This was a move I sometimes did at the gym, ending with my feet over my head, but Justin spread my legs as they rose into the air, then took another piece of the black stretchy material, clipped it to an ankle cuff, then looped the other end around the corresponding wrist cuff. Once he had finished I lay bent double with my legs in the air, my bottom high with cheeks and pussy lips wide and the backs of my thighs beginning to strain. The flexibility of the bondage rope meant that no injury was going to ensue but I couldn't claim to be in the most comfortable position nonetheless.

Justin placed a pillow beneath my coccyx, keeping my bum up without too much pressure on the spine. I imagined the view His Lordship must have of me now, splayed open with nowhere to hide. A shameful exposure.

'I'd like a picture of that,' said His Lordship. 'All that sweet, tender pinkness. A "before" and "after" shot would be good. But until we get to know each other better, I'll refrain. How do you feel, Keris, knowing that you have no private or intimate space any more, knowing that everyone here can see everything?'

'Embarrassed, sir,' I said in a tiny, shaky voice.

'I should think so. What kind of slut would let a man do that to her in front of witnesses? Hmmm?'

'A dirty slut, sir.'

'That's right. Justin, I think the dirty slut needs whipping. Nice and hard. I want to see that bottom squirming.'

The only good thing about my position was that I could see Justin ply the whip, an opportunity that was rarely to be had during a more conventional spanking. The novelty and thrill of being able to see his clenched hand, his knotted forearm, the look of grim determination in his jaw offset some of the discomfort and I began to feel alive and aroused again, rotating my hips and gasping with the efforts my restraint made me exert.

After a while, though, the heat and the pain overtook the enjoyment of the view. I began to whimper and try to kick, in vain of course, as the martinet strands flicked and stung, covering my helpless bottom with their pitiless needling.

'She's feeling it now,' said His Lordship. 'She needs more. Harder.'

The whoosh of the lashes was loud and the crack as they landed explosive now. Justin was beginning to sweat and grit his teeth. My wrists and ankles strained like mad, succeeding only in marking themselves with red rings. I howled and blurted incoherent pleas. No safeword, though. His Lordship would not hear me invoke that.

'This is what you need, Keris, isn't it – good, hard whipping? Regularly. Frequently. I would see that you got it.'

I wanted to touch my clit, I wanted to buck and rear and kick the whip from Justin's hand.

'I need her arse bright red and hot to the touch,' His Lordship continued. 'It's how it should be. It's how she should be, all the time.'

Please, come and touch me. Come and fuck me. Fuck me with the whip handle. I don't care. Just do it.

Justin laid one final killer blow and then fell on to his knees, dropping the whip on the bed, exhausted.

His Lordship approached my whimpering form and sat on the bed to inspect the damage at close quarters.

One fingertip brushed each inner cheek of my bottom. The way they had been spread had meant that the flicky tips of the martinet had got right into the tender flesh around my anus, and I knew it was going to throb and hurt there for a long time. He dragged a fingernail along the welts, bringing them to even more painful life and I moaned, my sphincter twitching at his touch.

'One day we'll do this with a plug inside you,' he promised me. 'Perhaps a ginger one. Then this will seem like a gentle stroke in comparison.'

'Ohhh, you're cruel,' I sighed blissfully.

He smiled.

'Thank you.'

He patted each sore cheek, harder and harder, until he was spanking them and I was soaking and begging for an orgasm, twisting my hips this way and that, trying to push out my clit.

'I know what you want, Keris,' he said, still smiling. 'I can see that you've no shame and you don't care who knows getting whipped makes you need to come. Tch tch. Look at her, Maz. Have you ever seen a slut like it?'

'No way, sir,' said Maz enthusiastically. 'Not even that chambermaid you had last year.'

Chambermaid?

'She's in Zurich now,' said His Lordship contemplatively. 'With a banker.'

He stopped spanking me and pinched the tip of my clit. My howl sounded heartrending, even to me.

'All yours, Justin,' he said. 'For now. No foreplay, please, just use her.'

I watched Justin shrug off his toga. The whipping was as much foreplay as he needed, his cock curving out before him, the harbinger of his whippet-thin, tight-muscled body.

He only paused to slip on the condom, then he landed on the bed on his knees, peering down at me through my awkwardly spread thighs.

'Hey there, slave girl,' he whispered. 'You've had your punishment and now it's time to do your duty to your master. But I want you to ask me for it.'

My voice was shredded and my lungs felt bent out of shape from the uncomfortable position but I managed to rasp out the necessary plea.

'Please fuck me, master.'

There was no preamble, just a hard shove into the yielding flesh of my cunt. He steadied himself by holding on to my hips, which were sore in places where the lash had wrapped around the curve of my behind, lowered his stomach so our pelvises met, and began to thrust.

He didn't look at me, just stared at the headboard, banging away, hard and fast. I had to realise that this was not for my pleasure. I was providing a service, a duty, a *raison d'être*. If I couldn't be fucked, I was useless trash to be discarded. I was my cunt.

The thought kept my juices flowing, along with the raging prickling heat of my arse. I embraced the graceless violence with which Justin pounded at me, grunting for more. I was directly at the centre of my sexuality, whirling inside its layered rings, living my kink at last.

Justin came before me, just as the first stirrings started up inside, and he withdrew immediately, leaving my cunt trembling as if begging for more.

I moaned and thrashed while His Lordship laughed on the sidelines.

'Disappointed? But you've performed your service and satisfied your master. You should be delighted.'

I lacked the strength to reply. My entire body was consumed with the need for climax.

His Lordship came over to the bed, picked up the discarded martinet and bent down low over my pussy, examining its post-use state.

'Swollen and stretched,' he said. 'A properly fucked little quim. And you've already come tonight, you greedy girl. I don't know of a better treated slave. I should have you whipped again for your ingratitude.'

I rolled my eyes back in my head. A whipping, just the touch of those leathery strands on my clit, might be enough to bring me what I needed now.

'But I'm a kind master, really,' murmured His Lordship. 'I don't know why I'm such a soft-hearted fool. Come on, then.'

Heaving a sigh, he brushed the soft leather over my

pulsing clit, creating a sensation of exquisite torture – too light to satisfy, just enough to drive me mad.

He did this until I was a begging, panting mess and then gripped my face with pincer fingers, making me look up at him while he drove the thick, plaited whip handle up inside me. He pushed it slowly up, watching my expression all the while, then he began to thrust with it, very slowly, dragging it out all the way then easing it back in until the deed was done and my orgasm tore me in two, raging around that whip handle while His Lordship kept my face in his firm hand, giving me nowhere to escape his scrutiny.

He patted my head once I'd stopped shrieking, pulled out the whip handle and made me lick it clean.

'I want you,' he said. 'I'll be in touch.'

Maz and Justin rushed forward to release me from my bonds while I tried to lift my head far enough to watch his exit.

'He's gone? Where's he gone?'

My thighs ached and my feet and hands were almost numb, so it took some time for me to revert to a more natural position. Besides, I didn't want to sit on anything until the effects of the whipping were a little less recent. I rolled over on to my stomach and let the tension drop, down, down, a long way down. There was a lot of it to release.

'It's OK,' said Maz, massaging my shoulders. 'He'll know how to get in touch with you. You'll hear from him soon, I'm sure.'

'I'm not bothered about that. I just think … Why did he leave? He could have stayed.'

'I think he likes the drama,' commented Justin, yawning by my side. 'He tries to make everything as memorable as possible.'

'Yeah, that was memorable.' I winced as Maz's hands worked on my bottom. 'For lots of reasons. What was that you said about a chambermaid?'

'His Lordship has staff,' said Maz. 'So does Her Ladyship.'

I twisted my neck, squinting at her.

'Her Ladyship?'

'Yeah, his wife.'

'He's married?'

'Right. Don't sound so shocked, Keris.' She laughed. 'Their relationship's like mine and Justin's. They're poly. They both like the same things and they throw the best parties. If His Lordship wants you for a submissive, you'll be at the centre of the scene.'

Was that what I wanted? To be at the centre of a scene? Especially a scene it appeared I knew nothing about.

'Won't they want someone to live in, though? I couldn't do that. I could only be a weekend submissive at best.'

'Weekend submissives are fine. They have a whole stable of them.'

I thought of the ponygirl on the landing. Did I want to be one of many?

'So he has loads of submissives? I wouldn't be the only one?'

'Not by a long chalk. Most of them are just girls he shares with other doms, though, who come up for his parties every couple of months. He only has a few special ones.'

'Do you think he wants me for a special one?'

'Looks like it. A chambermaid, at least.'

'And his wife doesn't mind?'

'She has her footmen.'

'Right.' I wanted to laugh at the extreme role play absurdity of it all, but Maz seemed to take it all quite seriously.

'This is still so new to you, isn't it?' said Justin, propping himself on his elbow beside me, stroking my back and shoulder blades.

'I never thought this stuff really happened outside the

150

pages of dirty books,' I said. 'I mean, everyone's heard rumours of people who are into partner-swapping or kink, but nobody can ever substantiate them.'

'Well, private lives are private, aren't they?' said Justin reasonably. 'People aren't going to bring it up in day to day conversation. But I bet you know lots of people whose lives behind the bedroom door are much more interesting than you'd guess. I mean, who would guess it of you?'

Good point. Cherry Delaney, mousy music teacher in glasses and sensible shoes. Who would see Keris Delray the submissive fucktoy behind that?

'So next time I'm in the staff room, I'll be wondering which of them are pegging their husbands on a Friday night,' I said with a cackle.

'Staff room?' said Maz. My blood ran cold.

'It's a, like, an online forum. For tutors,' I lied, but the words came out too fast.

'Sure,' said Maz. She knew I was lying. 'It's OK, you know. Whatever you do is OK. Private. Nobody else's business.'

I thought of the new clause in the teaching contract. Bringing the profession into disrepute. Would the General Teaching Council see it that way?

I yawned.

'Whatever,' I said, channelling Kacey. 'I could sleep for a week. Think I'll just …'

I rolled over, too tired to cope with uncomfortable thoughts any more, and shut my eyes.

It was a week before I heard from His Lordship. In a way, every day that my inbox stayed empty of his imperious presence was a relief. Perhaps I wouldn't have to deal with this, after all. Perhaps I could make do with my playmates Justin and Maz until whenever Stuart the Seafaring Surgeon returned, or some other less baroque and bizarre opportunity for living my fantasies presented itself.

151

On the other hand, I was consumed with curiosity, and the memory of his behaviour that weekend made me squirm and weaken at the knees every time it crossed my mind. He had made me feel special in a way nobody had since Stuart.

To Justin and Maz, I was just another kinky friend. To him, I would be more than that. And yet, I knew I wouldn't be his only one. Oh, it didn't make sense.

Neither did Patrick Superhead. His attitude towards me ping-ponged wildly between inappropriately intimate and icily professional. One day we met to discuss equipment for the new music studio and his fingers kept brushing against mine as he showered me with compliments on my ideas and enthusiasm. The next day, at rehearsal, he barely looked at me.

I wanted him in the worst way, and yet I didn't want him. I didn't feel I deserved him. What was I, after all, but a trashy slut who let strange men do rude things to her in public? What decent man would want me?

It seemed that the whole world was engaged in a conspiracy to do my head in.

So when the phone rang that Friday night, after Patrick had bidden me a terse "have a good weekend" and left, I was hoping it was Lou inviting me for a wind-down curry, or maybe Maz with a suggestion for Sunday afternoon.

Instead, the instantly recognisable, rather thespian tones of His Lordship caressed my ear.

I almost dropped the phone, then wrestled it back to my ear.

'I didn't give you my number,' I whispered.

'No, Justin did,' he said. 'You sound a little shocked to hear from me.'

'I was expecting maybe an email or something.'

'I prefer to deal in person.'

'But this isn't in person. This is a phone call.'

'You're very cheeky, aren't you, for a girl I've fucked

152

with a whip handle?'

That shut me up.

He seized his advantage and spoke into the stunned silence.

'I've been thinking about you, Keris. What I saw of you last weekend impressed me very much. I want to take you and train you and make you mine. But I don't know much about you, or even whether it would be possible. I think we should meet and talk.'

'OK,' I said. 'When and where?'

'Where do you live?'

'Portsmouth.'

'Not too far. Can you make it up to town tomorrow?'

I pondered. I was supposed to be conducting the choir and helping at the school Christmas Fayre. I couldn't very well let them down.

'I can't. I have a work thing to do.'

'What about the evening? What if you book a restaurant and I meet you there? I'll pay.'

'Oh well, all right. What kind of place do you want? Upmarket, downmarket?'

He tutted down the phone at me.

'I'm sure you could work that one out for yourself.'

Brasserie Boizot then. If there was a free table.

'I'll try and book the best place in town then.'

'I'd recommend that.'

'What time? Eight?'

'Eight sounds fine.'

He gave me his number in case of emergency cancellations and rung off without further comment.

I stuffed my knuckles into my mouth and bit down on them, hard.

What the hell was I getting myself into?

Interestingly, Lou asked me the very same question the next day while I gave her a hand on her Glühwein and

Lebkuchen stall at the Christmas fayre. The choir had managed an angelic rendition of *Mary's Boychild* and I was feeling quite accomplished, so her sudden introduction of the subject fazed me a little.

'I hardly see you these days,' she said, making up another bowl of hot herbal-smelling brew. 'How's the online dating thing going?'

'It's going,' I said non-committally, then I emboldened myself to add, 'I have a date tonight.'

'Oh? A first date? Or second or third? I feel a bit weird that you never tell me any of this stuff. I thought we were friends.'

'Sorry, I just … You know.' I shrugged.

She shook her head. She didn't know.

'I don't like to mention it too much because most of it doesn't work out,' I persisted.

'But that's silly. I want to hear about all the unsuitable men you meet! I thought we'd have a laugh about it. But you never say anything about them. Don't you have any funny stories to tell?'

I fidgeted, threading more ribbons through the Lebkuchen.

'Not really. Mainly they're pretty boring. Like me.'

'Boring? You aren't boring!'

'Look, if you must know, I'm a bit embarrassed about it. The whole online dating thing, you know, it has a bit of a stigma attached.'

'Oh, not any more!'

'It does to me. I feel like a loser. I don't want to talk about it.'

She narrowed her eyes at me, then had to serve a customer.

'So who's this guy you're meeting tonight?' she asked with a dash of hostility.

'I don't know. Some guy from London. I think he's rich. Older.'

'Sugar daddy, eh?'

'I could do with a shower of gifts.'

'Yeah, well, make sure you know what the hell you're getting into. Men like that tend to have a vast sense of entitlement. They think they can buy you.'

Exactly.

The mournful howl of microphone feedback rent the air. Superhead was preparing to draw the raffle.

'Now if only he wasn't married …' She nudged me and winked.

'He isn't. I mean, he's separated. In the middle of getting a divorce.'

Lou gasped and poured herself a cup of the steaming wine – the fayre was about to end, after all. I joined her.

'Why didn't I know that? How do you know? Did he tell you?'

'Yes. A week or so ago.'

'Well … For God's sake, Cherry, why don't you … I mean, he likes you. That much is obvious. If he spent half as much time with me, I'd be on him!'

'Lou! It's not very professional, is it? Besides, I don't know how difficult his divorce is. He's probably got issues coming out of his ears. Baggage and all that.'

'Well, your rich older man is hardly going to be a virgin, is he?'

'It just seems too close to home. I'm off workplace relationships.'

We both looked over at Gareth, who was clearing up on his darts game stall across the hall.

'Fair enough,' sighed Lou. 'So you won't mind if I have a crack at him, then?'

'Crack away,' I said, trying to ignore the pang in my heart.

I looked at the clock. Ten past five. Less than three hours until my appointment with His Lordship.

I'd decided on a simple black dress, nothing too overtly sexy. It was demure enough, with a sweetheart neckline and a flippy skirt, beneath which I hid my best black underwear set, including a suspender belt and seamed stockings. Cherry on top, Keris underneath.

I walked through Gunwharf Quays, past the groups of over-perfumed, orange-skinned Saturday nighters, in my kitten-heeled patent pumps, wondering if he would be there already, or if he would make me wait.

And then I wondered, with a snorty giggle, if I would even recognise him in contemporary dress. Did he sport those whiskers as a matter of course? Would he be checking his engraved fob watch, shaking his head over my lateness?

Not that I was late. It was one minute to eight when I entered the restaurant, and I recognised him immediately. He sat at one of the window tables in the curving room, looking out over the harbour, minus whiskers but plus one fantastically well-cut suit and green spotted silk tie. He looked no less distinguished than he had in Victorian mode – in fact, a little more so for the lack of fancy dress.

In front of him stood a bottle of white wine and two glasses.

He looked up and waved two fingers at me. I gave my coat to the waiter and commended my soul to God. I had absolutely no idea where this evening would take me.

'Montrachet,' he said, lifting the bottle. 'I noticed you were drinking a Chardonnay at the ball. Will this suit?'

'Oh yes.' I slipped into my seat opposite him, staring fixedly at my wine glass while he poured.

I took a sip at his behest.

'Lovely. Strange, though, I had you down as a Lambrini type of guy.'

The frown this remark produced was terrific and tremble-provoking.

'And now I have you down as an impertinent little

156

minx. And we all know what happens to them.'

'Sorry,' I mumbled, wondering what had come over me. Flippant remarks were a safety mechanism for me, a habit I would have to work on if I wanted to sit down much in the near future. 'I wasn't sure you'd recognise me with my clothes on.'

His facial muscles relaxed.

'I wouldn't have been ungentlemanly enough to say so but now that you mention it ...'

I blushed.

'I've never been here before,' I told him. 'It's usually fish and chips on the harbour wall for me.'

'I wasn't sure what to expect,' said His Lordship. 'Most of the stories of nights out in Portsmouth I've heard have involved fights and strippers.'

'A bit like my sex life then.'

'Keris.' He was warning me.

'Sorry. My mouth runs away with me.'

'We can sort that out.'

'Can we?'

'Oh yes.'

I tugged at my ear, my nervous gesture of choice.

'I think it's the clothes thing,' I offered after the waiter had handed us menus.

'Clothes?'

'If I'm fully dressed, I find it hard to be submissive. Does that make sense?'

He put his head to one side and scrutinised me.

'Yes,' he said. 'That makes sense. There's a way round that, you know.'

'Is there?'

'Yes. A bit of an old chestnut, but works like a charm.'

I swallowed.

'Oh?'

'Go to the ladies' and remove your knickers. When you return, give them to me. Not furtively, though – no passing

157

them under the table. You do it blatantly and in full view of the whole restaurant.'

'In full view?'

'Yes. People hardly ever register it. They won't realise it's your knickers, for the most part. The people that do notice will think it quaint and a bit sexy. It'll spice up their Saturday night. Perhaps they'll do it themselves.'

I goggled for a moment, then he raised his eyebrows and made a nod of the head that meant business towards the toilets.

An act of disobedience wouldn't get us off to a good start. Besides, once the order is given, even implicitly, I find my inner good-doggy and it all becomes easy.

I stood up and took my leave.

The toilets were distractingly fancy and I almost forgot why I was in there, so busy was I admiring the perfume dispensers and dazzling glass and gilt. I frowned, thinking, But I don't need to go, then I remembered.

I backed into a stall and shut the door, reaching up under my skirt to lower the knickers. Problem. I was wearing stockings and suspenders, and the knickers could only go as far as the stocking tops. Annoyingly, I had to unsnap each suspender, move the knickers down, then refasten them, which was a slow process with my fumbly fingers.

The mere act of pushing the knickers down to my knees made me wet and I squirmed as the little suspender buttons clicked back into their slots, hoping I wouldn't be in a state of raging arousal for the duration of the meal.

I finished removing the knickers and bunched them up in my fist. Outside the stall I looked at myself in the mirror. How obvious was it that I was carrying a pair of knickers? To me, it seemed glaringly so, but then I was bound to be hyper-conscious of my situation. Would anyone notice? Would they double-take and whisper about me, knowing that I was naked under the dress and informing their dining companions of the fact? Would the whole restaurant know that my bare pussy was just a whispery skirt away from potential fingering? I bit my lip, trying to chase the blush from my cheeks. It wouldn't go.

I sprayed my wrists with perfume then, looking around to make absolutely sure I was alone in there, I put the atomiser under my skirt and gave my nethers a squirt. Bad idea. It stung.

I winced, put the perfume down, squeezed the knickers into as tiny a ball as I possibly could and sailed back into the restaurant, trying to exude inner confidence.

I was so busy exuding this inner confidence stuff that I forgot to look where I was going, tripped over a waiter's foot and stumbled forward. In the process, I lost my grip on the knickers which flew wildly over to the right, landing with perfect precision in the dead centre of a diner's bowl of soup.

I couldn't help it. I screamed.

The waiter, a man of sterling worth, whisked the bowl away before the diner had registered anything more than a piece of dark cloth in his consommé, and His Lordship leapt to recover me, helping me over to our table while I gibbered hysterical apologies to the offended party.

Had anyone seen that the article in flight had been a pair of my knickers? Everyone was looking at me, but it wasn't clear from their expressions. They all looked away politely about three seconds later and the restaurant returned to the discreet buzz of conversation I had so recently shattered.

'That was spectacular,' said His Lordship dryly. 'You went a little bit beyond the brief there. So to speak. Haha.'

Hilarious.

I pouted at him.

'Stop it. I feel like crying. Can we just go?'

'No we can't. We're staying. I've just ordered you the crab linguine.'

'But I might die of mortification.'

'You won't die. Nobody ever died of losing their knickers in the soup.'

He stifled a laugh with his pocket handkerchief, eyes bright over the exquisitely stitched hem.

'You're cruel. Making me stay here under these circumstances. Really, really mean.'

'Yes, I am. So, how does it feel?'

'This level of embarrassment, you mean? Awful.'

'No. Your cunt. How does it feel?'

He wasn't laughing now. The light in his eyes was pure lasciviousness. He looked as if I was the main course and he was just about to dig in.

I forgot my lingerie woes and felt a gush between my thighs.

'Ventilated,' I said.

'Wet?'

'Yes.'

'I'd like to feel it for myself. Perhaps I will later. In the meantime, why don't you put a finger in there?'

'I can't!'

'Yes you can. Or just rub your clit. Do it, Keris.'

I adjusted the heavy tablecloth above my knees and placed one hand in my lap, glancing around furtively. Nobody was looking at me, the knicker incident forgotten, unless it was what they were all discussing so avidly.

My fingers crept slowly lower, past the border of the tablecloth until they rested on my bare knees. With my other hand, I held my wineglass, sipping ostentatiously to deflect attention from any other part of me.

'Are you doing it?' said His Lordship, voice seductively low.

I nodded and sipped, sipped and nodded.

Under the hem of my dress now, my hand moved towards the slick target. I kept it down, careful not to make a bulge in the visible part of the skirt. I watched the muscles in my upper arm, trying to keep their movements

160

unobtrusive.

My fingertips bumped up against my pussy lips. My index finger made a leisurely upward stroke over my fat, wet clit. I held my breath, my eyelids feeling heavy. I tried not to look as if I was concentrating too hard. It was impossible

His Lordship chuckled.

'That's it,' he said. 'Does it feel nice? Touching yourself in a crowded room? Of course, they all know you aren't wearing knickers. They all know you're a filthy little bitch in heat.'

The breath gusted out of me, but I managed to keep it quiet. I took my finger away, regretfully, wondering how long I would have to wait for an orgasm tonight.

'Perhaps I should let them have you, one by one, over this table? Give me your hand.'

I removed it from my skirt and raised it to the table. He took it and lifted the fingers to his lips, as if meaning to kiss them, but instead he inhaled deeply.

'Delicious fragrance,' he said, more loudly than was necessary. Lowering his voice, he continued, 'You're juicier than the fruit meringues over there. I know what I'm having for dessert.'

The crab linguine arrived on cue. It smelled of sex and the very word "linguine" made me think of lapping tongues. There was no way I was going to be able to eat.

'Before you start,' said His Lordship, 'I want you to pull your skirt up at the back so your bare bottom makes contact with the chair seat. That's how I want you to sit for the rest of the meal.'

Somehow the idea of disobedience had become unthinkable. His Lordship's lack of sympathy over the knicker tragedy had convinced me that resistance would be futile, so I reached a hand carefully around the side of me that wasn't visible to other diners and hiked the skirt up, inch by inch, until I had pulled the back completely clear of my bottom.

This left my stocking tops exposed, so I had to cover my thighs with the tablecloth – how grateful I was not to be in Pizza Express or somewhere else that had dispensed with linens. The more expensive the restaurant, the better the opportunities for kinky behaviour, it seemed.

The seat was cool and smooth against my skin. I fidgeted, trying to ensure that none of my juices leaked on to its luxurious upholstery, and looked shiftily around the room. Did anyone know? Could anyone see?

'Now eat,' said His Lordship.

'What's your name?' I asked, thinking I couldn't call him "Your Lordship" here in this public place.

'Sir.'

'What's your name, sir?'

'No, I mean that, to you, my name is Sir.'

'Can't I know your real name?'

'In due course. But not tonight. Especially since you haven't told me yours.'

My jaw dropped and a length of linguine slithered off my fork.

'What?'

'I called your name earlier, before you noticed me. You must have heard it, but you didn't react. You thought I meant someone else. So what's your real name?'

'Perhaps I'll let you know in due course,' I told him sulkily.

'I see we have a hill to climb,' sighed His Lordship. 'But I like a challenge.'

'Speaking of which,' I said, 'what do you have in mind? I'll level with you – I haven't told you my real name because my job makes all this a little bit difficult. I need to protect my identity.'

'I understand. It's why I haven't told you mine. It could all get awkward, if some new sub on the block decided to make waves for me. I need to establish a relationship of trust first. I'm glad you appreciate that. I won't ask what it is that you do, but I will ask how it might impinge on your private life.'

'Well, in practical terms, my availability is limited. I work full time and can't even promise to be free every weekend. But I do get good holidays. I was thinking of some kind of arrangement where I could … y'know … organise a few visits a year.'

His Lordship considered this, twisting a forkful of linguine round and round.

'You work in education,' he said at length.

'Yes.'

'Long summer holiday?'

'Six weeks.'

'But it's December now. That's a long way away. How are you fixed for Christmas?'

My heart began to thud. Concrete arrangements might be in place by the time I finished off this crab.

'I'm spending Christmas Day with my mother. But after that, I'm free from Boxing Day until school starts again on 5th January.'

'That gives us a good week. A new year with a new submissive. What do you think?'

'You want me to spend the week at your house?'

'At one of them,' he said urbanely. 'My country house. There'll be other guests too, but you will be the only trainee.'

'You're going to train me?'

'Of course. You aren't ready for full submission yet, that much is obvious. But you will be, once I've put you through my programme.'

'What's your programme?'

'I can't tell you that. It's individually tailored. Some trainees want to express their submission differently than others. We will discuss your needs before you arrive and I'll draw up a plan accordingly.'

'How many have you trained?'

His Lordship's eyes rolled up to the ceiling. 'Honestly? I've lost count.'

'What does your wife think of it?'

'My wife was one of my trainees. She is an important member of my faculty!'

'Doesn't she get jealous?'

'No. Every single desire she has is fulfilled immediately. She can whip or be whipped whenever she pleases. She submits to me, but she has authority over our staff.'

'Would I be a member of your staff?'

'No, not at first. You would be lowlier than that. They would be considerably higher than you in the pecking order. A trainee is the lowest of the low.'

The thought of this made me shift my bare bottom against my seat, reminding me again of my lewd situation.

'So they could give me orders?'

'Oh yes.'

'Let's talk about safety,' I suggested, though at that point I was ready to sign my life away. 'I wouldn't be obliged to stay if I wanted to leave, would I?'

'No, of course not. We aren't criminals. False imprisonment isn't a turn-on.'

'Good. And anything I was uncomfortable with?'

'A no-no. We are in the business of pleasure, Keris. Everyone's pleasure.'

'Business? Would I have to pay you?'

'No. It was a figure of speech. Any more questions? I'll answer them all.'

'That's all I can think of, for now. I'm sure there'll be more. I'll email you with them.'

I could no longer tell whether what I was smelling was me or the crab. All I knew was that I wanted an orgasm, and I wanted it soon.

'Good,' purred His Lordship, raising his glass. 'Here's

to a good decision well made.'

He made me sit, wet and horny as fuck, through dessert, coffee and liqueurs while he outlined some of the different training techniques he might try on me. By the time the bill came, I was bent low over the table, feeling the burn in my cheeks and between my pussy lips. We had to get out of here and find a place, quickly.

I stood and took his arm, already far away in my imagination, getting myself well and truly seen to, but instead of heading for the exit, he walked me over to the kitchen.

'Madame needs to collect something,' he said to the gentleman at the serving hatch, and I gasped. I'd forgotten all about them!

'Ah yes,' said the kitchen porter, disappearing then returning to hand over, with a mortifying flourish, the stained and damp knickers.

I didn't look back, hurtling out through the doors like a bullet from a gun.

His Lordship, chuckling at my rear, ordered me to slow down.

'What's the hurry?'

'I never want to go there ever again.'

'Fine. We won't.'

I caught a breath, letting the tingly winter cold bring me back to earth. My cunt still wanted some undivided attention. I let His Lordship put his hands on my shoulders and squeeze them, then bend to kiss the spot behind my ear.

'Where … What next?' I whispered.

'I'm going home,' he said. 'I'll drop you off.'

'You can't drive – you've been drinking!' I wailed, disappointed in the extreme.

'My driver hasn't,' he said.

'But can't you stay … just for a while?'

'No, I can't. And I know what you want, Keris, but you

can't have it. Not tonight. Not until you arrive at my house after Christmas.'

I pouted, but I didn't realise the enormity of what he was asking until he spelled it out a moment later.

'And I don't just mean sex, Keris. I mean you are not to have an orgasm until then.'

'What? Are you serious?'

'Absolutely. Hands off. Nobody is going to touch you until I do.'

'But …'

'That's my condition. Take it or leave it.'

I took it.

Chapter Nine

I'VE DONE SOME DIFFICULT things in my life.

I've stood up in front of bottom set Year Nine and asked them to discuss their emotional response to excerpts from the *Peer Gynt* suite.

I've made a perfect soufflé.

I've walked away from a boy I adored and yearned for because I knew he wouldn't be faithful to me when I went to university.

But those three wank-free weeks were one of the greatest challenges of my life. I know SecretSadist had given me a taste – a few days was one thing. Three weeks though … And not just any old three weeks either.

Three weeks of Christmas build-up. Tension, panic-buying, chaos in the classroom, too much chocolate in the staffroom, tinsel and mistletoe and – the end of term party.

Our usual demob-happy slouch to a nearby pub, followed by a curry with paper crowns on our heads, had been officially ditched by Mr Marks in favour of a proper turkey dinner and festive dance in the garishly over-decorated school hall.

Year Eleven had been let loose on that final afternoon with tinsel, baubles and crepe paper and had transformed our usually dour and whiffy dining hall into a winter wonderland, if you like your winter wonderlands hallucinogenic and a bit frightening. At least it smelled of chemical snow-spray instead of vinegar, probably adding to the hallucinogenic effect.

Lou set off the snow-machine as soon as we were all assembled, making us shriek and flick blobs of polystyrene-like matter off our trusty teaching-issue corduroy. Gareth and a few of the laddish-lad PE crew slid on their tracksuited knees into the maw of the machine, belly laughing as their hair was quickly replaced by fake snow. Was this what Superhead had had in mind when he planned his sophisticated soirée? I doubted it.

By the time he made his appearance, flustered after fending off an angry parent, most of us were thrashing around beneath a steady shower of flakes to the usual Christmas classics.

He signalled to the DJ to put a stop to Slade and took the mike.

'I'd like to thank you all for your efforts this term,' he said, before treating us to ten minutes of propaganda about how great we all were and how the school was moving to a position of strength, including the inevitable "refloating the sinking ship" metaphor. When we were invited to take our places at the rather soggy table, he made a slick move in my direction, cutting in front of Jane the Textiles teacher to bag the seat next to me.

'Cherry,' he said, panting slightly. 'Friday night with no rehearsal, eh? Makes a change.'

'They wouldn't have been good for much today,' I said, warm inside at the implication that he couldn't bear a Friday evening without me.

'I'm sure you're right. But things are coming together, aren't they? By March, we'll be on top form, ready to knock 'em dead.'

'Yeah, I think so.'

He pulled my chair out for me. I knew every single eye in the place was upon us as I took my seat. On one hand, I longed for an intimate *tête-à-tête*, but on the other, I had no wish to be the talking point of the staffroom. So I made an effort to talk to others at the table and join in the general conversation, even when they made pathetic jokes about pulling crackers and parson's noses.

Once the brandy butter was safely on the Christmas pudding, though, I judged that the time might be right to excuse myself from the surrounding jollity and focus on the sex god with a tinsel buttonhole to my left.

'Where are you spending Christmas?' I asked him.

'Mostly here,' he said. 'I'll be in London for New Year, though I won't be diving into the fountains at Trafalgar Square. How about you?'

'Oh, at my mother's place,' I said vaguely. 'Then I might visit some friends. Same as every year, really.'

'It's odd, isn't it, how something that used to be so magical becomes a chore and a duty,' he said. 'I used to love this time of year.'

'Oh, it won't be that bad, will it?' I looked at him, concerned, then my teeth almost cracked on a hard, flat thing in my pudding. 'What the –?'

'You've won the lucky penny,' he said, smiling. 'The kitchen staff refused to put it in – said it was against Health and Safety regs – but I sneaked one in anyway. I'm glad it was you who found it. You deserve good luck.'

'Thanks,' I said, after removing the foil-wrapped coin from my mouth. 'So do you.'

'I try to make my own,' he said, staring bleakly along the table.

The wistful synth intro of Wham's *Last Christmas* drifted down from the speakers.

'Why don't we dance?' he said, requiring no answer. He stood and led me to the least slippery portion of the floor, encircling me without warning in his arms and lowering his cheek to mine.

A slow dance! At the school disco! With the headmaster!

I ignored the cheers from the dining table and shut my eyes, letting the song carry me into a world where we could do this all the time. The sound of shuffling feet indicated that we weren't alone for long, more and more people joining us to celebrate George Michael's festive heartbreak.

His arms felt so good. His cheek felt even better, peppered with the first traces of stubble, and he smelled of power – the good kind of power, that is used to benefit humanity. It was a blend of good suit, good aftershave and good man. I didn't dare breathe too much of it in, in case it intoxicated me to madness.

The song ended and I pulled myself away, rather forcefully. If I didn't, I might stay in his arms all night, and that just couldn't happen.

'I ought to go,' I said. 'I need to pack my stuff for mum's.'

'You're going already?'

I couldn't look at his face.

'I can't stay really. I'll see you next term – have a good holiday.'

He followed me to the cloakroom and helped me on with my coat and scarf.

'I've got you a present,' he told me, while I pulled on my gloves.

'Yeah, you got us all a bottle of wine,' I said, not understanding. 'Thanks.'

'No, not that. Here.'

He took a small parcel out of his inside pocket and handed it over.

'For me?'

'To say thanks. For making my first term a good one. Merry Christmas.'

He stepped back, looking over his shoulder at the dining hall doors, through which the thin strains of *The Little Drummer Boy* were leaking. Then he seemed to think twice, darted forward and kissed me, just once, just so quickly I almost missed feeling it, on my lips.

Then he went back to the hall.

That week in the Isle of Wight with mum was a strange one. Despite the fortnight of sexual frustration that had preceded it, I found I had lost the will to wank anyway. Masturbation was off the menu, and not just because His Lordship had stricken it through. I just didn't feel my kink.

Instead, I took long walks up to The Needles, looking wistfully out to sea and putting my fingers up to the sleek little silver necklace Patrick had given me. It meant something – had to mean something. But damn, it all felt like too little too late. He wasn't going to want me now, not when he found out about my life on the underbelly. I had kinked myself out of the market.

And yet I wanted him so much. So much that when, on Christmas Eve, a drinks guest of my mother's embraced me wearing a scarf that smelled of Patrick's aftershave, I had to go out to the conservatory and sit down until my legs stopped shaking. It was like my first ever crush all over again, complete with teen-style angst and kissing practice on the back of my hand. He was a decent, good, attractive, solvent man who wanted me – but I just couldn't give myself to him.

Maybe, I thought, the week at His Lordship's would put me off that path and open me up again to vanilla possibilities. Perhaps Patrick could be my "cure". No, I was kidding myself. I was what I was. I would have to live with it for the rest of my life.

The night before I was due for my sojourn with His Lordship, I lay naked on my bed and put a mirror between my thighs. I suppose I wanted to know that my vagina was still there, in a recognisable form, after three weeks of being severely ignored and knocked back. The little aperture was still there amidst the pink and glistening whorls – it hadn't yet sealed itself. My clit remained as cheerfully fat and red as ever. I thought about touching it, but touched Patrick's necklace instead.

Tomorrow, everything could change.

By the end of the week, perhaps Patrick would be out of my mind for good.

I wasn't to take anything to His Lordship's house. No suitcase, no handbag, no money, no clothes.

I had dressed according to his instructions – high heels, stockings, simple dress, full-length coat, hat, scarf, gloves, no underwear – and admired my reflection in my long mirror, adding an extra coat of lipstick while I waited for the doorbell to ring. My pussy seemed aware of the possibility that it might be allowed to have some attention today and was wet in anticipation. The lack of knickers made this all the more noticeable and I pressed my thighs together, trying to warm the dampness away.

I wasn't allowed perfume either, and I was worried about how much fragrance my excitable nether parts were giving off. I hoped my heavy coat and leather gloves might overpower it.

I was allowed my mobile phone, but had to keep it switched off unless an emergency arose. I put my hand in my pocket and felt the cool, slim rectangle, gripping it for reassurance. Now that the hour was almost upon me, it occurred to me how reckless I was being in giving myself up to a stranger's pleasures and disciplinary measures for a week. He had given me every assurance of his credentials, and I wanted to do this, I really did, but nagging fears clung to the back of my mind regardless.

The buzzer rang. My chest burned. I could ignore it. I could make it go away.

I walked over and pressed the button, breathing deeply.

'Yes?'

'Miss Delray?'

'Speaking.'

'Your car is waiting for you.'

'I'll be right down.'

Lights off, appliances unplugged, windows secured, door locked, Cherry life left behind.

Keris life activated.

At the door of my building stood a man in an old-fashioned chauffeur's uniform – well-pressed navy trousers, a navy jacket with a double row of shiny brass buttons, a peaked cap and leather driving gloves. I recognised him from my night out with His Lordship and I nodded and shot him a nervous smile.

He didn't smile back, but led me immediately down the path and out to the pavement, beside which His Lordship's black Bentley was parked.

With formal stiffness, he opened the back passenger door and watched as I climbed in and belted up.

Then, without saying a word, he took his seat, started up the engine and began to drive.

Somehow I had the impression that I was not supposed to talk, so I didn't.

I watched the cold, grey city pass by my window until we were in the cold, brown-green countryside then I sat back and stared at the ceiling, wishing I'd thought to bring a book. I didn't know how long this journey was going to take and it didn't seem that the driver was about to tell me.

I emboldened myself to ask. 'Where are we going?'

He didn't reply.

For a wild moment I wondered if he was an abductor dressed up as His Lordship's chauffeur, but I calmed myself by looking around the car and making a note of everything I recognised from my last short ride in it.

Within an hour, we were driving in snow. Nothing serious, just a few flakes whirling and skittering around the car.

'Do you know what the weather's like where we're going?' I tried again. 'Is it proper deep snow? I hope we don't get stuck.'

Again, there was no reply, but about ten minutes later,

he pulled into a layby, got out of the car and opened my door.

Snowflakes fell on my scarf and my eyelashes, but he was busy taking a pair of deckchairs out of the boot. He set them up beside the car, took out a flask and spoke his first words to me.

'Sit down. Time for a tea break.'

How civilised. A tea break in the snow.

I sat on the deckchair and drank a plastic cup of welcomingly scalding tea while the flakes grew bigger and fatter around me. The chauffeur's burst of eloquence appeared to be short-lived, for he offered nothing further in the way of conversation until the flask was empty.

Then he fixed me with a piercing stare and said, 'Now you need to relieve yourself.'

'What? No, I'm fine,' I said, clasping my hands in my lap, though actually I was feeling a little uncomfortable after all that tea.

'His Lordship's orders. I am to oversee you. Come on.'

He pulled me to my feet with his leather-gloved hand and led me through the scrubby bushes that bordered the layby, into a ploughed field beyond.

'Here,' he said. 'You won't be visible from the road.'

'I can't …'

'You'll do it, or I have His Lordship's authorisation to punish you.'

'Punish me? How?'

'You don't want to find out. Now lift your skirts and squat.'

His command made my throat dry and my clit pulse. I turned my back on him and dropped to a crouch, gathering the heavy coat-skirts up and raising them to my waist. Now only my black jersey dress concealed my thighs and sex. I rocked from side to side, edging my stupidly high-heeled feet as far apart as I could without losing balance – I really didn't want to splash the shiny patent leather, or my stockings.

I glanced over my shoulder at the chauffeur, who was watching impassively from a distance of about six feet. There was nothing for it. I would have to lift my dress and give him a flash of my pale bare bum.

God, it was cold, and snowflakes landed on my cheeks, melting straight away. I angled my body forward and let the liquid stream, thinly at first, then in a solid jet, down to the hard ground.

I was pissing myself in front of a strange man, with my bare arse on show.

It was uncomfortable and my bare skin was in danger of freezing, but I felt a surge of pure lustful joy as the last drops fell. I looked back anxiously. I had nothing to wipe myself with.

The chauffeur stepped forward, handing me a crisp white handkerchief.

It seemed a shame to spoil it, but I used it anyway.

'Put it in here,' said the chauffeur gruffly, passing me a zip-loc bag. 'His Lordship will want to see proof of your obedience.'

I had passed the first test. I stood and let my skirt and coat drop back over my nakedness, then followed him back to the car.

While packing up the chairs, he said, 'No more questions, or that punishment will still happen.'

'What sort of punishment?'

He sighed.

'Stand facing the car and put your hands up to the roof.'

Oh. That counted as a question. Now I'd earned the retribution. How easy these traps were to fall into.

I swallowed, putting my hands on the car roof. I could peer over and watch the traffic pass by on the nearby road. How much of what we did would be visible to them? Between the snow and the smoked glass of the car windows, probably not much, I guessed. All the same, here

I was, outside by a busy main road, facing an indeterminate punishment.

'Take off your coat,' he said.

'But it's cold!'

'Do it, or I'll stand you on the other side of the car.'

The road-facing side. I took off my coat, gloved fingers fumbling with the buttons.

'Good. I'm tempted to cut a switch from those bushes, but His Lordship doesn't want you marked. Hmm. Lift your skirt and hold it high.'

He had already seen my bottom, so I didn't hesitate to show it him for a second time. Cars swished by, windscreen wipers clacking. I shivered all over.

The chauffeur put his leather gloved hand on my cold bum, caressing it for a moment, then he withdrew it and the next thing I felt was a good hard slap in the same place. He spanked me for a minute or so, hard and fast, warming me up until the glow covered both cheeks and he was satisfied.

'Now. Inside, and no more questions.'

I sat down on my deliciously warm behind, but before he closed the door, he reached into a pocket and produced a length of black silk.

'It's not much further now,' he said. 'His Lordship does not want you to see the environs of his house until you arrive there. So I'm going to blindfold you.'

I looked up at him. His bright blue eyes were friendly. He wasn't much older than me, pale and freckly with a rather wicked smile. I felt suddenly much safer than I had done, and the sight of his brown leather driving gloves made me blush.

The smell of them was glorious and profoundly arousing as he tied the silk around my head, covering my eyes. I breathed it in, wanting it to stay, but all too soon he removed his hands. I waited for the car door to click shut, but it didn't.

'Put your hands in your lap,' he said quietly.

I placed them in front of me, and gasped when he picked them up and began binding them in what felt like another length of that same black silk. He tied an efficient knot, then did up my seatbelt and shut the door.

The car engine started up and the indicator clicked for a while until we headed back out on to the road, towards His Lordship's lair.

Time passed slowly, or was it quickly? I couldn't keep track of it in the dark. The road seemed very straight for a while, then there was a series of left and right turns that sent my tethered body leaning and jerking.

We stopped suddenly, then the chauffeur wound down the window, letting in a blast of cold and a few snowflakes, and I heard a sound I presumed to be the opening of electric gates. This had to be the place.

The crunch of tyres on gravel accompanied the car's slow crawl forward, ending smoothly with the faint creak of gears and the dying of the engine.

'I'll help you out,' said the chauffeur.

'Thanks,' I said, desperate to remove the blindfold, then, looking for a tiny moment of intimacy in the vast unknown, I asked him his name.

'You're not to ask questions, remember,' he said. 'Not unless His Lordship allows it. I'll have to report you.'

He released my seatbelt, put an arm around my shoulders and helped me, so gently, out of the car, then he put a hand beneath my elbow, guiding my blind and bound self up some steps. The snow seemed colder when I couldn't see it, the wind biting into my cheeks below the silk.

We stopped and the chauffeur clanged the bell.

I hoped we wouldn't be stuck there on that snowy doorstep for long, and my hope was not in vain. The door opened, but nobody spoke.

Instead, the chauffeur nudged me over the threshold, and my arm was taken my someone else – a woman, I thought, judging by her floral scent and the click of heels on beeswaxed wood. The other smell that struck me as I shuffled along beside the strange female was that of roasting meat. I was hungry! I hadn't had any lunch. Why hadn't I had any lunch? I could have kicked myself – it might be hours before I got to eat again.

A door opened and I judged from the acoustic that we had moved from a large lobby into a small or densely furnished side room. Skinny, poky fingers untied my wrists.

'You can take off your blindfold now,' said a flat voice.

I lifted the silk from my eyes, squinted for a few seconds, then looked at the speaker. She wore an old-fashioned maid's uniform, complete with frilly pinny and mob cap on a bony frame. She looked Spanish or Italian, with lots of black hair piled under the white linen, and sharp dark eyes.

We were in a small wood-panelled room that seemed to serve no particular function. It contained a long, velvet-upholstered bench and a huge wardrobe all the way along one wall. The only other furniture was a Victorian looking glass on a tilting stand. I felt too intimidated to speak, so I simply stood there, listening to my heart pound, waiting for the maid-person to say something else.

She sized me up in silence, keen eyes flicking from my feet to my woolly hat. She didn't seem very impressed.

'You should strip,' she said. 'Then I'll fetch His Lordship.'

'Strip?'

She made an impatient gesture. 'That's what I said. Get undressed.'

I took off my hat, scarf and gloves. She snatched them up, lifted the velvet top of the banquette and threw them inside.

My coat disappeared into the depths of the wardrobe, and my shoes followed them. Only my dress and stockings

178

remained.

I turned my back to the hard-faced maid and lifted my dress slowly over my head. She made a strange scornful noise, presumably finding my attempt at modesty amusing.

'You can't hide your body in here,' she remarked. I bent over a little to peel down the stockings and she laughed again.

'That's a good bit of colour on your arse. Did he have to spank you?'

None of your business bubbled up inside me, but I remembered what His Lordship had said about all staff being superior to me and just shrugged.

This wasn't going to satisfy my watcher, though.

'That's not an answer. Yes or no. Did you get spanked before you even got here?'

'Yes,' I muttered.

'His Lordship won't like that. He'll punish you.'

'Again?'

'If you get punished by staff, he likes you to feel his wrath.'

'Double jeopardy.'

'I suppose.'

I wondered what condition my bottom would be in by the end of the week. On the one hand, it didn't bear thinking about but on the other, it absolutely did. It bore thinking about long and hard, with one hand cupping my pussy and busy fingers on my clit.

I turned to face the woman, deciding that my breasts and cunt weren't offensive to look at, so she might as well see them. I handed her the dress and stockings, which she put away wordlessly again.

I felt a flutter of misgiving. I had thought this would all be crazy, horny, kinky fun. It seemed terribly sombre somehow. Was everyone going to be this joyless?

'Sit down and wait,' she said, pointing at the bench.

My bare bottom met the deep velvet pile and the woman

left.

It wasn't warm in there, and I shivered, gripping the edge of the bench, for about five minutes. In those minutes, I examined every aspect of the windowless room from its high ceiling with low-wattage light fitting to its polished wooden floor. I stood up and posed in front of the full-length mirror, trying to strike a note of bravado, but I looked small and cold and scared no matter what I did.

Purposeful footsteps approached and I sat back down abruptly, wondering if standing up had broken The Rules.

His Lordship opened the door, filling the little cupboard with his presence. Unfriendly Maid peered at me from behind his shoulder.

He was dressed in his Victorian gentleman mode again, fob watch and mutton-chop whiskers in full effect.

'Keris,' he said. He sounded so pleased to see me that I forgot how cold and naked I was and smiled. 'I've been waiting a long time to bring you here. Did my chauffeur keep you safe and well looked after?'

'Yeah,' I said.

He frowned.

'Yes, sir,' I amended.

He turned to Unfriendly Maid.

'Katerina, wait outside until you are called.'

She left, rather grudgingly, and shut the door behind her.

His Lordship joined me on the bench, wrapping my trembling body against his warm, tweedy side.

'I'm sorry it's so cold,' he said. 'I'll try to make this little introduction as quick as I can so you can get bathed and dressed and warmed up again.'

The idea of warmth struck the first cheery note of the day. I laid my head on his shoulder and listened.

'Since this is your first day, I'm going to break you in gently. The staff have been instructed to keep their hands off you, except Kat there, who will bathe and prepare you,

180

but no more than that. There will be no public training or use until tomorrow at the earliest. Once you are settled and in the right headspace, we can get a little more ambitious. But for the rest of the day, you will see only Katerina and me. Full introductions can wait until tomorrow.'

'What's going to happen this week, sir?'

'You are going to find the core of your submission, Keris. You'll be worked hard and at times you might want to give up, but if you persevere you'll find it well worth all the effort, I promise.'

'I feel very alone here,' I confessed. 'And a bit lost.'

'You'll be well looked after. And nothing will happen unless you want it to. You can invoke your safe word at any time. I should warn you, though, that if you use it more than three times, you will be sent home. That doesn't mean you've failed a test – it just means you probably aren't suited to our version of the lifestyle. Does that sound too scary?'

'No, that's good,' I said. 'Thank you, sir.'

Just saying the word "sir" made me feel better. The fear dissolved and re-formed into something else, a flickering thrill that still contained that germ of intimidation but was also composed of many other things – exhilaration, anticipation, lust. I decided to trust him, and with trust came confidence.

'Well, then.' He stood and beckoned me to my feet, inspecting my naked body from head to toe. 'You can't wear that.'

His fingers reached out to Patrick's necklace and I made a small sound of disappointment.

'Does it have sentimental value?'

'Yes, sir.'

'All the same, you can't wear it here. Turn around and I'll take it off. It'll be kept safe, I promise you.'

I wanted to disobey, to stamp my foot and pout, but I kept control of myself and presented my back view to His

Lordship.

He unclasped the necklace, removed it and then his hand landed on my bottom, taking a handful.

'I see my chauffeur had to attend to you. What was that for?'

'Asking too many questions, sir.'

'Hmm, that doesn't surprise me. But it isn't a good start, is it, Keris?'

'No, sir.'

'I'll have to address it myself later. Just before you go down for your bath, we need to choose a name for you.'

'Oh?'

'Yes. Well, I'll choose for you and, unless you have any strong objections, that's what you'll be for the week. Since you're at the bottom of the heap here, that's what we'll call you. Bottom.'

'Seriously?' An image of me with asses' ears came to mind. 'Bit Shakespearian.'

'Indeed. But, as everyone will have permission to top you eventually, it's rather appropriate, don't you think?'

'It's not very … attractive, sir.'

'No, but you need to know your place. And your place is at the bottom, Bottom. Understood?'

'Yes, sir.'

'You get your own name back at the end of the week, anyway. Now …'

He opened the velvet banquette again, put away my necklace and brought out a stiff leather dog collar with a leash attached to its silver clip.

I held up my chin and let him fasten it round my neck. It was uncomfortable, but that made it all the more effective. Once it was buckled, he tugged firmly at the leash a couple of times and I lowered my head.

I felt owned.

It had begun.

He opened the door and called Katerina in. She sneered

at me and took the proffered leash.

'Take Bottom below stairs, Kat, and make the necessary preparations. I will be down to perform her induction in one hour.'

'Yes, sir.'

I expected His Lordship to leave without further ado, but instead he grabbed my chin and subjected me to a passionate kiss before exiting without another word.

'So … Bottom,' said Kat with a scornful chuckle. 'Nice name. Suits you. Come on.'

She yanked on the leash so that I stumbled after her into the vast outer lobby, which I saw for the first time without my blindfold. Intensely conscious of my nakedness, I darted my eyes around in search of witnesses, but the hall seemed to be empty, though I could hear voices, laughter, the clinking of cups, coming from somewhere beyond.

'How many people are here?' I asked Kat, but she tugged on my leash and clicked her tongue.

'You don't speak to me, Bottom. Only when spoken to. Understand?'

'Yes, ma'am.'

She led me through a door behind the vast staircase and down some smaller, darker steps, into a plainly decorated corridor. I resisted the temptation to muse aloud that this must be the staff quarters, and just let her take me along the passage with its thin carpet and slightly damp air until she opened a door and showed me into a room with a huge old-fashioned tin bath full of steaming water in its centre.

'Get in and I'll scrub you down,' she said.

I stepped in, looking around me at the surroundings. The floor was tiled with granite and the walls plain and whitewashed, but set into them on opposite sides were two huge iron rings. Looking up, I saw a hook in the ceiling to keep them company. There was nothing else in the room but a metal cupboard – of the type usually seen in offices – in one corner. A barred window, high in the far wall, was the only source of natural light.

The water was hot and I winced as Katerina poured a jug of it over my head before setting to work with the shampoo.

'This is the preparation room,' she told me. 'It's also the punishment room. You'd better hope this is the last day you spend here. I wouldn't like to think how many submissives have had their bad habits corrected in this room.'

Have you? I wanted to ask the question so badly, but I couldn't. Her gnarly fingers dug into my scalp, then she poured steaming water over me again until my skin felt boiled and tight. She scrubbed me with the stiffest-bristled loofah in the world, until I worried I might bleed, but apparently she knew how to stop just short of damaging me.

'We need to get you clean, you dirty little bitch,' she muttered, and I wished I could ask what I'd done to make her hate me, but of course, all speech was off limits.

She swapped her loofah for a rough cloth and used it on my breasts until my nipples tingled, then she spread my bum cheeks and rubbed it in between until I squirmed. Finally, my pussy was subjected to the same unceremonious treatment.

'We'll need to shave you,' she noted, making me wish to heaven that I'd had the courage to wax it myself that morning. 'OK. You're clean. Get out.'

She picked up the towel that was draped over one end of the bath and wrapped me in it while I stepped onto a bristly mat. My toes curled and I shifted from foot to foot, unable to find a comfortable way of standing on it, but it didn't take long to dry myself and then I was able to put my soles on the cool, soothing tiles.

Kat wrenched the towel off me and threw it into the corner by the door. She fished a tub from her apron pocket and slathered me from neck to toe in some kind of scented, heavy lotion, probably moisturiser, until my skin gleamed, then she unclipped the leash from my collar and took it over to the cupboard.

The leash was stowed away, but she came back carrying a length of slim silvery chain and a strange contraption rather like a low stool in a triangular shape with padding at the base of each leg.

'Come here,' she said, placing the thing below and in front of one of the iron wall rings. 'Kneel so your knees are on each hassock.'

I placed each knee on one of the padded bases. The two tubular metal legs tapered up between my thighs, the seat part hovering just below my pussy lips.

Kat bent to adjust the height of the struts, extending them until the narrow leather seat first touched my lower lips, then sat directly between them, pressing against my clit. Next, she spread apart the metal tubes so that my kneeling stance was almost painfully wide-legged and my cunt spread open, sprawled on the leather.

'Put your hands on your head,' she ordered, then she clipped the metal chain to my collar and fixed it to the iron ring. It was just the right length to keep me taut and upright. I would not be able to lean forward to escape the persistent pressure on my clit.

She patted me, unnecessarily hard, under my chin, then went back to the cupboard for more. I tried to adjust my position, to get more comfortable between my legs, but it wasn't possible. I was tethered tight.

When Kat came back, she had a pair of nipple clamps, which she applied with a smile. I bit my lip and moaned, but she hadn't tightened them too far and they soon calmed down to a low throb.

'This is where you stay until His Lordship is ready to make use of you,' she said. 'There's a little camera – do you see it? – just by the ceiling hook, so if you take your hands off your head, he will know about it. Goodbye.'

She nodded formally and left the room, dragging the tin bath after her.

'Damian! Can you give me a hand with this?' I heard her shouting in the corridor outside, then there was a male voice – the chauffeur's! – mingling with hers as they hauled the heavy bath away from me.

Then, silence.

Chapter Ten

HIS LORDSHIP HAD SAID he would come in an hour. How long ago was that now? The bath seemed to have taken ages but in reality it could maybe have only been ten minutes. I couldn't possibly kneel here, pussy wedged against this padding, neck forcibly high, for fifty minutes, could I?

I shut my eyes and tried to fill the vacant time with fantasies of what would happen when His Lordship arrived. Guiltily, I hoped he would bring his handsome chauffeur with him, though he had already said that he would be alone.

But the chauffeur's blue eyes, crinkled at the corners, and his soft, commanding voice and the sandy-red hairline that peeked from his cap all stayed in my mind, and I found myself hoping our encounter in the car wouldn't be our last.

I was picturing a scene on the back seat of the car with lord and chauffeur either side of me when the door finally opened, along with my eyes.

His Lordship surveyed me from the doorway for a moment while my cheeks glowed with the secret knowledge of my indiscreet thoughts and I tried to dismiss their after-effects.

'Bottom,' he said. 'By name and by nature.'

He shut the door behind him, walked up to me and took off the nipple clamps. I saw stars and gasped while he pulled the kneeling device out from under me and ordered me to stand.

My legs felt shaky but I managed a wobbly kind of stance while he inspected the leather seat of his contraption.

'My goodness,' he said. 'Soaked. You are a little whore, aren't you, Bottom? I don't know if anyone's managed to get it this wet before.'

He smirked and put the thing aside before running his hands all over my body. My hands were still fixed on my head as if glued there – I wasn't sure I'd be able to remove them now if he asked me – so he had an uninterrupted path along my body from armpits to thighs.

'Perfect,' he said. 'Kat has done a thorough job. But I'm afraid you didn't behave yourself on the journey, did you? I've spoken to my chauffeur and he said he had to spank you for excessive curiosity. Oh dear. So, before we can start on our training, there is a punishment in store for you.'

He tutted and shook his head for a moment before heading to that dreaded cupboard and retrieving another strange device – this one more like a stepstool with two padded levels. He placed it in front of me.

'Bend over,' he said.

But the chain was too short, and he had to let out a few links and refasten my collar first.

Once I was in position, arse high, head held up, he took some shiny black tape and wound it around my wrists, securing them in the small of my back, a few inches above my coccyx.

'Once your training is complete,' he said, going back to the cupboard and fetching a wide leather tawse, 'I won't need to keep your hands tied. You will be able to keep them there of your own accord. But for now, my concern is safety. You don't want this falling on your knuckles, believe me.'

I wanted to ask him how many strokes I was getting, my

stomach now coiling in fear, but I wasn't sure it was wise. Would an unsolicited question add to my total?

'I'm very sorry, sir,' I say instead. 'I didn't mean to break the rules.'

'Curiosity is natural,' he said, laying the split end of the strap across my backside and flapping it gently over the skin. 'But part of submission is subsuming your natural urges for the pleasure of another. It's a lesson that needs learning, Bottom. If I spare you, I'm not really doing you any favours. Now, I'm going to give you twenty.'

I winced, then exhaled. Twenty was a lot with a heavy thing like that tawse, but knowing the number was still better than not knowing.

His Lordship raised his arm and let the tawse fall with a terrific splat that conferred an immediate sting and then a slow, deep blaze that made me suck in the air around me. It was going to be hard to take this, very hard.

'You count the strokes when I chastise you,' His Lordship explained. 'And at the end of the session, you thank me for taking the trouble to administer discipline. Do you understand?'

'Yes, sir.' My voice was weak already and he'd only laid one stroke.

I remembered to keep the count, mostly. At seven I had to take a really long breath before I was able to speak. At 11, I begged him to stop, but I didn't safeword, and only numbered the stroke when he suggested repeating it.

At 15, I forgot, and then he did repeat the stroke.

At 16, I could feel the sob coming.

At 18, it came.

At 20, I was crying, but it was a weird kind of crying, a sort of cathartic triumph, a falling away of tension while my body floated in fire. His Lordship had whipped the grouchiness of the day out of me and I felt purified by the pain, new and clean and ready for submission.

'Have you forgotten something?' he asked, his voice

gentle. He crouched beside me and put a hand on my shoulder.

Had I? I couldn't for the life of me think what it might be. In fact, I couldn't think at all. Nothing existed in my life except my throbbing bottom and my need to be praised and petted by this man, because I had pleased him. Oh! That was it.

'Thank you, sir,' I said.

'No, Bottom, you must look at me when you say it, and you must be clearer about exactly what you're thanking me for. Try that again.'

I had to work up to looking him in the eyes. The words wouldn't be easy, but the steadfast gaze was a cruel thing to demand. I had a feeling I might need a lot of training for that.

I twisted my neck and let my eyes glaze a bit, softening the effect of his piercing look.

'Thank you for teaching me my lesson, sir,' I said. 'I will try to behave myself better.'

'That's a start,' he sniffed, chucking me under the chin. 'We'll work on a more eloquent rendering next time punishment is required.'

He stroked my bottom with one hand, making the most of its heat.

'I didn't go easy on you,' he said. 'I had a feeling you could take quite a good thrashing, from what I've seen of you.'

'Thank you, sir,' I said, though it was one of the more bizarre compliments of my life. Perhaps I should add it to my CV. Grade Eight piano, Cycling Instructor Qualification, takes a good thrashing.

'How do you feel now?'

'Cleansed. And hot. And sore. And a bit … y'know.' I squirmed illustratively.

He chuckled.

'But do you feel the need for closeness, reassurance?

Many submissives do. They want to be held. Don't you?'

'May I answer honestly, sir?'

'Of course. Always.'

'I want to be fucked.'

He chuckled.

'That's the other common reaction. And you haven't come in such a long time, have you? Hmm?'

'No, sir, and I've been so tempted, so often, but I held off.'

'Well, such obedience merits a reward, I think. I'm not completely heartless.'

He reached down between my wobbly legs and began to move his fingers over and around my clit, fattening it up, dipping deep into my juices.

'You won't take long,' he observed, delving, pressing, spearing my cunt.

His surmise was accurate – it had been so long since I had been touched there that I began to climax almost immediately. He had this way of manipulating me that spun the orgasm out, drawing wave after wave, moan after moan, commanding my body to perform against my will until I was finally spent and shivering under his hand.

Now I wanted the holding and the gentle words, now I felt the vulnerability that the whipping hadn't induced. I tried to nuzzle into him, and he stroked my hair and bent to whisper into my ear.

'Soon, Bottom, soon I can let you up and take you to my bed and feed you and take care of you. But first, there is one thing I must do. Be patient, sweet.'

He took the tawse back to the cupboard and swapped it for a bottle and an implement the length and width of a finger, made of pink silicone, tapering in at the bottom with a base in the shape of a heart.

I looked away quickly. It had to be a butt-plug.

'We'll take this slowly,' he promised. 'But it must be done. My submissives need to make all their orifices available to me – no exceptions. Are you ready?'

I had to be honest. 'I'm not sure, sir.'

'Well, you know the safeword. I'm going to trust you to use it if you need to. Try and keep relaxed.'

My wrists were still tied, so I wasn't able to do much more than shudder and shimmy my hips a little when his hand descended on my scorched cheeks to prise them apart. I heard a squelchy, sucky sound, then I whimpered as something cold and greasy was applied liberally to my virgin orifice. He spent a long time on lubrication, working his finger around and around, smearing and slicking, making sure I was thoroughly coated around the tiny hole before he put any pressure on it. I imagined it, shiny and explicit, tight and closed, waiting for that first prod.

I screwed shut my eyes and held my breath.

The oiled blunt end of a forefinger was placed squarely on the target. He began to turn it in half-rotations, slowly at first, picking up speed, pushing so very lightly that at first I didn't perceive it, but his motion gathered momentum and my muscles contracted in their first involuntary spasm, noticing rather belatedly that something was trying to breach them.

'Good, good, you're doing very well.' His Lordship's voice was a low murmur of reassurance. 'Don't fight it. You need this. It's coming to you.'

I hadn't realised that my spine was arched until he patted it down, leaving his palm flat on my back to hold me in position, arse thrust out as far and as high as possible.

'Tell me how this feels,' he said quietly, and then his finger had somehow wriggled clear of my protective muscular barrier and made its first ingress into my rear.

I tried to find descriptive words, but my powers of expression were not at their best.

'Oh, weird,' I whimpered. 'Unnatural. Invasive.'

'It will soon feel natural to you. It will be quite normal for you to have this area occupied when you are in my service. You will learn to offer it without question. Your arse, my dear, is mine.'

He screwed the finger further in, right up to the knuckle. It wasn't painful exactly, nor was it entirely uncomfortable, but it just felt so powerfully wrong that my body couldn't seem to adjust to it but continued to try and expel it despite my desire to please His Lordship.

He didn't seem unduly concerned by this, however, and he certainly made no effort to withdraw the finger or pander to the regular spasming of my sphincter. Instead, he let it mimic the thrust of a cock, pushing it up and pulling it down for about half a minute until he was satisfied that my resistance was wearing down.

'Good,' he said again. 'Now I am going to insert this plug – it's the slimmest of my training plugs. You will be required to keep this in all night – I will give permission to remove it if circumstances necessitate, but otherwise, you are to retain it until morning. Failure to do so will incur punishment. Do you understand?'

'Yes, sir.'

He removed his finger, replacing it swiftly with the sleek, cold tip of the plug, which slid in quite easily at first, being no wider than the lately-inserted digit – until it reached a halfway point, where it became clear that it flared out towards the middle before tapering off again. I let out a low moan, feeling myself stretch a little further, experiencing a pang of discomfort, but before it could register much more deeply, the moment had passed and the plug was fully seated.

I could not exactly ignore it – its presence would be an insistent sensation – but it could have been so much worse. In fact, my reading on the subject had led me to imagine an unpleasantly stretched and sore feeling. That's what you get for reading on the websites I tend to frequent, though. It served me right.

The thorough job His Lordship had done of lubrication

made me worry that the plug might even slip out without my noticing, but he prevented that eventuality by covering the base in bondage tape, so that a shiny black rectangle of the stuff must have interrupted the uniform redness of my bum, sticking the plug inside and making it absolutely obvious to any viewer that my arsehole was well and truly occupied.

He completed the job by smacking my bottom two or three times, hard, so that the plug jiggled inside me, letting me bask and bathe in the humiliation of it before slapping my thighs wide apart, unbuttoning his fly and penetrating my cunt with swift and unexpected vigour.

He fucked me without a word, slamming hard into me four or five times before coming and pulling out, setting himself to rights and bending to inspect the state of my pussy.

Our correspondence prior to this weekend had included comprehensive tests of our genito-urinary health and fitness, so I was unconcerned by the lack of a condom. The feeling of his juices, trickling down my thighs and drying there, added a deliciously shameful edge to my predicament, bound and plugged and visibly fucked for anyone to see.

'I needed that,' he panted behind me. 'Never could resist a plugged bottom. Now, I think you must be hungry and ready for some less harsh treatment, am I right?'

'Yes, sir.' I heard the happy sighing quality of my voice as if from afar.

He bent to untie my wrists, then helped me to my bare feet, holding me against him for a moment, stroking my hair.

'I have high hopes of you,' he said, before leading me out of the room and making me walk with him, naked, plugged, scarlet-bottomed and dripping spunk, along the corridor and back into the Great Hall.

A head peered round a door before we made it to the

staircase, but His Lordship clapped disapprovingly and the head disappeared. I recalled his promise that nobody else would be involved in my training today and drew a breath of relief.

The stairs seemed never-ending, but at length we arrived at the top floor of the house and I was ushered into a breathtaking suite of rooms, apparently decorated by the set dresser for *Downton Abbey* or *Upstairs, Downstairs*.

Not sure if I had permission to speak, I simply goggled in the doorway while His Lordship untied his cravat and removed his frock coat.

'While you're in my rooms, we are equals,' he told me, taking my hand and drawing me further in to the room.

I tried to listen, but my brain was busy absorbing its surroundings, so I might have missed a few things.

'Are you listening?' His tone sharpened, and I snapped to attention.

'Sorry, sir. This is amazing.'

'All right, I know it's quite impressive.' He rested on his laurels, pulling out a chair for me and waiting for me to sit – gingerly – before continuing. 'What I was saying, Keris, is that here in this room, we are no longer master and submissive. Our time spent here is on an equal footing and gives us a chance to get to know each other as people. Unless we do that, the trust which is so vital in our kind of dynamic can't be properly established, in my experience. Does that make sense?'

'So I don't have to call you sir? And I can say what I like?'

'Exactly. You're as unsubmissive as a naked girl with a plug in her whipped behind can be.' He chuckled darkly and I squirmed on said whipped behind. 'For a start, while we're up here, you can call me Marcus.'

'Is that your name?'

He raised his eyebrows at me. OK, maybe it was a silly question.

195

'You look hungry,' he observed. 'For your first night, I'll have dinner sent up and you can eat with me. It's a privilege I reserve for my most promising beginners – it won't be repeated this week.'

I watched him make a call, presumably to the kitchen.

'How many staff do you have?' I asked, once he'd put in his order for game terrine and a cold turkey platter.

'It varies,' he said. 'This week, I have half a dozen house guests, so I've hired caterers for the week – non-kinky, but kink-sympathetic, if you catch my drift.'

'So you don't get to spank the chef if the meat's overdone?'

'No. But we have three maids, including yourself, and a couple of footmen-cum-stable lads. There's my chauffeur, but he's not submissive – he looks after my wife if she's missing my firm hand.'

The food arrived, brought in by Kat on a trolley under a cloche. She didn't even look at me, but kept her head bowed and left swiftly.

'About your wife,' I said, spearing the terrine and shoving it down my throat. I had forgotten all about being hungry, and now my stomach was reminding me with some insistence.

'What about her?' He regarded my famished behaviour with amusement.

'Is she really and truly OK with all this? With you entertaining various random women in your bedroom and all that?'

'First of all, they aren't random. They're very carefully selected. Second of all, we have an open marriage and always have had. It works well for us.'

'So she can shag whoever she likes?'

'No, she can't shag whoever she likes. She can shag carefully selected partners who have been approved and tested for sexual health, as you have been.'

'Is she a domme?'

'She wasn't, when we met. As the years have passed, she has begun experimenting with that side of herself.'

'Funny, that.' I chewed ruminatively. 'I keep coming across these women who started off as subs and switched when they got older. Is the BDSM scene ageist, then?'

'Ageist?' He sounded surprised.

'It's just that I can't imagine ever wanting to switch. Will nobody want to top me when I'm past thirty? Because if so, I've only got three years to cram a hell of a lot of submitting into.'

'I'm sure I don't know what you're talking about.'

His voice was cold and my hackles rose. I wondered if I'd unwittingly uncovered a big old flaw in this little scene.

'It would be a shame,' I mused, daring to pursue the theme, 'if that were the case.'

'It would be a shame if you wittered on about something you have absolutely no evidence for.'

Ouch. Acid splash. I abandoned the topic in favour of the cold meats and pickles.

'How old is your wife?' I asked after a few minutes of détente.

'Thirty.'

I almost snorted into my wine.

'How old are you?'

'Fifty-five.'

'What about your chauffeur? Is his name Damian?'

'Yes, what about him?' His Lordship, or Marcus, or whatever, seemed very curt now. I wondered if I ought to change the subject to something obsequious or flattering. But he had said I could say what I liked in here, after all.

'He's quite fit.' I sipped my wine delicately. 'Does he work for you full time?'

'Yes, he does. Well, for me and others of my circle. You have an eye for him, then?' His Lordship pursed his lips.

'Just like I said – he's good-looking. I bet he's popular.'

'Yes.'

'Like you.' I relented and released a bit of the flattery.

'Oh, I wouldn't say –'

'Yes, you would. Everyone says you're like the superstar DJ of the dom world.'

'I'll take your word for it.'

'You should. I know I'm very lucky. I feel I'm joining an elite.'

Mollified, His Lordship poured me some more wine.

'It's true. People come from all over the world to spend time here and avail themselves of my highly trained submissives.'

'Do they? It's like a kinky jet-set?'

'Yes. Just this week, I have a couple from New York and some Germans. Most nationalities have been represented here at one time or another.'

'Who are the kinkiest?'

'I think we English, if I'm honest.'

'Well, yeah, but this is England, so English people would be over-represented, wouldn't they?'

He sighed and put down his glass.

'I know I said you could say whatever you wanted in here, but I think I'm going to ask you, very nicely, to finish the meal in silence. And then I have a treat for you.'

'Oh, sounds good.'

I was a bit annoyed at having to hold my peace – I wanted to ask how one becomes a dom of international repute, but it would have to wait. I didn't want to mark myself down as a troublemaker on my first day.

So I downed the wine, scarfed a bit of cold Christmas pudding and tried to ignore the butt-plug, without success.

In lieu of an after-dinner mint, His Lordship's treat for me was a massage, face-down on his four-poster bed, the oils sinking into my weary skin until, absolutely contrary to my plans, I fell fast asleep.

*　　*　　*

Before my eyes even opened, my first thought of the new day was what's in my arse? I remembered as my eyelids unglued and put a hand to the taped-in flange, checking that it was secure.

Once I'd managed to get my head out of the covers, I saw His Lordship, fast asleep on the far side of the huge bed, and sighed contentedly, figuring that another hour or so of quality shut-eye was on the menu before I had to start bowing and scraping in unorthodox bodily contortions.

Maybe, I thought optimistically, burrowing back down, I would get to see Damian again today. Perhaps he would even take me for a drive that ended up on the back seat. I was contemplating this pleasant eventuality when my reverie was cut short by a wholly unexpected female voice.

'Good morning, Bottom.' The "Bottom" was spoken with such plosive derision that I sat bolt upright, regardless of the plug, and stared. It had come from the corner.

Sure enough, seated regally on a chintz armchair, was an Amazonian blonde of roughly my age, dressed only in a corset and those Victorian-style drawers. My eye was drawn to the luxuriant spillage of flesh over the top of her tightly-strung bodice, and the firm jaw. She was like a boudoir Boadicea. Or is it Boudicca? Never sure on that one.

'Good morning, um …,' I said.

'Ma'am,' she helpfully supplied. 'Did you sleep well?'

'Yes, I did, thanks … ma'am.'

'Well.' She stood and clapped her hands. 'Time to get cracking. You have so much ground to cover today.'

Her clapping awoke His Lordship, who sat up and rubbed his eyes.

'Darling, what time is it? It's still the middle of the night, surely?'

'Six o'clock – time for staff to be hard at work.'

'You want to handle this?'

'Yes, you go back to sleep, love. I can see you're

199

shattered.' His Lordship lay back down and the woman – whom I presumed to be his wife – clapped her hands at me again, visibly annoyed that I hadn't leapt up and started scurrying about like one of the three blind mice.

I put a toe out of the toasty warmth and shivered. The heating had only just come on and Ma'am couldn't be warm enough in just her underwear.

'Come into the bathroom and I'll shower with you,' she said, yawning. 'Then you can dress me.'

'Yes, ma'am,' I whispered, following her through a door.

'Right, well, you're the maid, so you'd better unlace me,' she said.

She presented her back view to me and I got to work on the ribbons, wondering if she had been wearing this all night long.

'I've been up all night,' she answered my question. 'Entertaining our German gentlemen. So I'll set you off in service this morning, then I'm off to bed until at least noon.'

'This is a beautiful corset, if I might be allowed to say so, ma'am.'

I laid it gently down on a footstool, then I pulled down the drawers and gasped.

Her bottom was a mass of mad red welts that looked as if they were pulsing.

'They wanted to try out a birch,' she said matter-of-factly. 'Have you ever been birched, Bottom?'

'No, never.'

'Ah well, that pleasure will come. Maybe I'll get to do it. Now, you'd better turn around. I'm going to unplug you.'

I hesitated, suddenly coy at the idea of allowing a complete stranger – and a woman at that – access to my most intimate area.

But she yanked me round by the shoulders, fingers

digging impatiently into my skin and bent me over, ripping off the bondage tape so that the plug gave a rather worrying jolt.

I cringed as her fingers fished the long, slim invader out of my bottom with exquisitely lingering tenderness.

'There, all done,' she said, putting it in the sink and running the tap over it. 'You can clean it up properly later. There'll be a bigger one for you tonight.'

I can hardly wait.

She stepped into the wet room and turned on the jets, comfortable with her nudity and unconcerned at whatever my thoughts might be. She was rather magnificent, I thought. I could see why His Lordship had married her.

I stepped in after her, sighing with pleasure at the warm spray.

'Here, girl, wash my hair.'

She handed me a bottle of shampoo, and I reached up to lather it into her head of long, thick hair. The obvious enjoyment she derived from my actions was pleasing, and I worked hard to sustain it, happy to wash her body too, sliding my hands over every curve of her body. Her breasts were bruised, so I was careful with them and, of course, with her sore bottom. When she parted her thighs to grant me access to her cunt, I was interested to see that she had pierced labia which could be linked shut if required. I was extra careful around the jewellery, trying to imagine how it must feel to have rings hanging down from such a sensitive spot.

'You have a gentle touch,' she said. 'I've had three hefty cocks up there tonight. God knows what they feed them in Lower Saxony, but they're like bullocks.'

'May I ask you a question, ma'am?'

'Depends what it is. Go on.'

'Do you like dominating? Or do you just do it because you think you should?'

She was silent for a moment, then she said, 'Tell you

201

what. Why don't you work it out for yourself? You'll get plenty of clues over the course of the week, starting with drying and moisturising me.'

Drying was easy enough, but I'd never prepared another woman for bed, especially one who appeared so high maintenance. She led me out to her walk-in wardrobe and made me lace her into a frothy confection of old lace she claimed was a nightgown – this was a long and complicated process and my ineptitude resulted in a number of slaps to my bare behind and thighs which she apparently enjoyed dealing.

'Useless slut,' she snarled, laying on another when the laces slipped from my hands for a third time. I had to admit that perhaps I'd been off-base with my theory about her reluctance to dominate. Or, of course, she could just be venting her frustration with the situation.

By the time she was gowned and nightcapped, I was a living collage of handprints.

'Finally,' she sniffed, admiring her reflection in the pier glass. 'And now I suppose we should get you dressed. You'll have to come downstairs for that.'

I looked down at myself with some dismay. I was naked, damp hair coiling down between my shoulder blades. And it was freezing. Did I really have to trudge about the cold house in the nude?

It seemed I did.

I followed my mistress all the way down the stairs, back towards the little room in which I had been subject to His Lordship's disciplinary attentions. But she didn't take me in there – instead, she took me further along the corridor, to the end room.

Inside, three women were dressing and preparing for the day ahead.

'Kat,' said Her Ladyship, 'get this one uniformed. You know what the newbies wear.'

'Yes, ma'am.' Kat smiled cruelly.

'She's to be given all the most demeaning duties today. Make sure you don't let a single thing slide – she needs to be watched like a hawk. You have my permission to discipline her when necessary – please keep a note of each occasion for myself and His Lordship.'

'Yes, ma'am.'

'Very good.'

Her Ladyship nodded and left. Alone in the centre of the room, being sized up by six strange eyes, I suddenly felt more vulnerable than at any point since my arrival. What would I give for Damian the chauffeur to walk through the door now?

No sign of him, though – instead, Kat took hold of my hair and dragged me over to a large chest that lay at the end of the room, beyond the beds and drawers. She took out a tiny sheer white lace apron and told me to put it on.

'This is my uniform?' I picked up the insubstantial scrap and frowned. 'Isn't there more?'

'Yes, there's more. Shoes, stockings and suspenders. Plus your collar, of course.'

'Right.'

The other women wore proper Victorian maid uniform – the only difference being the way their long black skirts were slit up the front and back. I longed for some of their coverage. This piece of woven air was hardly going to solve my goosepimple problem. I put it on, though, and tied it round the waist. The bib did nothing to conceal my breasts, gauzy as it was, and my bottom was completely exposed. I took the frilly suspender belt Kat offered me and clipped it to a pair of sheer black stockings, completing the look with high-heeled patent pumps. I looked nothing like a maid, everything like a whore.

The other maids lounged, smirking and watching, while Kat fixed my collar around my neck and buckled it tight. Next she rolled up my hair into a neat bun, pinning it into place.

'What do we think, girls?' she asked, twirling me around by the shoulders. 'Is she ready for her lessons?'

'Nice,' they giggled in unison.

'You've all done this?' I asked them, on the verge of panic. 'You've all been trained like this?'

'Oh yes,' said one, a demure blonde. 'You're the latest in a long line. Don't worry, just enjoy it.'

'Right,' said Kat, 'I think you're ready. But one thing needs to be sorted out before you start.' She reached under my apron and tugged at my pubic hair. 'You need to get shaved. Damian will do it. Take her into the kitchen, Liv, and tell him he needs to get ready with the razor.'

'What?'

But nobody was going to help me. The blonde girl, Liv, took my hand and led me out of the dormitory and along the corridor to the kitchen, where Damian himself sat with his feet up on the table, polishing his boots.

'Well, good morning,' he said with a broad smile. 'Here's our new girl.'

'She needs your steady hand with the razor,' said Liv.

'Oh good. I was hoping for that.' He winked at me and beckoned. 'Come and sit on the table. I'll just get my tackle.'

He was as gorgeous as I remembered, freckly and pale with the filthiest glint I'd ever seen.

I positioned myself on the edge of the table. Liv went over to the old-fashioned range and set about getting the kettle on. I tried to adjust my mindset, to view all this as normal, but it wouldn't shift and everything remained obstinately bizarre. I'm not one for waxing – a neat trim is as much as I can manage when it comes to pubic topiary. I'd always been too shy to put my bush in the hands of a beautician – so it just seemed topsy-turvy in the extreme that I was now entrusting it to a bad red-haired man with a cut-throat razor.

He came back in with a bowl of water, a towel over his

204

forearm and a blade that made me think of Jack the Ripper and screw my eyes shut.

He laughed at my fear, setting the bowl down on the floor.

'I'm a dab hand at this, sweetheart,' he said. 'Don't worry. Raise your apron for me, doll, and spread your legs nice and wide. Here, lift up your bum.'

He slid the towel underneath me and waited until I was in position, wide-thighed with my apron bunched up in a fist.

'Good. Now lie back. Think of England, if you like. Or think of whatever you want. Sex is always favourite.'

Oh, he was a cheeky bleeder, but it worked for me. My crotch tingled as I pressed my spine down on the hard deal surface and looked up at the ceiling.

The range was beginning to bring some much-needed warmth to the room and behind me Liv clattered about with pots and pans, preparing for the caterers, I supposed. Not that supposition-making was easy when a sexy man stood in your foreground, sharpening his razor blade on an old-fashioned leather strop. I wished I could take some footage of it, to be replayed at a less nerve-wracking, more leisurely time. I would be happy to watch it for hours.

But he put down the strop and the razor on the table, took a shaving brush and began to lather me up, circling the bristles from the base of my abdomen and down until the whole area was a mass of foam, even as far back as the crack of my bum. His brisk, firm appliance was performed by an expert hand – not a bubble of the stuff landed inside my lips, which I kept wide open for him.

'That's a nicely swollen clit,' he commented, just at the moment that the caterers appeared, taking over at the range from Liv, who came to watch Damian's handiwork.

'She's enjoying it,' she remarked, bending forward to get a better view.

The caterers threw some bacon into a pan, oblivious.

The sizzle coincided with the first careful stroke of Damian's razor.

'You know you have to keep very, very still,' he murmured, holding a thigh steady with his unoccupied hand. 'You don't need me to tell you that, do you?'

'No,' I whispered.

'No, sir,' he reminded me gently. 'Everybody here is Sir or Ma'am to you, whether guests or servants. Don't forget, unless you want me to use my strop for something different.'

'Sorry, sir.'

He scraped, slowly and diligently, the sides of my lips while I held my breath and tried to visualise perfect stillness.

He had moved up to the pubic triangle when Kat marched into the room, carrying a large glass of water containing the butt-plug.

'Here's your plug from last night,' she said, banging it down on the side. 'You're to wash it when you've finished here, and then go and scrub the grates in the drawing room.'

She flounced out again, apparently annoyed about something, though who knew what.

'Butt-plug, eh?' Damian's voice held a wealth of quiet amusement. 'Are you new to backdoor fun then?'

'Yes, sir.' My face flared and my clit throbbed at the embarrassing subject matter.

'Unusual – usually the girls who come here are pretty experienced on that score. His Lordship must be overjoyed – he gets to break you in. He loves that.'

Somebody behind me cracked a series of eggs into a bowl.

'Must admit, I'm a bit jealous,' Damian continued. 'I wish I could claim that privilege.'

I kind of wish you could too. You're about fifty times more attractive than His Lordship.

'Maybe another time, sir,' I said.

He chuckled.

'His Lordship will want to keep that for himself, unless he gives permission. Shame.'

He removed the last of my pubes with a flourish and patted me dry with the towel.

'There. You dare to bare. Nice job, if I do say so myself.'

He flashed me that filthy grin and winked.

'I'd love to stay and, uh, chat, but you've got work to do, missy.' He picked up the strop and flicked it lightly but stingingly between my thighs. 'Get to it.'

Chapter Eleven

WASHING THE BUTT-PLUG at the Belfast sink alongside the caterers, who kept their eyes politely averted throughout, was one thing, but scrubbing a grate quite another.

Naked for all intents and purposes, bent double, scouring out the ash and soot, I felt like a slave. I'd expected to be put to work, but I hadn't expected the work to be this dirty. This was not the kind of filth I was here for.

My blackened fingernails and knees dismayed me, especially when three men entered the room, speaking in loud and confident German and taking their seats in positions that afforded the best view of my wriggling bum. These must be the men who had kept Her Ladyship up all night. Perhaps they would be too exhausted for anything other than breakfast and chat.

I looked up to see Liv enter the room with coffee, which she poured for the men. They continued to talk in German, as if they hadn't noticed her, but from the corner of my eye I saw one of them slide a hand inside the slit of her skirt and keep it there until she had put the cafetière down on the side table. He pulled her over his lap, lifted her petticoats and proceeded to spank her, almost listlessly, until she couldn't stop herself from crying out. Then he pulled down her drawers, spanked her some more and fingered her until she came with a tiny sigh and a gasp.

'What are you looking at?' one of his companions asked me suddenly.

I spun back around, furious with myself at getting sucked into this moment of voyeurism.

'No, no, no,' he said. 'You can't pretend. You were watching. Come here, girl.'

I exhaled defeatedly and put down the scrubbing brush. When I stood up, ready to present myself, he clicked his tongue and shook his head.

'What a mess,' he said. 'I can't let you near this suit. Tell you what, since you watched this girl get spanked, I think she gets to spank you. Get on to your knees on the rug. You'll have to clean it after, though.'

I got on to all fours and saw Liv, from the corner of my eye, adjusting her skirts before coming to kneel beside me. Her hand was small and soft and the spanking she gave me didn't really hurt, but the German guests seemed to appreciate it, and so did His Lordship when he entered the room in the middle.

'What's her transgression?' he asked idly, sitting down and picking up the newspaper.

'She was not paying attention to her work.'

'Oh dear. We will have to address that at dinner time. We have guests for a formal supper tonight – there will be twenty of us, all told. They'll enjoy a little show.'

My cunt spasmed at his words and I pushed my bottom back into Liv's line of fire.

'That's enough, Liv,' said His Lordship. 'You, Bottom, get on with your work. I want that grate spotless. When it's done, you can get cleaned up and serve at the breakfast table.'

During the course of that morning, it became startlingly apparent just how dull complete submission could be. I spent over an hour standing, holding a tray in the drawing room, while the guests lounged about chatting about the snow.

After that I was sent to the kitchen to polish some silver. No matter what the context, polishing silver just wasn't going to do it for me, and there was no sign of Damian, just Kat, Liv and the other girl yammering on and ignoring me.

But, just before lunchtime, I was finally summoned and told to present myself outside beneath the large oak tree.

'Outside ... ma'am?' I asked Kat, staring out at the snowscape. 'Do I get a coat to wear?'

'No. Go on, they're waiting for you.'

The guests, all wrapped up in scarves and huge long coats, stood clapping gloved hands and glowing by the old tree. I stepped out of the French windows and almost screamed. It was so cold my nipples turned to instant bullets, tight with pain at first before numbing. But I tottered over on my high, high heels until I stood before them, head bowed and hands at my side, as I'd been instructed, making sure I didn't cover any of my accessible orifices.

His Lordship wrapped a length of rope about my wrists, then looped it over a low branch of the tree.

'An endurance test for you, Bottom, and a bit of fun for us,' he said, tugging the rope until my arms were high above my head. 'Keep your feet wide apart. Like that.'

He patted my rump and stepped away from me, turning to the guests.

'Right then. Target practice. Five points for her tits, ten each for her arse or cunt. Who's going first?'

They spent ten minutes pelting snowballs at me until the impacted ice slithered down my thighs and over the curve of my breasts, torturing my nipples, thawing on my clit, soaking my apron and stockings. I shivered and squealed, trying to twist away from the onslaught, but they were merciless, laughing and comparing scores, scooping up more snow the more I moaned.

Before I turned blue, they took pity on me, untying me and supporting my shivering body back inside. His Lordship laid me down on a sheepskin rug in front of the now roaring drawing room fire and caressed me gently while I warmed back up, crooning that I was a good girl and had done well and 90 per cent of other submissives would have safeworded after a minute.

Pride seeped through my heating blood, along with the relief of warmth. I was going to beat this. I was going to win. I was going to be the best trainee he'd ever had.

'I think you've earned your lunch,' he said. 'I'll send down to the kitchen for a bowl of something for you. But first, when you're warm enough, I have a little appetiser for you.'

The appetiser was the cocks of all four of the men, followed by the ladies' juicy pussies. I sucked and licked at them all, on my knees between theirs, draining every last drop until each was replete and red-faced and ready to dine.

While they ate, I was made to stick my face into a bowl of sloppy pasta salad and eat it like a dog, with my hands behind my back, which was messy but possible.

'She's good, Marcus,' commented one of the Germans. 'Where did you find her?'

'At a slave auction, showing herself off like the whore she is,' he replied. 'We'll have fun with her tonight. Stand up, Bottom. Christ, what a mess you've made of yourself. Go and wash it off, then you have permission to take a two-hour nap. After that, you have a lesson with me.'

The nap was just what I needed, but I woke after an hour, shivering under my scratchy prison-issue blanket while the bedsprings creaked. Outside the barred window, the sky had that iron-grey cast that presaged more snow.

I sat up and looked around. The other maids must all be busy; distant kitchen noises travelled from one direction while I could hear music floating down from the floor above. I got up and the bedspring creaked again, then again.

Except that couldn't have been my bedspring. I was on my feet, looking for something properly warm to wrap around myself. It must have come from the room next door.

That must be the men's sleeping quarters.

Throwing the blanket over my shoulders, I tiptoed to the corridor, wanting to investigate. By "investigate" of course I mean "find Damian".

It was easily done. I knocked on the neighbouring door, concocting a story in my head about needing a dressing gown. Within seconds, Damian stood there, tall and draped in a long cotton robe that showed the freckles on his chest.

'Oh,' he said with an inviting smile. 'It's you.'

I forgot my cover story in an instant.

'I'm so fucking cold,' I told him.

'Need warming up? Step right in.'

He peered out into the corridor, pulled me up to his chest and whisked me into the room, shutting the door smartly behind us. Within seconds, I was against the wall, crushed into a kiss that stole the reason from my brain, stole the cold from my bones, stole everything except my need for Damian's body.

'What about His Lordship?' I gasped, letting him lead me over to his narrow bed. 'Isn't this against the rules?'

'It's me that'd get into trouble,' he reassured, bundling me down and kissing me again. 'I'm in the position of authority. You're just obeying me.'

'I don't want to get you into trouble.'

'I don't care, babe. I want you. I'm going to have you. His Lordship only comes down here when there's someone in the punishment room anyway. We're safe. Even if the staff find out, they won't snitch, I promise.'

'You're very sure of that.'

'I'm very sure of them. They won't want to get me into any strife. Now shut up and kiss me.'

I was happy to do so. Here was a feeling I had almost forgotten amidst the formality and strictures of my D/s couplings. Spontaneity, passion, lust that was triggered by the man rather than the situation. This was what I had felt with Stuart, and what I had been reaching towards ever since. I didn't want an either/or. I didn't want to be vanilla or kinky. I wanted to be both, but with the same partner.

Lying beneath Damian, luxuriating in his hard, male body, I was so struck by this revelation that my tongue stopped pushing, fingers stopped pinching, hips stopped gyrating until he extracted himself from my lips and blinked down at me.

'Are you OK? Did you hear something?'

'No, no. It's fine. Just … had a thought, that's all.'

'Don't think, love, that's always fatal. Thought is the enemy of fucking. What do you think of that? Just made it up – might have it monogrammed on my chauffeur gear.' He grinned, devilish and much too attractive to blow off in favour of navel-gazing. I pushed my self-analysis to the back of my mind and replaced it with his taut chest and shoulders.

'You're right. Less thinking, more fucking. I don't want to waste a minute.' I pushed him back down with a hand to the back of his neck and let him have his way with me. His way involved much less pinching or slapping than I had become used to, though he managed a good few bites before his hungry mouth found its way to my hungrier pussy. He sucked at my clit and made a strawberry-coloured mark on my thigh, licking me until I almost came, then he pulled away, flipping me on to my stomach and driving hard and fast into me.

Hard and fast, feverish and disordered, this was the way sex hadn't been for so long. He braced a forearm beneath my stomach, grabbed a hip and pounded, grunting behind me while I jolted and wobbled on my knees, trying to keep my bum up while the pillows edged further and further into my face.

He's really having me, I thought with delirious joy. He isn't going to stop until I can't walk straight. I moved a hand to my clit and stroked it slowly, letting the sweet sensation mingle with the brutal stretching above it, trying to find the perfect balance. He removed his own hand from my hip and made me cease my strumming, which was disappointing until it became clear that he meant to do it himself. Thrusting vigorously, he dipped his fingers deep into my well of juices, rubbing up and down. I tried to strain against him, to get my release, but unexpectedly he stopped fingering me and put my own hand back on the needy button of flesh. I waited a moment before starting again, needing permission.

'Go on,' he whispered. 'Touch it. I've got a surprise for you.'

I was so close, so close, almost there, and then his slick forefinger slid up the crack of my arse and pressed at my newly-trained hole, testing it for give and tension. I yelped and contracted my muscles.

'Tch tch,' he said softly, holding me still with his cock fully seated inside me. 'You're going to get this, aren't you? From His Lordship, by the end of the week. I just thought I could help with preparing you. What do you think?'

'Oh God,' I moaned, horribly turned on by the thought, despite my anxieties. 'I thought you said he wouldn't let anyone else … You know.'

'Not going to put my cock up there, am I? Just a finger. Or two. Just give you a taste … of how it feels to be double-penetrated. Don't you want to know?'

'Ohhhh,' was all I could say to this. Of course I did.

'Is that a yes?'

'Go on, then,' I whispered furiously. He had no right to know how to push my buttons this well. He was a cheeky bastard. But oh God, I wanted him to do anything and everything to me, until I passed out.

He took his time inserting the first finger, pausing every time I squeaked or shot forward or tensed my ring to utter soothing words and sounds. It was really no worse than that butt-plug anyway – in fact, it was better because the finger was flexible and warm and responsive to my body's cues.

He slid it in to the knuckle and twisted it around, his broken sighs of, 'Ohhh yeah,' calming me, turning me into clay beneath his expertly moulding hands. Then he chose to resume his thrusts and my forgetful cunt tightened around him, greedy for more of his cock, more of his energy, more of his mastery, more of everything.

By the time he got the second finger in, I had come, a long, sobbing, wailing kind of orgasm that made him chuckle even as he fucked and up his speed, up his rutting cock and delving finger-play until he too had had his fill and poured himself into me, uttering obscene endearments until he was wrung out.

We lay together for a while, limp and thirsty and wordless while the snow fell outside and the room grew darker still.

'That was a fuck and a half,' he said at last. 'What's your name?'

'Am I allowed to say?'

'Of course. Well, not really. But you have my permission.'

'Cherry,' I said, and then I bit my lip. Why had I told him my real name?

'Cherry? That's a sexy name. Suits you. I'm Damian.'

'I know. You're allowed to have a name. It's just me that isn't.'

'Listen, Cherry, thanks. That was seriously fucking incredible. I wish we could do it again.'

I turned to him, pouting. 'Can't we?'

'Probably not a good idea. Fuck. Listen, I'll see what I can do, OK? But we'll have to be careful. Really careful.'

Something occurred to me.

'Why?'

'Why? Because we'll both get booted out on our arses if

215

His Lordship gets wind that we're fucking without his dispensation.'

'And? So what? We're here voluntarily, aren't we?'

'You're saying you want to leave?'

I pondered this proposition. Did I want to leave?

'I ... don't know, actually. When I got here, I really thought it was what I wanted. But now I'm not sure.'

'The reality of kink is different from the fantasy. A lot of the girls find that. More than half don't make it through the week.'

'How many have you seen come and go? How many have you had?'

Damian smirked. 'I've never had one without His Lordship's knowledge before. But a fair few, yeah, when there's been a scene I'm part of.'

'Is it just me, or is there a bit of tension around Her Ladyship's role in all this?'

Damian bit his lip and sucked in a breath.

'You think?' he said eventually.

'I can't say anything for certain, but ...'

'Things change, relationships change,' said Damian vaguely. 'What you want changes. What you need changes.'

'So this set-up isn't how it used to be?'

'Sweetheart, I've been doing this on and off for five years. Obviously I've seen some changes. I don't know if they're good or bad. To be honest, I'm a little bit worried about Her Ladyship.'

'Really? Why?'

A bell rang, somewhere along the corridor.

'Shit. Nap time's over, babe. We'd better get clean, get dressed and get out of here.'

'Fuck!'

I leapt towards the old-fashioned sink and scrubbed at my nethers with the rather harsh cloth that hung over the side. I grabbed my blanket and ran for the door, but

Damian stopped me just before I reached it for a quick but indecently thorough kiss.

'Take care, babe,' he murmured. Then he opened the door and threw me out into the corridor.

I barely had time to brush my hair and try to tone down the flush on my cheeks and the swollen, stretched throb of my nether regions before His Lordship rapped sharply on the door before entering.

His total lack of resemblance to Damian irritated me and I kept my eyes to the floor while he stalked up and around me, inspecting my naked body. Suddenly I became horribly conscious of the tiny red mark Damian had left after sucking on my thigh and I contrived to hide it as unobtrusively as I could, hoping upon hope that His Lordship wouldn't notice. He didn't.

'Lessons, then,' he said briskly. 'You will need to put on your uniform and follow me to the study.'

Some laundry fairy had put a fresh, unsnowballed apron in my drawer so I put that on along with the stockings and suspenders and followed my master out of the servants' quarters and back to the main house. This time, I was not so conscious of my near-nudity, but I was highly conscious of my recently fucked state and sure it would be picked up upon. I kept my buttocks clenched, although they were itching from their recent attentions, and my thighs almost clamped, walking slowly in a geisha-style shuffle along the corridors to the study.

'Kneel,' said His Lordship, before he had even turned to face me. I fell to my knees on the Persian rug and watched him open a bureau and rummage inside.

When he turned to face me, he was carrying a leather flogger and several pairs of cuffs.

'Today's lesson covers positions. In some ways, it is a test of endurance and stamina. I need to know that I can place my submissives in certain positions and expect them to maintain those positions. If they are unable, of course they earn a punishment. The discipline side of our relationship is very important to me. I need to know that you will accept it without question. Indeed, I will want you to embrace your corrections and to accept them in a meek and joyful spirit, because you know that they are merited and deserved. Do you understand?'

'I think so, sir. It's difficult to be joyful about a whipping, though.'

'Yes. It's difficult. That's the whole point, Bottom.'

I nodded sagely. Testing of limits, pushing oneself, finding strengths one didn't know one had. It all sounded disturbingly reminiscent of a pep talk I'd given my tutor group last year. This BDSM stuff was really just life, sexualised.

'So, let's start with the kneeling position. Your knees should be apart, Bottom, at least a foot's breadth.'

I shuffled them wider, grateful for the minimal coverage of the apron which would at least hide the evidence of Damian upon my body.

'Now, I need your hands to be clasped on the back of your neck, elbows out. Yes. Back absolutely straight, to enhance your breasts. I need your breasts to jut, Bottom. That's what everyone will want to see. Firm, prominent tits. Of course, we usually want good hard nipples too. Ah, you can oblige. Marvellous. Sometimes we might help them along the way with a pair of clamps, but that doesn't seem to be necessary today. Now, I am going to sit at my desk and do some work. You are going to maintain that position until my timer goes off. I'm not going to tell you when that will be. If I see any sagging of the spine, or adjustment of position, I will use the whip. Do you understand me?'

'Yes, sir.'

'Good.'

It might have been ten minutes. It might have been an hour. My knees began to ache and so did my nipples. My arms shook and my toes froze, but I didn't break position. The trick of it was to be somewhere else. I took myself to bed with Damian and stayed there for as long as the timer ticked, reliving the length of his cock and those rude fingers in my backside, his soft, dirty words spoken like caresses, his lean, fit, freckled body.

When the timer went off, my pussy was wet again.

His Lordship put down his newspaper, picked up his flogger and used the handle to check the perkiness of my tits and the width of my thighs. He found nothing to punish. I thrust out my chin and took a deep breath.

'Good girl,' he said. 'Impressive. Are you wet?'

'Yes, sir.'

'Even better. You may stand and shake yourself out a little. Our next position is rather more difficult.'

I followed his order and rose, my knees creaking a little. I wriggled and writhed until he called time and beckoned me over to his desk.

'Because you seem to have excellent stamina, I'm going to fast forward you to one of our most challenging positions. Lie flat on the desk, please.'

I climbed up and let my body take up the full length of the desk, smoothing the flimsy apron rather compulsively over the spot Damian had stupidly marked.

'Now I need you to lift your bottom and put your legs in the air.'

I braced my hands in the small of my back and levered my coccyx up, watching my knees rise above my face. Fortunately, this position caused the little strawberry mark to disappear into the fold of skin it created at the crease of my thigh, even though my apron rode straight up and pooled in my belly.

'Now spread those legs in a good wide V shape. Show me everything you have there.'

I parted my knees, opening my cunt and, lower down, my anus. I shut my eyes briefly. Would His Lordship be able to tell that certain fingers had been there recently? If he noticed, he said nothing.

'Now, bend your knees. I want you open to the very fullest extent.'

I strained to bend myself into the required pose, completely and inescapably displayed.

His Lordship made me grip my ankles with my hands and ordered me to hold this pose – which was already telling on my thigh muscles – without moving until the timer went off.

'We call this Full Display. It's what you'll be doing at tonight's supper party. You'll be the centrepiece. Of course, it'll be a little more complicated than this. Penetration of orifices may be involved, and you'll be available for all the guests to handle and toy with.'

Now I was seriously wet, leaking down into the crack of my arse.

He noticed, and leant over to breathe hot beads of steam into my cunt. I longed for his tongue to dart out and flick my clit, but he wouldn't do that.

He took a long sniff and stood up, frowning.

'Very ripe,' he said. 'I'd almost think you'd been recently fucked. But of course I know that can't be the case. Can it?'

'No, sir.' But my heart was banging and I momentarily lost grip on one of my ankles, letting it wave wildly in His Lordship's face.

'That's one fail,' he said calmly. 'We'll deal with that at the end of the session.'

To my utter relief, he dropped the subject of the state of my pussy and sat back down, inches away from my rude exposure, and began fiddling about with his android phone.

The pose was much harder to sustain than the kneeling. My thighs and arms began to shake in pretty short order, and hard as I tried to concentrate on breathing, I was soon struggling.

Before the timer went off, His Lordship remarked that I seemed to be having difficulty, but I shouldn't worry because tonight I would be cuffed into position. He rattled the metalware on the desk in a sinister fashion.

Just as the timer blared, I let my ankles drop with a resounding thud, letting out a gusty sigh.

'The timer is a signal for me, not for you,' admonished His Lordship, transporting me eerily back to my classroom again. 'That's two fails. Get up, stretch, and then I have some homework for you.'

From a large walk-in cupboard, he dragged an old-fashioned school desk and bench affair, complete with inkwell, slate and chalk.

'You'll need your school uniform,' he noted, dragging out a plaid skirt and white shirt.

'Oh … no!' I froze in mid-stretch and shook my head. 'I can't do schoolgirl role play. I'm sorry. It's just too weird for me.'

He stared.

'Because of my job,' I explained, though I hadn't ever told him I was a schoolteacher. 'It feels too wrong. Too taboo.'

'That's a safewording then,' he said after a stunned pause.

'Fine. So be it.'

'You don't mind sitting at a desk, though?'

'We don't have them any more,' I said. God, I was giving myself right away, but I felt I owed him the truth. 'Tables and chairs.'

He stared at me and I subsided into the desk and clasped my fingers, waiting for the black cloud that had settled over us to pass.

'Right,' he said eventually. 'I have here a diagram of all the different positions you will be called upon to take and maintain. You have twenty minutes in which to memorise them, and then you will be tested.'

221

He handed me a laminated card with twenty different positions. The one I had recently held was number twenty.

I said, 'Thank you, sir.'

He nodded abruptly and left the room.

I contemplated leaving my desk and snooping in his drawers, but after all, twenty minutes wasn't such a long time to learn all these poses, some of which were hellishly complicated, so I resisted temptation and applied myself to the task.

When His Lordship returned, he made me stand and demonstrate ten of the poses chosen at random. I scored six out of ten.

'Not the worst score I've seen,' he noted, 'but not the best either. You have amassed a total of six fails. For each fail you will take ten strokes of the flogger. Now, put yourself into the fourth position.'

The fourth position was the classic touch-your-toes, with the slight variation of having to keep your feet wide apart. Grabbing of ankles was also permitted, and I decided to avail myself of this steadying tool.

The backs of my thighs already ached from the earlier practice and I wasn't sure I'd be able to keep myself in position for sixty strokes, unless he decided to give them very quickly.

As it happened, he did. The flogger flew, speedy and stinging, across my bottom, a stroke landing every couple of seconds. It was an easier pain to take than some of the other implements – lighter, although it built to a substantial and steady burn after only the first ten. I was moaning and complaining within a minute, but His Lordship flogged on, ignoring my oohs and aahs.

Finally he finished and I took my hands from my ankles.

'Ah ah ah,' he said, indicating that I had presumed too much.

Gasping, I re-clasped, conscious of my aching calves as

well as my sore bottom.

'We have one more thing to attend to,' he said.

The cold kiss of lubricant against my anal pucker soon gave the grand finale away. I held my breath and screwed my eyes shut, suddenly convinced that he would know Damian's fingers had been inside that sacred orifice, but he said nothing, simply inserted a slightly larger plug than the previous night's, twisted it for luck then stepped away with a final smack of my bum.

'You're to keep that in until the banquet,' he said. 'Kat will remove it for you before bringing you in. Now go to the bedroom – they're waiting for you. They need to get you ready.'

I went back down to the servants' quarters feeling strangely unenthusiastic about the evening's prospects. Yet I had planned this with His Lordship over the preceding weeks, working with him on every detail. Why would I not want to do it?

Sex with Damian had unleashed a craving for a more immediate intimacy, I realised. The formality and coldness set out for me had its place in my needs, but those needs weren't playing ball tonight. I just wasn't in the mood. I wanted more monkey sex with the red-haired pervert, much more, all night long. The unlikeliness of getting it threw me into a kind of existential sulk.

Liv and the other girl – Sukie, I think – were indeed waiting for me in the maids' bedroom.

'Come on!' said Liv. 'What kept you so long?'

'Lessons with His Lordship.'

'Let's see your bum then – oh, I see. I love lessons with His Lordship,' grinned Sukie, prodding my butt-plug with a malicious fingertip.

'What's that, though?' Liv frowned, crouching to peer at the love bite on my thigh.

I shrugged.

'I didn't think His Lordship fucked a new sub on debut

day until the banquet,' she continued. 'But this looks fresh. Have you got a boyfriend at home?'

'She didn't have it this morning,' said Sukie, who'd come round to investigate. 'Is it a birth mark?'

'Deffo a love bite,' said Liv with a frown. She leant further in and sniffed my cunt, mortifyingly. 'You smell of spunk. You've been fucked today. Jesus, woman! Was it one of those Germans? Didn't you know you were meant to wait till tonight?'

'His Lordship will go crazy.' Sukie sounded satisfied.

'No, no, you're wrong.' But my heart wasn't in the denial. So what if the stupid rules stated I was supposed to do this, that or the other. I was here by choice. If I chose to shag the chauffeur, so chuffing what?

Perhaps rigid discipline and unquestioning obedience weren't for me after all.

'Wrong, my arse,' said Liv. 'Kat, come and look at this.'

The terminally unfriendly chief maid had arrived through the doorway, appearing dissatisfied with our rate of progress, grabbing nipple pasties and body glitter from a cupboard.

'Look at what? All I can see is a naked girl who needs to be prepared. What have you been doing?'

'She's got a love bite on her thigh,' said Sukie.

'Really? Show me.'

A third woman busied herself with the close inspection of my crotch area. Just as well I'm not shy.

'Look – totally a love bite. Quite a hard one too. And she reeks of sex. Naughty girl.'

Kat straightened and stared me in the face.

'Who have you been with?'

'Nobody.'

'Liar. I'm taking you to His Lordship. Explain to him.'

I recalled Damian's words – that the staff wouldn't split on him if we'd been discovered together. Perhaps if I told them the truth, they'd soften.

'Listen, OK, it was Damian.'

Sukie and Liv looked at each other. Kat slapped me so hard across the face that I staggered backwards.

'Liar!' she said again. 'He wouldn't. Not without telling me.'

'I'm not … lying,' I panted, clutching my jaw, aghast. 'Ask him.'

'You little slut, he's my husband.'

Oh shit.

'Take her to His Lordship,' urged Liv.

'I will,' said Kat. 'They'll all be in the drawing room by now. Let's get this sorted out there.'

'I'm not standing before any kangaroo court,' I told them, backing away, but Kat and Liv caught me and yanked me, one on each arm, out of the room, Sukie following behind.

In the drawing room, at least twenty people sat and stood, chattering and drinking in the glamorous golden glow of the chandeliers. When I was dragged through the door, all conversation stopped.

Damian, acting in the capacity of butler and master of ceremonies, turned paler than ever and looked away.

Her Ladyship, resplendent in an ostrich feather head dress, was first to speak.

'What's the meaning of this?'

'I have to report a rule break.' Kat was trying hard to keep calm, it seemed, her voice low and contained.

'Put Bottom on her knees before us,' ordered His Lordship, 'and explain.'

They pushed me down on to the plush rug. My awareness of so many pairs of eyes studying my naked body, my open cunt, my flogged and plugged bottom failed to arouse me. My throat was dry and I suddenly felt endlessly vulnerable. If they decided to murder me … Was that possible? How wrong could this go?

'She has allowed herself to be taken by another man before Your Lordship performed her debut,' explained Liv, because it seemed Kat was all out of speech.

'Is this true?'

I nodded.

'Which man? A member of our staff?' asked Her Ladyship sharply. When I didn't answer, she addressed the maids, none of whom replied.

'She won't say,' said Kat. 'We think it might be somebody from outside the house.'

'Stop this. It was me.'

Damian's voice.

'Shut up!' screamed Kat.

'I'm sorry, I'm sorry,' he said, but she had leapt at him and was slapping him about with abandon. 'I'm sorry, Kat. And I'm sorry, Cherry. I should have controlled myself.'

'Who's Cherry?' Now His Lord and Ladyship were confused.

'If you want me to leave, I'll understand,' said Damian, putting my own thoughts succinctly into words.

'What about me?' shrieked Kat. 'What if I don't want to leave?'

'Then stay,' said Damian. 'Stay and be His Lordship's favoured submissive, since that seems to be what your life is all about.'

'You did this deliberately,' she spat. 'To get away from me.'

Damian finally managed to extricate her, his face a mess of scratches.

'Sorry, love,' he said quietly. 'It suited me for a while. But I can't live with you like this any more.'

'I did this for you!' Kat was beside herself.

'No you didn't. You always pushed things further and further. Just being your husband and your dom would have been enough for me. It wasn't enough for you, I see that now.' He shrugged. 'I should go.'

'Wait,' cried Her Ladyship, rising from her chair.

'What for?' he asked gently, then he left the room.

'I should go too,' I ventured. 'God, what a mess. I wish I hadn't come here now.'

'So do I,' said Her Ladyship. 'And what's this Cherry business? Did you even give us a false "real" name?'

'I'm sorry. I didn't want to risk my vanilla life, my career, any of that stuff.'

'Because you're a schoolteacher,' said His Lordship. 'Not a piano tutor.'

I looked around the room, at the avid faces of the guests. They might not be getting what they had expected, but this would entertain them at least.

'Look,' I said. 'I don't feel I can stay, under the circumstances.'

'I think you should stay.' Her Ladyship's voice was uneven with rage. 'I want to thrash the living daylights out of you, you fucking whore.'

'She was fond of Damian,' remarked His Lordship. 'But she'll get over him.' He reached over and gave her wrist a very firm squeeze. 'Now get out, Bottom, and don't darken our door again, eh? There's a girl.'

Chapter Twelve

DISORIENTATED, I WANDERED about the house for a good few minutes before I got my bearings and remembered the location of that little cloakroom where all my clothes were stashed.

From somewhere not far away I heard Kat's screeching voice, then Damian's, lower but getting louder and louder until a door slammed.

My heartbeat was too intrusive, pounding in my ears, interrupting my thought processes. A primitive need to escape was the only real item on my agenda. All the processing, reasoning, brooding and analysing could come later.

I found the room and fell on my knees before the velvet banquette, lifting its seat to peer inside. The interior was divided into little sections. My belongings were tucked into the slot at the far right. I dipped my hand in. The first thing I found was Patrick's necklace.

I couldn't move. I could only stare at it. Then I held it up to my cheek, bent over into a foetal position and wept my heart out.

There was no way I could ever have Patrick. He was too good for me. I suppose I had known this all along, and chosen to deliberately ignore or misread his signals accordingly. I just didn't deserve him. And I should probably resign from my job as well. How could a mindless slut like me be a suitable role model for children? Especially the troubled children of St Sebastian's.

Everything was hopeless.

The door handle turned and my shoulders froze mid-shake. I gathered a shuddering breath, preparing to tell whichever jeerer or mocker it might be to take a running jump.

But the voice, when it spoke, was soft.

'Thought I might find you here.'

'I'm going. Just getting my stuff.'

My head was dull and achey from all the sobbing and my eyes were sore. I didn't want him to see that I'd been crying. I held my position.

'Yeah, looks like it,' he said with a small chuckle. I heard his footsteps move towards me. He crouched down by my shoulders; I could see the shiny tips of his chauffeur boots, smell the leather and polish. He put a hand on my back. My spine sagged.

'Damian ...'

'C'mon, doll, get dressed and I'll drive you home.'

I braved the raising of my face to his, hurriedly dashing the wetness from my face with the heel of my hand.

'Is that a good idea?'

'Is anything we've done here a good idea? How else are you going to get back? Hitch a ride? You've no idea where you are.'

In the extremity of my angst I hadn't considered this. He was absolutely right. My best guess was somewhere in Wiltshire, but it could as easily be any of six or seven other counties.

'Well, where are we?'

'The middle of nowhere, sweetheart.' He sighed. 'Malmesbury's the nearest town.' Score! I was right. 'You'd need a taxi. There's no railway station and no bus service back to the coast. You'll have a fucking nightmare, darling, not to mention the snow's played havoc with public transport anyway. Let me take you.'

I was too tired to resist, plus his apparently pathological

flirtatiousness always hit something squarely at my centre.

'Is it safe to drive?'

'Snow's starting to thaw. If I take it slowly, we'll be fine. If the worst comes to the worst we'll book the nearest hotel room for the night.'

'God, Damian, what about your wife?'

'Even she wouldn't cast a lone woman out into the frozen wastelands. Besides, all that's over now.'

'I'm sorry.'

'It was on the cards, love. Don't blame yourself.'

I snorted. 'I don't! I blame you.'

His hand patted my shoulder. 'There. That's better. No more weeping and wailing, eh? Get your kit on.' He chuckled. 'Never thought I'd say those words.'

He helped me to my feet, then inhaled sharply.

'Ah, hang on,' he said. His hand brushed down my spine, landing firmly on my bottom. I felt a weird sensation, then squealed as I realised what it must be. He had tweaked the flange of my butt-plug. The butt-plug I had somehow completely forgotten I was wearing. 'I think we need to make sure we don't leave with any of His Lordship's property. Imagine if we were pursued all the way to Portsmouth by cops investigating the theft of a butt-plug.'

Despite my woe and shame, I giggled at the image.

'Hmm, bend over, Miss Delaney,' he growled. How could my clit throb at a time like this? How? The use of my real name instead of the fictitious Delray made it all the sweeter. I bent, grabbing the edge of the banquette.

'Do you want one quick yank or a slow screw?' The man was incapable of saying anything without making it sound filthy. Actually, this was kind of filthy, wasn't it? He was gearing up to pull something out of my arse. Does it get much filthier than that? 'It's probably going to feel a little bit uncomfortable, darling, either way.'

I screwed my eyes shut. 'Make it quick, like ripping off

230

a plaster.'

'Good decision. I promise I won't damage you. I'm an expert at this.'

He put a steadying hand on my coccyx, holding me still. My knees trembled. He hooked two fingers underneath the flange and spent a few seconds twisting it gently.

'I'd love to do this under happier circumstances,' he murmured. 'Pulling it out so I can replace it with my cock, for instance.'

'Do you ever stop thinking about sex?'

'No. OK. Are you ready?'

'As I'll ever be.'

He pulled it out, swiftly and seamlessly. My sphincter muscles contracted in confusion and tried to clench it tight, but Damian's sure technique outfoxed them and I was empty before I knew it. All the same, I needed a few moments to pant and squirm while he wrapped the thing in a handkerchief and tossed it into the banquette.

'Come on, then,' he said with a brisk smack of my bottom. 'Get cracking. I want to be out of here before midnight.'

It seemed unfair to expect Damian to chat whilst trying to negotiate endless twisty-turny snow-filled country lanes in the pitch dark, so we sat in near-silence for the first half hour of the journey, the car's purr only interrupted for the occasional, 'Shit, was that a deer?' or 'Christ, it's deep here.'

Once we pulled out on to a main road where the shovellers and gritters had been at work, though, I made a tentative gambit.

'Is the car yours?'

'Yep. I bought it off His Lordship a few months ago. In some ways, it feels like I've been planning for this day, though not really consciously.'

'Aren't you upset? About Kat?'

231

He flicked his eyes briefly towards me. 'No. She's impossible. I don't want to go into it all, if you don't mind, but we've had issues pretty much from day one of our relationship. She's in love with His Lordship anyway – oh, for fuck's sake, why am I calling him His Lordship? Marcus. She's in love with Marcus. We haven't fucked since October.'

'Really? Why is she still so possessive of you, then?'

'Because that's what she's like. Not saying I'm blameless – I'm not. But I've never made out like I own her, or she has to have my permission to sleep with certain people.'

'Perhaps that's what she wanted you to do.'

He sighed. 'Perhaps. But I'm uncomplicated and I don't play mind-fuck games. We just aren't right for each other.'

'How did you get together? Do you mind me asking?'

His lips curled into a rueful smile. It felt wrong to be finding him as sexy as I did after all the furore, but my pussy couldn't be reasoned with.

'I followed her up the escalator at Waterloo station. She had the pertest little arse I'd ever seen and she was waving it in my face, in this tiny denim miniskirt. When we got to the top, she looked over her shoulder at me and gave me the most blatant come-hither I've ever seen. She made me follow her all the way across the station concourse, wiggling that booty all the time until we got behind a shelf in Tie Rack and she said, "I bet you want to smack it, don't you?" I said, "Among other things," and she said, "Go on, then," and bent over there and then. How was I meant to resist an offer like that?'

'Wow,' I said, impressed. Damian was definitely an arse man, if I'd been in any doubt whatsoever. 'So you spanked her in the middle of the Waterloo branch of Tie Rack?'

'Yeah. And then I got her number and then I had to get my train. But things went from there, obviously.'

'Obviously.'

'And just thinking about that has got me horny. Or hornier, I should say, since I've been thinking about how much I want to fuck you for the past twenty miles.' He turned his face to me, suddenly anxious. 'Sorry, sweetheart. Sorry, that was inappropriate. You must be all over the place. Forget it. The last thing I want to do is put you under pressure.'

'No,' I said with determination. 'Sod appropriate. A really good hard fuck might clear my head.'

He put a hand on my thigh. 'You're a bloody marvel. Why didn't I meet you at Waterloo station that time, eh?'

We found a layby and got ourselves laid in it while the car heater pumped out noisy warmth. I reclined on the reclining passenger seat and pulled up my skirt. As on the journey to His Lordship's house, I had no knickers to worry about.

Damian, trousers around his knees, cock out and proud, slid above me, wetting the tip of his tool in my juices.

'Mmm, you don't need warming up, do you, love? You're soaking wet already. Why's that, then? You need cock that bad?'

I forced a hand between our pelvises and wrapped it around his good hot stiffness. Oh, I was ready for that. More than ready. We had only fucked a few hours ago, and yet it seemed like days and days since I last had him.

'Yeah,' I gasped. 'Please.'

'Oh fuck, this is good. If you were mine, I'd never let you wear knickers. I'd have you ready for my cock at a moment's notice, always.' He rubbed his tip round and round my clit while his hands groped beneath my dress, stimulating my nipples. 'I'd fuck you by the side of the road every day of the week.'

'Want you to …'

'Yeah?' He aligned his blunt cockhead with my well-lubricated cunt. 'What do you want, babe? What do you

233

need?'

'Filled up. Ridden. Hard.'

'Mmm.' He was inside, stretching me, gliding into the space he'd already occupied that afternoon. I felt a profound, base-level joy, as if I was where I should be. 'You will be, doll. Hard as. Mmm, and you're still so tight, even though I was in here before. You fit me like a dirty little glove, don't you, babe?'

'Oh God, yes.' He had started to thrust, urgently, bearing down so that he moved that fraction closer to my G-spot with each foray.

'That's it, babe. Ride it. Take it in. Feel it.' His litany of filth poured into my ears, provoking me to heights of erotic abandonment. I bucked my pelvis upwards, wanting to be impaled as deeply as possible, I grabbed his arse and dug in.

His ferocious tempo and technique drew an orgasm from me almost immediately, but he wasn't finished, not by a long way. He meant to make me take this ride to the end, until I was steaming and broken and yanked out of shape.

'Get those legs wider, I want your ankles around my ears,' he ordered, slamming into me, lifting my hips high so that my toes scraped the car roof.

I thought sparks might be struck from our skin. His cock plunged in and out in a blur; the windscreen behind him was opaque with condensation.

'You won't be walking far tomorrow,' he vowed, and my G-spot erupted into a fountain of wild celebration. He ploughed and ploughed and roared his climax into me, his red hair slick and damp, his pale eyelashes dark with sweat.

We lay, fused together by heat and perspiration, limp and used up for a long while, listening to the cars on the main road swish by, churning up the slush.

'I like you,' he said at length.

'Yeah, I like you too.'

'If things were different …'

'I know. It's not a good time for me either.'

'You're hung up on someone else?'

I shifted beneath him, looking him in the eye.

'What makes you say that?'

'The way you were hanging on to that necklace earlier.' He put a finger to my throat, tugging the fine silver. 'What's he got that I haven't?' he said with a wink.

I couldn't answer, didn't want to.

'Yeah,' he said with resignation. 'Your heart. OK. We should get back on the road.'

He hauled himself off me and began putting his clothes to rights.

I had little to do in the way of dressing, so I simply tilted the chair back up and smoothed my skirt back down over my lap.

'Keep it up,' said Damian suddenly, flipping it up my thighs. 'If you sit on it, you'll stain it. I can just wipe the seat clean, no problem.'

'How, er, practical.'

'Nothing practical about it,' he said, pinching my thigh. 'Just like the thought of you, naked and oozing my juice over there. It'll add a certain something to the rest of a tedious journey.'

'Pervert.'

'Pot, kettle, black.'

He turned the key in the ignition and crawled to the end of the layby, easing out on to the quiet road again. Pleasantly exhausted now, and relieved of all the angst-related muscular tension of earlier, I threw my coat over me and shut my eyes.

When I opened them again, it was nearly midnight and we were in Portsmouth.

'Christ, was I asleep all that time?' I jerked upright and looked through the windscreen at Albert Road, decked out with snow and Christmas trees and staggering drunks – a heartwarming scene indeed.

'Sleeping Beauty,' confirmed Damian. 'I was going to wake you with a kiss, but you've spoiled my fun now.'

'I'll go back to sleep,' I offered, scrunching my eyes.

'I'm going to kiss you anyway. Might as well stay awake now. Your place is only around the corner, isn't it?'

'Yeah, second right.'

The huge Victorian villas split into flats loomed against the flat, dark sky until we reached mine. Unusually, there was space to park outside and Damian pulled up, took off his chauffeur gloves and said, 'Well, then.'

'Well, then.'

'This is where your adventure ends. Alice has left Wonderland.'

'More like Blunderland. And who are you, then? The King of Hearts?'

He smiled, a little sadly. 'Off with her head,' he said, reaching out to stroke the back of my neck.

I didn't know how to leave him. Actually, what the hell was I thinking?

'Surely you aren't planning to drive all the way back there tonight?'

He shrugged.

'Stay the night at mine. You're more than welcome.'

'Are you sure? Would that be OK?'

'Of course it would. Seems like the least I can do, after you've brought me all this way in the dark and the cold.'

All we did that night was sleep, after a tot of whiskey each and a bit of snogging on the sofa that we were too tired to take anywhere.

We even forgot to eat, and consequently I was awoken the next morning by the rumbling of Damian's stomach, which my head had somehow ended up right beside.

'Breakfast?' I asked him, popping my head out of the covers and catching him in a huge yawn. About three seconds after suggesting it, I remembered that I had no bread, milk, or anything, having expected to be enjoying His Lordship's hospitality for the whole week.

'Don't mind if I do,' said Damian, but instead of demanding a fry-up he reared up, pinned me down and slithered his way along my body until his mouth found my pussy.

He feasted and gorged on me, laughing a dark laugh every time I came, which was three times in total, before moving back in for more. I could barely see straight to return the favour, but by the time we thought of showering I had swallowed a substantial mouthful of his juices, while mine glistened all over his chin.

'I'm sorry, I can only offer black coffee,' I told him when he appeared, dressed and washed but gorgeously ruggedly unshaven in my kitchen. 'I can pop up to the Co-op on Albert Road if you must have milk –'

'It's OK. I should get going.'

'Oh.' I couldn't quite mask my disappointment. 'Lots to sort out today, I guess.'

'You said it.'

'Well, good luck with it.'

He was behind me at the kitchen counter, wrapping strong arms around me and clasping my hands in his. He kissed my cheek and then my earlobe.

'Thanks,' he said. 'I'll need it. I'd love to stay on but … Well, y'know.'

'I know.'

I twisted my neck up to him and let him kiss my mouth, a long, sloppy smooch that melted me all over again.

Breaking away, he took the pen off the magnetic strip of my kitchen organiser pad and wrote down a phone number.

'I'm not going to try and compete with Mr Necklace,' he said. 'But if you ever find yourself fancy free and footloose, give me a call.'

'I will.'

'Do you promise?'

237

'I wouldn't dare disobey.'

He growled a little, pulled me close and patted my bottom.

'Good,' he said. 'See that you don't.'

There was more kissing and maybe a few tears from me and then he left.

It was all over.

What next?

What came next was a trip to the Co-op, breakfast and many, many cups of strong coffee.

And after that, I switched on my computer.

In my inbox, the most charming email from, presumably, Kat.

'Bitch, we know your name now and we know where you work. We are sending photographs to your headteacher, your board of governors and your local newspaper.'

I shook for a few minutes before firing back. 'I know HL's real name too. Tit for tat, anyone?'

I didn't know his real name, of course, apart from the Marcus part.

The reply came ten minutes later.

'You don't know HL's real name. I don't believe you.'

'Try me and see.'

Nothing more after that.

I sat in my armchair for two hours, neither moving nor reading nor watching TV nor listening to music. All I could do was stare ahead.

A text message tone from my phone made me jump. Christ, it was from Patrick.

'Good Xmas?' Neutral enough.

'Interesting.'

'Are you still on the Isle of Wight?'

'No, back home.'

'Would you like to meet up?'

'Yes. Something I must tell you.'

'Really? I'm intrigued.'

'Don't be. It's not worth being intrigued by.'

We texted back and forth, arranging eventually to meet that afternoon outside the castle.

The common was still knee-deep in snowdrifts and I watched as a giant ferry made its stately progress up the Solent towards Bilbao or Le Havre or some other foreign port that seemed a better place to be than here. Perhaps that was what I should do. Get on a boat, be an anonymous woman in a busy city, teach English as a foreign language or something. It was one plan, and the best I'd come up with so far.

It was cold, so cold. I stamped my feet and huddled, but the wind whistled along the sea front until I considered giving up and going home. As soon as I turned, I saw him, hurrying through the slush in Hunter wellies. Was he a gardening man? I wondered. Not that it was any business of mine. Not now, not ever.

'You must be perishing,' he greeted me, grinning and puffing out steam. 'Why didn't you choose an indoor place to meet?'

I supposed I felt I deserved to suffer.

Drawing closer, he reached towards me, noticing the necklace.

'You're wearing it,' he said. He was very close, too close.

'You'll probably want it back.'

'Oh?'

We began to walk, across the common towards the boarded-up funfair at Clarence Pier, a place that looked as desolate as I felt.

'I'm thinking of leaving teaching,' I said.

Patrick stopped in his tracks and put hands on my arms, spinning me forcefully to face him.

'You're what?'

'I'm not the right kind of person for the job.'

'But … You're … Cherry, you're exactly the right kind of person for the job. You're competent, caring –'

I cut across the bluster. 'My private life isn't compatible. I'm a bad person.'

He shook his head, so stunned that I wanted to pull him close, tell him I was only joking. Could I pass this off as a joke? No.

'Somebody tried to blackmail me today,' I said, more gently. 'It made me realise that I could expose you and the school to scandal. I don't think they're going to do it really – but if they did …'

'For God's sake.' He took my elbow and marched me over to the garish blue and yellow façade of the funfair.

Below the trashy plastic awning, a sad-looking greasy spoon café was open for business against the odds.

Patrick ordered us two teas and sat me down at a Formica table. I picked up a tomato-shaped ketchup dispenser and began picking at the green plastic frill around the stalk mouth.

When the tea arrived, steaming and more welcome than any other cup of tea in the history of history, Patrick leant down low and said, 'Now, what's this nonsense?'

I wanted to cry. He sounded so – oh, so everything I'd ever wanted. But then I shifted on my chair, feeling a residual burn that reminded me of all the sex I'd had with Damian over the past 24 hours. I wasn't worthy, and I was never going to be.

'I have an unconventional sex life.'

He blinked, shook his head again, but quicker this time.

'What's that got to do with leaving teaching?'

'Oh, don't be naïve.'

'Are you telling me you're a paedophile? A necrophiliac? Anything else illegal?'

'God, no, of course not. Jesus, Patrick.'

'Well, then, if it's no business of the law, it's no business of anyone else's. Is it? Or am I missing

240

something?'

'I joined this sex cult. Well, no, that's not how it was at all. Sorry, that sounds really lurid. What I did was … I surfed the net for people who shared my interests. Then I met up with a few. We did stuff. But it all got a bit elaborate and there was emotional fall-out and people got hurt, so … I feel awful and shit and like the worst human being ever.'

Tears were coming. I derailed them with a big gulp of tea.

'Oh, Cherry.' Patrick didn't sound shocked. He didn't even sound disappointed, or not much. 'Listen, I …' He looked around the room, as if the peeling paint might give him a clue what to say next.

'I might understand a bit more than you expect,' he said at last. 'I don't know what you've done, whether it's swinging or dogging or whatever, but as long as you can keep it out of school, I really don't give a toss. Well, I do give a toss, obviously, because I did have a few hopes, but don't mind me. Don't mind me.'

'I do mind you.' This was worse than shock and horror. He was writing me off, setting me free. I didn't want that.

'Thanks. Thanks for minding me, but please don't give up teaching. Though if you want to leave I'll understand … I'll give you a glowing reference. But, on the other hand, please don't go. Look.' He drew himself up, visibly manning up after this rather shambolic speech. 'OK. Tell me. Tell me the worst. What was this bizarre sex thing you were into?'

'If I tell you I'll have to find a new job. I won't be able to face you every day knowing that you know.'

'I'll take the risk. I'm just wondering …' He seemed about to make a grand confession, but he pursed his lips instead.

'It was SM,' I said, as casually as I could. 'You know. Whips and rubber and that. Just always been a bit drawn to

241

it and thought it would be fun to experiment. Experiment got out of hand.'

Patrick swallowed. He put a hand through his hair, disarranging the perfection of it.

'Right,' he said. 'Right. I see. And you, er, did the whipping, or …?'

'No, the other way round.'

'And you met people over the internet?'

'Yes.'

He sat back and stared up at a cobweb on the light fitting for ages.

'I want to tell you something, Cherry.'

'Oh?'

'After I applied for divorce, I registered with a website. I'd always wanted to explore this certain side of myself, but Lynn wasn't interested and I certainly wasn't going to force the issue.'

I put down my tea and let my eyes pop.

He smiled tightly, his eyes troubled.

'The site was called MasterMe dot com. I called myself SecretSadist.'

I squealed.

The tabard-wearing woman behind the counter stopped wiping down the tea urn. I apologised to her, flapping my hands, then pointed to myself and whispered, 'AtYourService.'

He put his hands over his mouth and caught his breath before removing them and mouthing, 'Seriously?'

'That was me! That was you? God, I loved you! You were amazing! Why did you disappear on me?'

'I was scared, Cherry. I've been in the local press so much. I was worried I'd be recognised and, well, you know. You've had this same dilemma. I can't believe it was you. I'm just …' Whatever he was just, he couldn't express it, except by shaking his head even more.

I put the ketchup dispenser down.

'Oh, the irony,' I said.

He looked up at me, eyes tired and bloodshot.

'If you hadn't buggered off,' I explained, 'I would never have got involved with the scene I ended up in. If you'd held your nerve, we could have got together and none of this would have happened.'

'You still haven't told me exactly what did happen.'

I looked over at Tabard-Wearer, who was feigning obliviousness to our conversation very badly.

'I don't really want to talk about it here. Can we go back to my place? Or maybe yours?'

Chapter Thirteen

'SO WHAT WILL THE New Year bring for us?'

I didn't hear what Lou said at first, since she'd bellowed it over the top of the Beatles tribute band we were dancing to at the Wedgwood Rooms New Year's Eve bash.

'No more dates with Physics teachers, I hope,' I yelled back at her.

She rolled her eyes.

'Yeah, that was a bad call.'

We carried on dancing to *I Wanna Hold Your Hand*. I tried to decide whether I should spill the beans about me and Patrick, but it just seemed too hard. I would get a load of recrimination and disappointment about not mentioning anything sooner, not to mention the possibility of gossip spreading through the staff room like wildfire. And, just for now, just until *West Side Story* was all done and the dust settled, we didn't want to go public.

Patrick was spending New Year with his children in London but, before leaving, we had met up for a pre-emptive celebration of our own.

Opening the door to him, I had been thrilled to see he was wearing his headmaster suit underneath the coat and scarf. We had shared a quick hug and a smooch and then he had ordered me into the centre of the living room with my hands on my head.

He needed to check that I had dressed as instructed in his earlier text. Tight T-shirt, teeny skirt, thigh-high socks, high heeled pumps, all present and correct.

'Mm, I can't fault your outfit,' he nodded his approval. 'Underwear?'

I lifted my top to show the push-up bra, then repeated the action with my skirt so he could see the high-cut knickers.

He put a hand on one bum cheek and pulled me close to him.

'So, then, New Year,' he said softly. 'And a new start for both of us. What are you hoping for?'

'More of this,' I said. 'More of you.'

'Snap,' he said, and he accompanied the word with a crisp smack of my bottom. 'I've high hopes for us, Cherry. I don't want to put pressure on you, but I think we could see in the New Year in our own way and maybe the ritual will bring us luck. Start as we mean to go on, so to speak.'

'Oh? What ritual?'

He took out his mobile phone from his pocket and fidgeted with it for a moment.

'I've got a recording of the chimes of Big Ben on here,' he said. 'I know it isn't midnight for another 14 hours, but let's pretend for a while, shall we? It's midnight. The old year is ending, the new about to begin. And I'm going to drive all the old, bad stuff out in my own special way.'

I smirked up at him, having an idea of what he might have in mind.

'How are you going to do that?'

'Bend over the arm of the sofa, and I'll show you.'

The arm of the sofa. Where it all began, with Stuart, only a few months before. I snuggled myself into position, legs out straight behind me, a cushion beneath my stomach performing the dual purpose of protecting my abdomen and pushing up my rear end.

'This is an unusual ritual,' I said as he flipped up my skirt. 'I haven't heard of this one.'

'I invented it,' he said. 'Though I daresay plenty of

other secret sadists across the land are doing something pretty similar today. Maybe the entire constituency of MasterMe dot com.'

He was probably right. The sadistic mind did seem to be a highly creative one. He took something from his briefcase which I identified as gym shoe – a large one, size ten at least.

'The teacher's weapon of choice, back when I were a lad,' he said, whacking it down alarmingly so that dust flew up from the armrest beside me. 'The rubber sole confers a very particular kind of sensation. You'll see. But first, we need our soundtrack.'

He pushed a button on the phone, then yanked down my knickers to my knees. The dignified chimes boomed out, making me think I was in Westminster, looking up at the iconic clock tower.

'Out with the old,' intoned Patrick. 'Let's get rid of the doubts and the fears that held us back.'

The first stroke. Bong. Thwack. Ouch!

It was perfectly true. There was something about a gym shoe. The rubber burned and sent aftershocks of pain through every fibre of my backside and beyond.

Each stroke was a redefinition of pain, exquisite torture mingling with something more profound – a sense of security, of comfort, even. Despite everything I'd done, I'd never been spanked by someone with an investment in me and our relationship. The feeling that I didn't have to hang on to every second of sensation in case it was my last was an enormous bonus. This was one spanking, there would be more. This was just one moment among many.

I was home and dry.

Well, not dry exactly …

As the twelfth chime died away and the twelfth stroke of the shoe sank into my burning skin, Patrick reached between my legs.

'In with the new,' he whispered and, before I knew it,

the condom was on and I was filled.

I rocked to and fro over the arm of the sofa, welcoming his fat, hard cock, spreading my thighs for him, loving the way he slapped up against the warmth of my arse as he thrust.

'Happy … New … Year, Cherry,' he grunted, working me hard.

'Happy New Year, sir,' I panted in reply.

'Happy New Year, Chez,' blurted a worse-for-wear Lou as the countdown began and balloons fell from the ceiling.

'It will be. And Happy New Year to you.'

As we sang about auld acquaintance being forgot, I thought about Stuart. I hoped he was giving some lucky girl in some faraway port the new year spanking of her life. I thought about Justin and Maz, who were celebrating the season in Australia, getting kinky on the beach. I wished them well. Perhaps we would stay in touch. I thought about His Lordship and that little coterie. Had things been different, I would have been at their masked ball, exhibiting my submission skills. Finally, I thought about Damian. My ghost lover, my might-have-been. I hoped, sincerely, that he would meet his match too, as I had met mine.

And then I cut him loose from my preoccupations, freeing him to find his dream submissive. Auld acquaintance might never be forgot, but this year would be all about new acquaintance.

Also by Justine Elyot

The Business of Pleasure

If one call could set you on a trail to the heart of your darkest fantasy, would you make it? Charlotte does, and her bold decision propels her into a world where no desire is too outrageous, decadent or extravagant to be satisfied – for a price. Her own fantasy life merges with reality when she is hired to work for the shadowy organisation she first encountered as a client. She organises an array of wild set pieces involving banquets, film productions, mansions full of pleasure slaves, as well as thoroughly researching those requests that chime with her own kinky tastes. Two men, one woman, and every sexual fantasy imaginable – these are the ingredients that make up the business of pleasure.

ISBN 9781907016257   Price £7.99

Also from Xcite Books

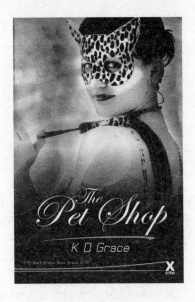

The Pet Shop
K D Grace

In appreciation of a job well done, Stella James 's boss sends her a pet – a human pet. The mischievous Tino comes straight from The Pet Shop complete with a collar, a leash, and an erection. Stella soon discovers the pleasure of keeping Pets, especially this one, is extremely addictive.

Obsessed with Tino and with the reclusive philanthropist Vincent Evanston, who looks like Tino, but couldn't be more different, Stella is drawn into the secret world of The Pet Shop. As her animal lust awakens, Stella must walk the thin line that separates the business of pleasure from the more dangerous business of the heart or suffer the consequences.

ISBN 9781908006790   Price £7.99

Xcite Books help make loving better
with a wide range of erotic books,
eBooks and dating sites.

www.xcitebooks.com
www.xcitebooks.co.uk

Sign-up to our Facebook page
for special offers and free gifts!